the MONOLOGIST

"To punish the oppressors of humanity is clemency; to forgive them is cruelty."
	-Maximilien Robespierre

"The first lesson a revolutionary must learn is that he is a doomed man."
	-Huey P. Newton

Book design by George Cotronis
Editing by Gabriel Hargrave

ISBN 979-8-9868455-3-1 (Paperback)
ISBN 979-8-9868455-2-4 (Digital online)

First paperback edition July 2024

Published by Third Estate Books
https://www.thirdestatebooks.com/

Introduction:

The lights flickered, if only for a moment. Their worlds paused, as a power that could end them permanently was laid bare. Martini glasses filled with substandard wine rested upon lace tablecloths. Anything to give the appearance of sophistication, anything to bring their money to the desolate desert. It was bad enough that Mother Nature had given them such meager tools for the modern world.

So they paid her back in kind. They did not protest when men in olive jumpsuits came and stuck their chain-link fences and barbed wire into her flesh. They had done the same when they built their oasis in the desert. They did not turn away the gifts of The Dam, no matter how much of their blood was spilled upon its masonry as it was erected—The Hoover was even hailed as a modern engineering marvel.

Now, the aristocrats of the Golden Coast drove from far and wide, scurrying between desolate outposts just to see the latest accomplishment of Man, the destruction of worlds—just not THEIR world. At least that's what they told themselves behind tinted goggles as the explosion lit the sky a bright red in the distance. Some, so removed from the possibility that they were playing with fate, hadn't even noticed the earth shake beneath them. That they were witnessing Man play God without fully grasping the consequences of their hubris never crossed their minds as the eruption bloomed.

The shaking of the earth had become undeniable now as the cheap wine spilled on the ground, splashing onto the shoes of one particularly bourgeois film producer.

"Fuckin' prick, you know how much these shoes cost?" he seethed. "Do you know how much these cost? The cobbler died in Tuscany in the war. You can't get these anymore! HEY! You! I told you to put it in the MIDDLE of the table. Where's your boss?"

A poor waiter, who hadn't even served him, stood frozen in fear as the middle-aged tycoon chastised him. He hadn't been afforded goggles like the wealthy, so he'd taken the risk of looking at the explosion head-on, ignorant of the potential implications. What did it matter if he couldn't put a roof over his head?

Never mind the display of human ingenuity behind him, the film tycoon's shoe had been damaged, and he demanded retribution. The waiter caught a glimpse of his supervisor on the outside deck, a single finger beckoning him with the seduction of a lover and the implication of something far more sinister.

"Don't come back," his supervisor warned. "Don't you ever come back."

The waiter peered deep into his supervisor's eyes, but the older man quickly averted his gaze as he hurried towards the producer sitting at a table by the railing, watching a mushroom cloud in the distance slowly dissipate.

The supervisor practically tripped over himself in his attempt to grovel. "I am so sorry, sir!"

The appeasement was earnest enough, but the waiter didn't wait to hear the rebuttal that would inevitably follow. Instead, he shuffled down the stairs and out the front entrance onto Fremont Street. The chaos of Sin City's streets was much more his speed, anyway. It was the only home he'd known. He'd slowly but surely watched it grow from a backwater into what it was today, doing anything it could to remain relevant in the changing landscape of post-war America.

"It's only going to get worse," someone said. "One day, those tests will stop, but this city will keep evolving, doing anything to draw them in. Only when it's a carcass will they stop and move on to the next place. Parasites."

The waiter turned to see a man in a silver suit smoking a cigarette and leaning against a light pole, staring at the crowds.

"Who are you?"

"An idealist." The stranger smiled. "A man with a plan. A man who's seen the story too many times. They think themselves God. They think of you as nothing more than a nuisance, a price to pay to sustain their complexes. If they could erase you, they would. But there's a better way. There's hope yet. It won't come without sacrifice. It won't come without work. But there's a better way."

The waiter took a step back, then looked at the sky for a moment. The air had been rent by the splitting of trillions of atoms, and the cloud left in the aftermath was gorgeous, magnificent even in its terror. And yet, within a minute or two, the crowds had returned to their daily lives, the rush of euphoria as fleeting as it was sudden.

The waiter returned his attention to the stranger. "How do we fix it? What do we need to do? What do you need from me?"

He wasn't sure why he was ignoring his urge to run away. Typically, he'd have put his guard up, but something about how the man spoke, his thick out-of-town New York accent, proved to soothe him.

The Man-In-The-Silver-Suit lowered his head, his cigarette falling to his shoe, ash landing in the crease of its leather forefoot. He paid no mind as he stomped out the butt, offering his hand to the waiter. His eyes glowed an unnatural yellow, and a twisted smile formed on his lips.

"Everything. I need everything."

1.

The dry air of the desert was a far cry from the sticky variety Pat had grown accustomed to in the foothills of Central Massachusetts. Hours had gone by without another vehicle on the road. Once he passed Utah, the lack of others became more common. His car shot through the clay-pocked road like a red bolt as Jerry Lee Lewis played through his speaker—not that he could hear it over the air slicing its way into the cabin through the windows.

Pat didn't know what awaited him on the other side of his country-wide trek but hoped it was opportunity. He was a self-ascribed monologist, a comedian; the gift of the gab had been bestowed upon him much like it had been for his ancestors from the old country. Unfortunately, places like Worcester had no space for him to grow unless he wanted to play small show after small show. He'd considered Boston or New York but thought it wasn't far enough away, not an actual fresh start. Then he'd considered Los Angeles, but he wasn't going into the motion pictures. He wasn't John Wayne, and while he had convinced people he was Paul Newman's red-headed cousin once or twice while out drinking, nobody would mistake him for being a film star.

That left one city, the oasis in the desert: Las Vegas, where dreams became a reality, where you could be anybody you wanted to be. Once you stepped out into the neon glow, who you were didn't matter, just who you wanted to be. With so many casinos looking for acts, it was his chance to shine. He didn't need to be Patrick Gallagher. He could be Pat, the bee's knees, the cool cat everyone wanted to be.

Nodding to himself, he said, "Patrick's dead. He died that night I left. Pat's all there is now." It wasn't all that different to anybody else, but to Pat, it was everything.

One thing he hadn't expected on his road trip was falling in love with the sunset. Back home, the trees obstructed the pink glow of the sky. It was beautiful there too, but with nothing but pillars of sandstone and the occasional cactus or shrub shaping the backdrop, sunsets took on a whole new meaning in the West. In Colorado, he pulled over to watch it crawl behind the mountains. Today, however, he knew only a few hours stood between him and Las Vegas and its promises of opportunity, its promises of escape.

While he wasn't opposed to rolling into town as the city came alive, he'd be anything but. This was his fifth hour of the day on the road. Adding a few more to that would ensure a rough night. Pat knew Las Vegas was no stranger to wild nights, nor was he, but first impressions were everything. He'd rather experience it with a proper sleep behind him.

There was also the issue of which motel he'd stay in. Ramshackle lodgings weren't rarified air in America's heartland, and he suspected more of the same in the western frontier. So long as there was a pool and air conditioning, he'd make the best of it. Besides, he'd heard stories of unsavory characters patrolling the arid foothills outside the city. Pat Gallagher wasn't a coward, but he wasn't foolhardy either.

A night of rest would do him good. Of that, there was no question. As he sped past the mundane yet hypnotizing landscape, he could see a building with a faded pink stucco façade in the distance. Mirage or not, he'd take his chances that it was a place worth staying.

As he got closer, he gawked in surprise. Despite the tacky exterior, the lot was nearly full of vehicles from all over, the state plates ranging from Georgia to California. His car shifted as he took the keys out of the ignition, his radio having turned to static as now he was truly far from civilization. Yet, the hotel shone like a beacon against the harsh wilderness of the unforgiving West.

Pat stepped outside the car, his brown leather shoes toeing the sand and gravel beneath his feet. The dry air filled his lungs as he sighed and stretched, happy to be standing once more. He felt the air escape in the discs of his back, audible crunches coming from beneath his tan blazer. Heat or no heat, he was dressed to impress. He reached back into his car for his matching hat, then placed it upon his head as he tried to find an entrance to the pink fortress of solitude that had laid claim to the otherwise unremarkable stretch of barren land.

He spotted a screen door and, behind it, a secondary door. He closed them as quickly as he opened them, not wanting to let any potentially cool air escape out into the arid wastes. Standing on the other side, he found himself in the humblest of lobbies, nothing more than a few chairs on either side of a marble-top desk, from behind which the sound of an air conditioner radiated. He didn't notice the woman behind the desk at first—or notice when she started speaking to him.

"Welcome to Sunny Side Inn. We don't have much for rooms available, but if you don't mind a single bed, we'll take good care of you."

He shook his head as he snapped out of his daze. "Sounds good to me, miss." Pat flashed a toothy grin at the woman behind the desk. "Lovely place you've got here. I don't have anything against the Sunny Side, but I am hoping the room has some reprieve from the heat."

She gave a dry laugh. "I assure you, we have the coolest rooms in the area. Not that there's much competition."

It was Pat's turn to laugh.

"How many nights did you plan on staying?" she asked, getting down to brass tacks. Her blonde hair fell down to her shoulders as she stared at him. "I reckon probably one night, but I just want to be sure, as we have some reservations coming into the weekend."

"Thought the only reservations out here were for the Indians." He expected her to laugh, but when she didn't, he said, "Just kidding. I'm heading to Las Vegas in the morning. I should like to tell you I am something of a comedian—a monologist."

This was met with an eye roll as the woman scribbled the information into her logbook. "We have a pool in the central courtyard. On your left is a door to the rooms. Icebox is here in the lobby behind me and available upon request." She grabbed a key on a red leather key chain with the number *6* inscribed in the middle and handed it to him. "I'll let you get settled in."

"Thanks ma'am." There was no humor in his voice this time; his first few jokes falling flat had shaken his confidence. "Say, what town is this, anyhow? I'd like to see how far I am from Las Vegas, for the morning."

"You're on the outskirts of Lund, Nevada. Not much more than a few hours north of Las Vegas." She looked down at her log. "I almost forgot; the room will be two dollars for the night."

"How about the day? Or are they charged together?" A last feeble attempt at humor.

This time, she didn't do him the courtesy of feigned bemusement or just plain ignoring him. Instead, she let out a deep groan. He rushed to hand her two one-dollar bills to move the situation forward.

"Room number is on the key," she said. "Do us all a favor, eh? Don't practice your jokes too loud. Sheriff ain't too far from here. Doesn't take kindly to anyone disturbing the peace."

No amount of desert sun could approximate the burning of Pat's cheeks. He gave a curt nod and made his way back toward the heat to grab his luggage.

Outside, he stared out at the desert beyond his two-tone car, with its cherry red body and pearl white roof on top. With a sigh, he grabbed a worn linen suitcase out of his trunk. It wasn't much, but it did the thankless task of carrying his clothes from one ramshackle lodging to the next. He was used to tossing that suitcase onto creaky, broken beds and threadbare chairs.

Tonight, however, luck was favoring him, as if it knew the haven of all gambling was near. While the receptionist hadn't been receptive to his jokes, that wasn't treading new water. And it didn't speak to the quality of the place...just the bad tastes of the staff. The lobby was clean and bright, so though he hadn't seen the rooms, he doubted they'd prove to be as rough as some places he'd stayed on his journey.

The woman was watching him with raised eyebrows when he went back inside. "Surprised you came back in," she said. "Thought I might've scared you off. Sorry to come off so harsh, but the heat makes me so very irritable."

"Don't sweat it." He waved his hand dismissively. "Nothing to be done. I was being cheeky. Sometimes you have to remind someone who's the boss. Your inn, your rules." Throwing a thumb over his shoulder, he added, "I'll get out of your hair."

He made his way to the doorway that led to the pool and the courtyard where all the rooms were. As he stepped back outside into the heat, he was met by the joyful sounds of a child splashing in the pool. A shrill yell escaped the child, the ecstasy that came from a youthful disposition that time had yet to erode. Pat's own childlike wonder had lingered, despite the harshness of reality. Sometimes, he still felt like a kid, optimism brimming with each step he took.

"Which room?" he muttered, staring around him at the doors before spotting the number 6. "Ahh, there it is."

He stepped out of the sun and under the second story of the inn. They weren't built directly upon each other. Instead, the upper floor jutted out, creating merciful shade for those below. He put the key into the lock and opened the door, which creaked as he quickly made his way inside, the buzzing of the air conditioner beckoning him to cooler pastures.

The room was basic enough: a thin, yellowing sheet draped over a small twin bed with a pillow in a floral pillowcase, complete with shaggy worn brown carpets, which he'd wager had been a more neutral color once. He put his bag on the bed and pulled out his map, carrying it to the desk and unfurling it until he could see the entire nation before him. A moment passed as he scanned for Lund, Nevada, eventually finding it north of Vegas.

"Maybe four hours, then." Pat tapped Las Vegas on the map. "Should be there by early afternoon, finally home."

His mind drifted back toward Massachusetts, a place he had long thought to be where he'd grow old. But things changed. He shuddered as he thought about the night he fled, the night the illusion of a quiet, unremarkable life had been broken.

He made his way to the window in his room, a thick curtain taking the brunt of the solar rays and keeping the room cool. Peering out at the pool, he noticed the kid swimming, parents watching as they sipped on their beers. Perhaps this was a vacation for them. He couldn't imagine Sin City was the most family-friendly of destinations.

"To be young, if I could have a do-over," he mused.

Nobody could hear him. He was alone, but saying it out loud brought comfort. A reminder that even if he wanted to change it, time did not afford the opportunity to do so.

The shower seemed inviting. While Pat would turn in early, he didn't see that as a bad thing. Driving for as long as he had came with its drawbacks, namely sore backs. These thoughts served as a distraction from more macabre ruminations. Las Vegas was a place to start anew, but that didn't mean the past would haunt him any less.

"Didn't give me a choice," he reminded himself. "Was me or him. You didn't even do it. Simple as that, Pat. You know it."

It was a feeble attempt at assuaging the deep-rooted guilt that was a constant facet of his upbringing. How he longed for the innocence of that child he watched from afar, splashing in the pool with little concern for the harsh reality of the world they shared.

It was in that moment he realized how bizarre he was acting. If the parents or the child glanced over, they'd know him to be no different from a peeper. He moved away from the blinds and sighed.

"Just practice your set, Pat. Just practice the set until you get tired. Never you mind what anyone else is up to."

He made his way to his bag, pulling out his notepad full of jokes.

Pat practiced for hours until the inevitable feeling of drowsiness found him in the Sunny Side Inn, waiting in the shadows of the silent desert. Only when he stopped reciting the same jokes repeatedly did he realize it was quiet, save the buzzing of his air conditioner. No crickets, no owls, no sound of cars passing by. He wondered if that kind of silence was what Randy felt, and with that troubling thought, he slept.

2.

Another dreamless night. Pat would've been worried about that at one point in his life. However, it was a blessing now, given everything that had brought him here. He got up and dressed in a clean shirt but the same suit, as the space in his luggage was limited. Then he stared at himself in the mirror, red hair glinting in the artificial light as he smirked.

"It's going to be okay. We're coming home. New start, Pat. New start."

He splashed water onto his face before packing up the meager belongings he had brought inside.

Stepping outside, he couldn't help but notice the pool was empty now. The only sign anyone had been there at all was the cigarette butts on the ground. The heat hadn't come on fully yet, but Pat had little doubt that it was a matter of time. He went back into the lobby, past the pool, noticing how vacant the place felt. Once inside, he saw the same receptionist from the night before and braced himself for more ribbing.

"Sorry about last night. It was a long day in the heat. Your jokes weren't half bad." Pat raised a brow, which shot up even further when she added, "We had a commie scare yesterday morning. Agents came looking around. I don't know if they made any arrests. Been like this almost weekly since the Embargo. Just had me on edge."

Pat stared at her, not knowing what to say. While he wasn't complaining about the validation, people didn't share so openly back home. Finally, he settled on, "Only thing red 'bout me is the hair, ma'am. Skin, too, if I stay in the sun too long."

That was met with a genuine chuckle, which made Pat smirk. Not a bad joke to add to his routine. He put the key down on the front desk, and she quickly grabbed it.

"Say, I didn't get your name for the log," she said. "Must've been more flustered than I thought last night." She looked up at him, waiting for his answer, pen ready to jot it down.

"Name's Pat Gallagher," he said, but it came out *Gallagah*, his accent on full display. If the red hair hadn't given it away, his cadence did. She nodded along as she wrote it down.

"Well, Pat Gallagher, you got a good shot down there. Seen a lot of would-be entertainers come through those doors. Most of them don't have your confidence. Go get 'em, kid."

He could tell she was working overtime to make up for her deflating of his ego the night prior. And it was working. His confidence ballooned.

"That's the idea, anyway. Have a swell weekend, miss. Sunny Side Inn has been very good to me throughout our long journey together. But I gotta hit the road, Jack." He flashed a toothy grin and, without another word, was out the door and in his car.

Not long after, he was back on the road, the pastels of the hotel fading into the distance as the sun slowly ascended to its apex. There was nothing left besides dusty peaks, shrubs, and his thoughts to keep him company. The radio was intermittent, sometimes playing portions of a song and other times cutting off altogether, leaving the only sound the wind that ripped through his opened windows.

With no music and no company, his lingering thoughts manifested front and center, the metaphysical silver microphone staring out back at them, daring them to be heard. *Always wanted to grace the stage, always wanted to hit the big time, Pat. No time like the present. Just need to take it and make it. Give nothing back.* The words didn't mean much. There was no way of knowing what he'd have to give up. The internal monologue went on nearly as long as the empty stretches of highway, which became curvier the further south he went.

After a sharp curve, he noticed a large tuft of gray smoke coming from the side of the road in the distance. "That doesn't look good," he said under his breath as he approached. His car stopped behind the smoke plumes, which appeared to be dying off. It was another car on the side of the road.

"Really hope there ain't a body in there."

He stepped out of his car, slamming the driver's door with a thud, almost hoping somebody was in agony inside the vehicle. The alternative wasn't something Pat was prepared to ponder. There was no odor of burning flesh that he could smell. When he was a child, the apartment building across the road caught fire, burning everyone inside. It was a smell he wouldn't forget, and it was mercifully absent from the air he inhaled now.

Upon inspection of the burned car's driver seat, he saw there was nobody inside, just a briefcase sitting on the passenger's side, only the frame remaining as heated leather peeled off.

"That doesn't look so good."

His mind jumped to the Mob. He'd heard rumors that Las Vegas was the brainchild of that shadowy organization. While he didn't know how much truth was in the speculation, this burning car on the side of the road didn't do much to deter suspicion. The view on the passenger side only affirmed the lingering anxiety that radiated up his spine. The brush to the side of the road descended into a gulch. He could see footprints moving toward it in the sand.

"Oh, brother."

A sharp pang of nervousness moved from his spine to his stomach. He turned back to his car, hand resting on the door handle. He debated the merits of leaving the situation in his rearview mirror. It was clear something unsettling had occurred here, but strange things happened every day. That didn't mean he had to get involved. He was a fish out of water, in a desert, no less. But Pat was no coward. His mother had taught him better.

While his gut told him the vehicle's owner was long since dead, there was a glimmer of hope. His conscience held on to that slight possibility, refusing to relinquish its grasp on his thoughts. *He came back for you, Pat. He came back for you. Now is your chance.* The inner battle was over. Instead of sitting down, starting the car, and being on his way, he reached into his glove compartment.

Silver glinted in the sun, exposing his Smith and Wesson revolver to the sun's rays. A weapon of cowboys and bandits. He pictured himself going to a saloon after he escaped the gorge.

"C'mon, Pat, ain't too late to keep going."

There was no conviction in the plea to himself. It fell on deaf ears. Before he knew it, his gun rested at his side as he carefully trod down the brush, following the footprints.

The brush scraped at his pants, stabbing at the cloth shielding his legs from worse damage. Within half a minute, the decline leveled out. He looked out at the Nevada wilderness, pensive as he tried to make sense of the arid alien landscape.

"Nothin' out here, silly Pat. Nothing out here. Somebody just wanted to look at the view. It might have nothing to do with the car. No wind out here, so it could've been days ago."

Smooth-talking himself, he was lulled into a false sense of reassurance. Something had happened with the car. There was no doubt something had happened, but once again, insensible fear propelled him to jump to the worst conclusions.

Raaaaaaaatttttttttleee. Hisssss—raaatttttttttle. Pat knew of that sound by reputation but had never encountered one face to face. He turned back toward the incline, and there it was. A rattlesnake snarled at him, blocking the path he had taken down. He shuffled his feet as he lifted his pistol, knowing in his heart the gun did little to deter the aggressive serpent.

"Hey there, fella, no need to be so wound up. It's a beautiful day out, plenty to be jolly about."

Smooth-talking did nothing for the snake, which crept closer to him. He held his gun before him, knuckles turning white as he gripped his salvation.

The snake lunged, the hiss filling the silence as he fired his gun once at it, a bullet whizzing through scales and flesh, followed by a thud. The snake danced, convulsing across the landscape, erasing the footsteps that Pat had followed down. His heart thumped in his chest as the echo of the bullet filled his ringing ears. Thanks to the Eagle Scouts, he had long since learned to fire a gun. Back then, they used air rifles for marksmanship. While the pistol was a vastly different beast, the training took over, and it was over quickly for the snake.

"I need to get out of here."

He looked around, and a glint caught his eye. While he knew this part of the country once drew many in hopes of jewels and gold, he thought that excitement had long since died down. Yet, the greed of human nature drew him to the glint even as his stomach and mind pleaded.

As he made his way over, he realized it wasn't raw gold but a piece of jewelry: a gold ring, a clover with emeralds embedded in it. His eyes lingered on a patch of dirt just a few feet away from the ring, almost brown compared to the red-orange clay of the landscape in front of him. He gulped as his mind came to terms with exactly what had transpired. He'd suspected it to be so, but his vindication was soured by the tang of panic in his throat.

What if whoever'd done this was still here?

Rushing back up out of the gulch, he tried to erase the image of the discolored soil. That there was no shovel beside it did little to assuage his fears. A person had recently perished, and somebody was aware. The burning of the car implied guilt, a means to cover up the deed. With enough time, nobody would know; it would be just another nameless skeleton in the vast ocean of bones, populated by mishaps that'd become fables told to children in sleepy East Coast hamlets, not unlike the one Pat grew up in.

Pat knew if it weren't for the rattlesnake, which had left him shaken, he might never have taken a second gander down that way. He climbed toward his car, leaving the brush and the ring behind him. A brief wave of relief came over him as he saw the road was empty and the other vehicle's smoke had died down, leaving a burned husk. The last thing he needed was a sheriff driving by and thinking he had something to do with the mishap. He threw his gun into his car through the open passenger window and went to the driver's side. Paranoid, he looked around the road despite it being empty.

Pat rested in his cloth seat, the sweat sticking to the back of his suit and headrest. He closed his eyes and let out an exasperated breath. "Ain't the way I wanted the day to play out. Will tell you that."

Who he was telling was not apparent, as he was alone. Despite that isolation, he couldn't help but feel everything seemed too coincidental. Perhaps the paranoia and anxiety of starting anew was clouding his judgment. As he opened his eyes, that thought was pushed back by a fresh surge of fear.

On the dashboard, he could see a black book of matches.

"What the hell?"

He reached toward it, dirty, caked fingers caressing the matches as he glanced around him. There was no sign of anyone watching him, yet the matchbook stared at him despite having no eyes.

"Louie's Lounge, Las Vegas." He bit his lip as he eyed the wording in bright red block letters with what appeared to be lightbulbs drawn on the inside of each letter. After the name of the business, there was a number. He looked around once more, convinced he was being watched, but all that met him was the silence of the sands.

"Time to go, Pat." He risked a glance back at the makeshift grave. "Before they dig up a matching plot."

He started his car and made his way down the road as he tossed the matchbook next to his firearm on the passenger seat. The name "Louie's Lounge" ran through his mind again as he tried to distract himself from the stress of coming upon a burial and a venomous snake. It was already an eventful day, and as soon as he was properly hydrated, he thought he might find himself drinking in a lounge—just not Louie's. As his mind wandered, he couldn't help but imagine the circumstances which led to the Clover Ring Man's death.

"At least he got buried. They didn't leave him to the vultures."

The image of a man floating in a lake flooded his mind, open eyes staring into nothingness as fish glided through strands of blonde hair that swayed like golden kelp.

"At least they buried him."

3.

Pat often wondered when exactly it was people began to realize Vegas was an adult playground. Even from a distance, he could see the luminescent lights pushing upward toward the blackness of the clear desert night. Stars weren't a new concept to him, but they shined all the brighter in the desert.

It wasn't long until he was in the city, Elvis Presley blasting all around, brightly colored buildings lining the highway corridors, and revelers spilling out of motels and casinos filled to capacity.

"Home, sweet home."

Thoughts of the snake and the buried man were thrown aside. They were still there but hidden by the allure, by the display of gratuitous opulence. There was a dark side of the place known as Sin City. It was inevitable people would get involved in things they shouldn't. Pat just had bad luck in coming upon the aftermath.

The matchbook rested in his blazer pocket, a reminder that *somebody* had seen him there, even if he hadn't seen them. Pat had since decided he would go drinking after checking into his hotel. He might even gamble with what little pocket change he had.

Before he knew it, he had passed the strip on the city's outskirts and made his way downtown. The streets were filled with music and laughter, people enjoying their evening. The hotels were full up from what he could see, even though it wasn't the weekend. But Pat finally found one with a bright neon *"vacancy"* sign.

He pulled into the lot, and while it was far from empty, it was clear the place wasn't packed. The inn was painted red, reminiscent of a hotel from the Swiss Alps, a precarious choice given the location. Eclectic venues were a staple of the city, and yet this one toed the line of believability. However, beggars couldn't be choosers, and with his budget, it would have to do.

As he parked his car, he looked in his mirror, noticing how dirty his suit was from the sand. "They won't care, Pat. This is Sin City. Way more characters than you out here." His pep talk geared him up to go inside. But first, he eyed his passenger seat, moving his revolver underneath it, just in case.

As he walked into the clearly marked lobby, a couple smoking out front gave him a curt nod, which he reluctantly returned. In the lobby, the low hum of Frank Sinatra filled the air from a radio in a corner. The front desk was unattended, save a silver bell resting on the top, facing the entry door.

Ding.

Pat lightly tapped the top of the bell as he looked around the lobby. It looked put together, new even, even if Sin City wasn't what he associated with a ski vacation.

A young Latino man in Lederhosen approached the front desk. "Welcome to The Slippery Slope. My name is Lars. I'd be happy to help you, sir."

Pat stifled a chuckle. "I have a feelin' you aren't a Kraut, but your secret is safe with me. Do you guys do week-by-week rates? Plan on staying here a bit."

Lars looked through his logbook, flipping through the pages before looking up at Pat. "I got a room that'd work. Rate weekly is ten bucks. That work for you?" Lars was already jotting notes into the room's slot as though Pat had agreed.

"Yeah, that works for me. Say, are there any lounges nearby? I am not from around here, and the chatter about this city is buzzing over on the East Coast. I figured it couldn't hurt to get a drink and see the nightlife myself."

"There's Louie's Lounge," Lars said, his eyes trailing up and down Pat's suit and coming to rest on some of the dirt and sand caked onto it. "It's the hotspot in town. Just opened a few months ago. Looks like your kind of crowd."

Pat's eyes widened as he reached for his wallet to pay for his room for the week. That was the last place he wanted to check out, but he also didn't want to draw attention to himself, so he elected to play it off. "Sounds lively, but you know, I want a place that has character, feels worn. Authentic. Y'know?"

Lars raised his eyebrows. "Authenticity? In Las Vegas? Golly, sir, are you sure you picked the right town to visit? Vegas…it's a lot of things, but genuine? I don't know if that's in the cards."

"What can I say? I want my cake and to eat it too. I'll just go out and about myself." Taking the key the receptionist was holding out to him, he smiled. "Thank you, Lars. And call me Pat."

This time, he'd snagged a corner room. He was sure there was a pool somewhere on the property, but his appetite for people-watching had diminished. He did, however, need to make a phone call, as he'd told the others he'd let them know when he arrived.

He pushed open the door to his room, taking the time to embrace the ski lodge aesthetics, especially the rustic-looking fireplace that was clearly for show, as there was a sign asking people to not use it. He stifled a chuckle as he approached the bright red rotary phone by his bedside, then dialed a number he had known his whole life, calling across the country.

On the third ring, a voice answered on the other end. "Pat? Nobody's up this late phoning me unless he's across the country or the Devil himself." It was the voice of Tommy Brunwell, an older man Pat had known since he was nothing more than a child. "You got red hair but not much else. You make it there okay, pal?"

Pat tried to fill the words with his normal charm, but it landed flat. "Hey, Tommy, I'm doing swell. Just fixing to go out drinking tonight."

He owed himself that after his long trek through the heartland. Liquor was a quick remedy for stress. For proof, one only needed to look down the long line of Gallaghers who'd turned to the bottle. Pat wouldn't be the one to break that cycle, especially since the nature of his stupor turned less externally vitriolic in favor of a more subdued inner turmoil.

"I figured since I got here," Pat continued, "I'd call to see how everything's going back home."

"Things are going as well as they can," Tommy said. "Everyone misses you. Told them you got the chance to leave earlier than you thought. A fresh start, ain't nobody even talking about Randy."

Pat's heart skipped a beat. He'd known the topic would come up. How could it not? But the mention of the man's name still filled him with fear.

"They think he skipped town, too," Tommy was saying. "Nobody knows anything. I reckon they won't, either. Everyone else is looking the other way."

"Somebody must know, Tommy," Pat insisted. "He wasn't popular, but guys don't just disappear. We'll be the first ones in line for questioning."

"Nonsense, Patty. Randy wasn't known for making friends. They can blame it on Korea if they want to, but he was a nasty fella long before they shipped him out to Seoul. There's a long list of suspects before they'll think it was you. Not for nothing, Pat, but nobody thinks of you as much of a hooligan." Tommy was quiet for a moment, then he said, "As for me? I never had a reason to get in a squabble with him until...until that night."

The less said about that night, the better Pat would feel. Guilt was a powerful weapon, and he wielded it against himself.

"I know, you're right." Pat sighed. "Just have the jitters. Ain't never been involved in anything like this. You know what, I was going to come out here before. I have my first audition tomorrow; I think I'll get it. I'll be a proper Jack Benny. Just you watch."

"Focus on the jokes, Patty," Tommy said soothingly. "Ain't no reason to worry about Clinton. I'll let you know if things change, but as far as it stands, you're in the clear."

Pat paused, taking a deep gulp of dry, cool air in his faux-ski lodge hotel room. "Thank you. I wish I could explain... Thank you, Tommy. It means the world. I'm going to do right by you. Thank you."

There was silence on the other line for a moment, followed by a deep sigh. "Be safe out there, Patrick. I hope you never have to use that gun."

The phone clicked right before the call ended. Pat put the phone down before looking over at the curtains obstructing his hotel room window.

He pulled open the curtain. The bright lights of the city and cars passing by filled his senses. It was a vibrant world—much more colorful than he was feeling. Pat, however, was not one to allow doubt or fear to linger. The taste of liquor was in the back of his mouth.

"Salvation at the bottom of a bottle," he said, eyes resting on his suitcase before sweeping back to the city beyond the window. "The Irish way, isn't it so, Patty?

"Fuck it. Tomorrow you work; tonight you play."

With that, he made his way to the shower. After disrobing, he looked upon his reflection, his pale skin a pink hue from overexposure, dirt stuffed under his fingernails and caked on his stubbled cheeks, nearly unrecognizable even to himself.

"Tonight? Yeah, tonight, you play."

4.

It never ceased to amaze Pat how much a shower could change everything. The stress washed away, slinking down the drain along with the dirt and grime. He felt like a new man when he stepped out onto the Vegas strip, the Louie's Lounge matchbook in his pocket.

He hadn't even bothered to check in with Lars, the Lederhosen Latino, for recommendations. But he also didn't make his way to Louie's. Instead, he found himself in a casino on Fremont Street, which he'd seen while aimlessly strolling and indulging in a cigarette, taking the dry air into his lungs alongside the smoke.

The casino floor was full of the extravagance one expected out of Sin City. The carpets were a mix of maroon and gold, making an intricate pattern that reminded Pat of childhood stories about Rome. Opulence. That was the word swimming around his brain. The men traded out the vestments of the legionnaires for tapered suits, their helmets replaced with slick backs and their weapons replaced with the fistfuls of poker chips. Yet, the warriors' scowl of determination remained, only in place of conquest was a fetterless appetite of greed.

He hovered near a blackjack table, watching a man in a velvet blazer throw chip after chip in. He rested against a pillar across from the table and lit his fourth cigarette of the night.

"You're here, kid," he reminded himself, puffing as he put the matchbook away in his pocket. "You made it."

He heard another voice say, "You think he's bluffing, or he's got the juice?"

Standing beside him was a tall man with a crooked nose that suggested it had once been broken. Despite his olive complexion, his eyes were hazel. He was of a huskier build, and yet his gray suit accented all his features.

"Old guy like that?" Pat considered the gambler the man was pointing to. "I reckon he's trying to impress some lady, hoping she'll link up to his arm. Plus, ain't this the low-stakes table?"

"Yeah, now that you mention it," the tall man said, "I think it is. Say, you ain't from 'round here. That accent's a giveaway. Plus, not many redheaded Indians."

"Really? Well, that's going to be an awkward conversation with the parents," Pat deadpanned. "I'm from Boston. Name's Pat. And you?"

The tall man looked on, and sure enough, the gent in the velvet blazer won the hand, no bluff involved. He cheered as he puffed his cigar and pulled the chips in. The groans of the other players only seemed to strengthen his joy.

Pat's new companion shook his head. "Well, I will be damned. He wasn't bluffing. I'm from Phoenix. Decided I wanted to go somewhere colder." Pat raised a brow, then stifled a chuckle as the man went on, "Kidding, kidding. Name's Lorenzo. Nice to meet you, Pat. What say you and I get a drink? Two strangers in a town of transients."

"You buying?" Pat asked Lorenzo as they left behind the low-stakes blackjack table for a bar near where some not-so-friendly games of poker were going on. "I'll get the second round if you should like to stick around."

"Must be new in town," Lorenzo said as the bartender brought them both drinks without either of them ordering. It was clear Lorenzo was a frequent patron of the bar and a fan of rum. "The only people who offer to pay for drinks are either allergic to gambling or just passing through."

Pat wasn't really listening, though, still preoccupied with Lorenzo's apparent pull here at the casino. "Wow, they sure know how to roll out the red carpet for you. You connected to the head honchos or what?" he asked between sips of his drink. The familiar burning liberated him from the drawn-out events of a chaotic day.

Lorenzo looked around shiftily before breaking into a chuckle. "No, I just spend enough money here that the bartender should know my preferences. I always get the same drink for my esteemed company—as a suitable host *should* do."

"A host? If this bar's your domain, what do you do for work? I assume you must be a showman of some kind. Too much charisma for anything else."

Pat glanced at the man's face, lingering on his eyes longer than he meant to. Then he shifted away, clutching his glass and focusing on the TV on the wall behind the bar. It was a story about Cuba, something to do with Castro condemning the United States. Pat wasn't terribly interested in the discourse surrounding the island, and he certainly didn't understand the purpose of being involved.

Lorenzo sipped his beverage as he, too, watched the news story unfold. "I work in waste management. Casinos like this? A lot of garbage to take care of. It ain't much, but it's an honest living." Without looking at Pat, he asked, "What about you? If you just got into town, I assume you don't have work lined up."

"I'm a monologist," Pat said. "Working on getting some gig work tomorrow. Got a few auditions lined up. I know show business can be cutthroat, but I think I got the skills to knock 'em dead and leave them wanting more."

Lorenzo didn't say anything at first, just sipped in silence. Then, "It's a tough town, Pat. But I believe in you. I don't acquaint myself with just anybody. You seem like a good guy." Setting his glass down, he added, "Where are you trying out? Heard Louie's Lounge is hiring big time for people."

Pat sighed as he took a drag from a newly lit cigarette, puffing it toward a passerby. "Everyone keeps talking about that place. Is it really all it's cracked up to be?"

Lorenzo shrugged. "Want my opinion? It seems like a good place to lose yourself. And there's nothing wrong with that. Tons of people come to the city, running from the past, from their present, delaying their futures. I don't pass judgment. I'm just another sinner."

The glass felt somehow colder in Pat's hand. The rest of his senses however dulled, his own curiosity, amongst other things, taking hold. "How about you? Are you running from anything? Not judging either—not until I've paid you back for this drink, at any rate."

Pat laughed at his own joke, but Lorenzo didn't, just stared introspectively down at the bar. "No, sir. Just figured it was time for new scenery. Fresh start does a lot of men good." He paused, but it was clear he had more to say from the way he spun his glass around. "I promised myself I'd never die where I was born. Mi papi served over in Europe. Told me even the days when there was nothing but mud and sludge, he was grateful to see the world. Even in places like that, there's beauty." Then he cracked an uneasy smile and huffed sheepishly. "I don't know. Think the liquor's talking a lot. I'm a lightweight. Say, you never told me where you were auditioning."

"I can't remember the name, but it's a tiki-themed casino down the road. You know, next to the other casino with a gimmick." Pat grinned, but he was being overly vague on purpose, a mixture of distrust and wanting to test the waters.

Lorenzo smiled back at him. "I don't bite. I leave that to the liquor. I can see in your eyes it's already hitting. Must've had a long flight, coming in from Boston."

Pat shook his head. "That's the thing. I drove here. Crazy, I know, but there's something beautiful about driving through the heartland. Eisenhower did an amazing thing with those roadways. I'd have voted for him for a third term, but he decided against pulling a Roosevelt."

"Yeah?" Lorenzo knocked back the rest of his drink. "I don't care much for politics, but Kennedy? Golly gee, can he talk up a storm. Can see why he won. We finally got a Catholic in the Oval Office." As he ordered another round, he said, "You must be tuckered out from that long drive. How's your first night here treating you?"

Pat was feeling the liquor, his heavy hand indulging him in deeper sips. One drink had already led to another, and he was barely listening to the man sitting beside him. "You know, I always wanted to come here. Dad told me you could see atom bomb tests from the rooftops back in the day." Pat shook his head, rambling on, his words slurring. He felt comfortable with Lorenzo, something he hadn't felt recently. "Crazy to think about that. The world's changing. Like you said, look at Kennedy. Irish guy like him, running a former British colony? That's incredible. Wonder what Washington would say."

Despite his claim of being a lightweight, Lorenzo seemed considerably less drunk than Pat. "Have a hard time thinking Washington could get over us integrating colored folk. A lot of people, even today, can't get over that one. But your dad was right. I remember when those tests were the attraction."

Pat's stomach growled, though he wasn't sure if anyone else could hear it. "Say, I think we should grab something to eat. I've never had a taco before. Are they good? I heard they're good."

Lorenzo bellowed a laugh as the bartender chuckled and wiped off a glass. "Never had a taco? What do you people eat up in Boston? Beef stew? Boiled cabbage? Haven't lived, not yet, mi amigo." Lorenzo clapped a hand on his back and helped him out of his bar stool before throwing a five-dollar bill on the counter. "C'mon, I know a place. You'll like it. Least...I think you will."

As they made their way across the carpeted casino, Pat shook his head, the bright lights overwhelming his dulled senses. Cool, dry desert air pushed itself upon him the closer they got to the exit. Elvis Presley echoed through the streets as the night consumed the Spring Mountains in the distance. The only sources of light were lit cigarettes and the bright neon lights advertising that their respective casinos were the premier spot to piss money away.

Pat looked around him in amazement at the hustle and bustle of the strip. "It's not even the weekend. Everyone sure likes to party here. Is that the real reason you came? You strike me as a partying man, Lorenzo."

"You know, I wasn't when I moved here," Lorenzo said. "I needed work. In a city like this, lot of trash needs to get put out. Somebody's gotta do the dirty work. Seemed like a fair trade: a fresh start for me, clean streets for Vegas. Plus, I get to meet nice people all the time. Never could do that back in Phoenix. Not like here."

Lorenzo wrapped his arm around Pat's waist as though he was helping his newfound friend from keeling over. The scent of the man's musk stirred a beast within Pat, and he found himself wondering what was underneath Lorenzo's clothes.

"Yeah? Y-you sound like a good guy." Pat stumbled a little over his own feet. "Sorry. I must really be that drunk. Where was this taco place?"

"Just around the corner." Lorenzo smiled at him. "I forget sometimes that booze knocks a man on his ass. You'll be right as rain in no time, Pat. Just need some good ol' barbacoa in you, mi amigo. Say, you never did tell me what they eat out in Boston."

"I'm from outside the city, a small town called Clinton," Pat explained. "We've got a few local pizza places. And some Greeks moved to town after the war. Other than that, it's just your usual burger and malt shoppes. How about Phoenix?"

"We have burgers," Lorenzo said. "Everywhere in the good ol' US of A does. But there's a lot of Mexican food, too." He chuckled as he added, "Shame about Boston. Can't imagine my life without tacos. Maybe they'll never catch on up there, but we'll see, won't we?"

Pat doubted they wouldn't catch on; he could smell the mouthwatering aroma of beef and pork in the air and could imagine the people back home going mad for whatever he was about to experience.

"Looks like there's no line, rare, I reckon. "I suppose that means we should get in while the goin' is good."

Pat wasn't one to wait when immediate gratification was within reach. The world was his playground, even back in Clinton, that small town with its disproportionately big stresses. His earlier conversation with Tommy faded as his lust for food—and for Lorenzo—took precedence.

Lorenzo hadn't oversold the life-changing impact of a well-made taco. Words escaped him with each bite, but the imagery of an angel floating with tortilla wings and a grilled avocado halo filled his brain. The Catholic in him shuddered at the thought of eating such a holy thing, but the realist in him was doing just that without the faintest trace of penance. Only instead of St. Michael the Archangel, he was consuming St. Barbaoca the patron saint of tacos, and cuisines worlds beyond the emerald pastures of Killarney, where his lineage began.

After a filling and delicious meal, Pat started to sober up a bit. He and Lorenzo were making their way down Fremont Street towards a nearby lounge, watching vacationers and locals alike, taking in the scenery of an alien world, almost as though it was on the big screen. He imagined he was Leslie Nielsen in *Forbidden Planet*, the daring commander landing on a different planet. But instead of someplace new and foreboding, Pat was now exploring a place he had known about his whole life but never seen with his own eyes.

For the first time in weeks, he was engrossed in the moment, without thoughts of Clinton or the deed that'd expedited his trek across the country. He was also feeling bold as they sat at the lounge bar, a few more drinks behind them. It's why he allowed himself to voice the question that'd been plaguing his mind all night.

"Lorenzo," he hazarded, "how far is your place from here?"

The man looked at him over the rim of his glass, and Pat's eye's locked onto his own, revealing the intention behind the innocuous-sounding query.

A grin spread across Lorenzo's face. "Not much of a jaunt at all. We could get there quicklike, if you got a pep in your step."

Finishing off the rest of his drink, Pat said, "Lead the way."

5.

The grogginess after over-drinking proved to be no less intense in Las Vegas.

Pat woke up in an unfamiliar bedroom, sun shafts striking through curtains, giving his pale flesh stripes reminiscent of a tiger's. He blinked once more and realized the stripes were closer to a zebra's. *Always the prey, never the hunter.*

He chuckled as he realized he was not in the bed alone.

Memories of the night before came flooding into the brain as it understood the task at hand was no longer concocting dreams but rather recollecting. Lorenzo lay beside him, his musk consuming the room, save the faintest hints of marijuana. Pat could taste that smell, amongst other things, in his mouth. He shook his head and sat up, waking up more and more as each moment passed. Then he crawled out of bed, softly treading across the carpeted floor, making his way to his clothes on a chair.

As Pat dressed, Lorenzo stirred. "Leaving so soon? You told me you wanted to go at least three times." It came out as a barely coherent mumble.

Not one to be deterred from quipping, Pat was already upon him. "Liquid courage for me, liquid luck for you. Plus, there's no reason the first night should be the last."

Lorenzo groaned before chuckling, feigning disappointment. "Fine, you go knock it out of the park, kid. Be careful, though. A lot of those club owners talk fast and over-promise. I'm sure you can take care of yourself, but keep your eyes peeled. Never know."

Thanks, say, I was meaning to ask you. Are there any bars for people like us here? Or do they pretend we don't exist out here too?"

Lorenzo took a second and huffed out a sigh as he got up from his bed. His head tilted as he contemplated what to say next. "Well, that depends. Do you want something more discrete? If so, there's a few." There was a sleepy smile on his face. "Ironically, the bar I picked you up in caters to people like us. It's just quieter about its patrons' proclivities, being in a casino and all. None of which are comedy clubs, though. Afraid you'll have to keep the jokes relegated to husbands and wives." As he padded over to his own clothes, he asked, "What is it they find humorous up there, anyway?"

Pat shrugged. "You know, toilet jokes, Nixon, Kennedy's love life. Say, I wasn't asking because I want to monologue at them. I was asking because I liked last night. Back home, I had to hide. Didn't want to get killed. Was just hoping Vegas was different."

He shuddered as he thought about what'd happened back home.

Lorenzo tugged on his pants as he said, "It's better here. Good as it can be at least." Drawing his belt through the pant loops, he added, "I'll tell you this, though. Don't matter what we do in this town. If you're with me, you're safe."

Pat raised a brow, wondering if the conviction in Lorenzo's voice was warranted or not.

"I am in waste management," the other man reminded him. "Everybody has rubbish they need to put out. Garbage to be collected. Out here in this heat? You don't want it out in the sun. They comply. Nobody gives me any trouble. Would like to say the entire city knows about me, but that could just be the ego talking."

Pat wasn't entirely convinced. Lorenzo sounded as though he had rehearsed that speech countless times before. He didn't, however, feel worried. If anything, he felt comfortable around Lorenzo, which wasn't something he was used to—especially not this soon after meeting someone. It took him a long time to trust, but perhaps Vegas was truly bringing about a new era in his life. The Patrick of Old, the skeptical and jaded one, had been left behind in Massachusetts.

Still, despite how good he felt, he couldn't get the shamrock ring out of his head. It haunted him like the image of a man floating in water, his blonde hair mimicking the ripple of kelp rooted to the seabed. Only this body was in a lake. He knew that for certain.

He looked back at Lorenzo, realizing he was waiting for Pat to say something. "I, uh, I left my car and stuff over at the Slippery Slope. Could I ask you to jaunt over there and take me back?"

"Sure thing." Lorenzo's next words were mostly said with confidence, but there was a definite hint of nerves underlying them. "You want to meet later for dinner? You know, tell me how you did at the auditions? I wouldn't say no to the company."

Pat blushed, not used to being courted. Often, he was the one who did the talking, the prodding, the inviting. The script had flipped, and he was here for the creative team's new direction.

"I'd like that. I'd like that a lot."

"Last thing before we go, Patty, I just need a favor from you."

"Sure. Just don't ask me to sort out garbage. That's what they pay you the big bucks for."

Lorenzo smirked. "Don't let those judges bring you down. Talk their ear off. You're in charge. That stage is yours." He rested a hand on Pat's shoulder, his smile growing. "Pat, the monologist. Has a nice ring to it."

* * *

Lars had been replaced with another poorly befitted Latino in Lederhosen. This one's nameplate read, "Gunther." Obviously, this place was trying too hard to immerse their patrons in the Bavarian theme. It wasn't landing how they'd hoped, but he admired their dedication to the bit.

"This city really has everything, huh?" Pat leaned against the desk. "Did Lars end his shift? Liked that kid. Big shoes to fill, Gunther. Up for the task?"

The young Latino man seemed disinterested in Pat's inquiry and just glumly nodded. "He'll be back this evening, sir. In the meantime, is there anything I can do to be of assistance?"

Pat shook his head before heading back outside toward his room.

As he pushed his door open, he couldn't help but notice how clean he had left everything. He sat on his bed, looking at himself in the mirror. There was a relaxed assuredness to his face, as though one nighttime escapade had suddenly reversed time and eroded the wrinkles of stress. He'd been running ragged for days as he trekked across the country; last night was the first time in weeks he could remember sleeping through the night. Lorenzo was either a good luck charm or Pat was more stereotypically Irish than he realized. His relatives often joked about the medicinal benefits of liquor, especially for those of the Celtic persuasion. But he'd always assumed it was just an excuse they used to get rip-roaringly drunk. He'd never considered there might be some truth to it.

He shook his head. *Nah, it's not the booze.* Between finally hearing Tommy's voice and meeting Lorenzo, he'd had a decent first day in the city; that was all.

"Let the good times roll," he murmured as he opened his suitcase, trying to find an outfit for his auditions later in the day.

Not long after scouring through his limited selection, he conceded that perhaps a shopping trip was in order. That was a problem to face tomorrow, however, as he'd managed to find an outfit he wasn't entirely dissatisfied with.

As he got ready, he looked over at his nightstand, and the matchbook with the Louie's Lounge logo emblazoned on it stared back up at him with a taunting gaze. He could feel an energy radiating from the matchbook, an aura of something that did not belong, unlike anything he'd ever experienced. When he first came into town the night before, he thought he should avoid the lounge like the plague, but now morbid curiosity set in.

"Maybe after the auditions," he decided, still nervous about the prospect.

Lit cigarette in his mouth, he went outside to his car. The red of his vehicle was dulled by the clay and dirt of the Nevada desert, a clear marker of the journey he'd taken to get there.

Pat sat in his car, psyching himself up. "It's showtime, kid. Show 'em what you got."

Looking around, he caught the silver glint of his gun from beneath the passenger seat. He looked around to ensure he wasn't being watched before bending over and pushing it further underneath to avoid being exposed. With that, he drove off to his auditions.

Vegas was a whole different place in the daytime. Gone were the neon glows and women in cocktail dresses arm in arm with men in blazers and cowboy hats. The daytime crowd looked decidedly rougher, locals who had grown disenfranchised with the rapid growth of the only place they had ever called home. Pat and his Massachusetts plates stuck out like a sore thumb, garnering dirty looks from more than one resident walking along the dusty roadway.

There amongst the locals, he found his first pit stop, his first audition. *The* Djinn's Lamp glowed in its dulled daytime glory, the gold lettering suggesting the place was rather lively at night. He pulled into the lot and momentarily stared at the doorway, taking in the scenery.

It's everything you ever wanted, right here, he reminded himself. *If you fail, it's on you. It's showtime, Pat. Dazzle them.*

He sighed before shouldering his door open, the leather beneath him squeaking as he slunk out of the car. He looked up once more at the sign for the casino, noticing the gigantic lamp. He stifled a chuckle before marching his way inside.

The atmosphere was less gluttonous than he'd envisioned, but again he had to remind himself that the city really only came alive when the sun went down. The crowds in the morning were mostly of the elderly variety playing card games. As he caught sight of a sign pointing toward the theater, he hoped whoever was in there had a good sense of humor and more vitality than the old people narrowing their eyes at him.

He had called ahead a few weeks before leaving, scheduling his audition. They seemed confident he could fit, that he *would* fit. Of course, they'd made lofty promises—their premier location, the heart of the city, full capacity shows, and crowds 24/7—all of which he'd taken with a grain of salt. While embellishment was to be expected, he could see now that they'd really oversold this place. The casino reeked of mediocrity, not allure. Still, he argued internally on their behalf, desperate for any chance. The casino was not alone in embellishing its resume. That was a dance he knew just as well.

Standing outside the theater was a doorman. He towered over the small ginger comedian. "How can I help you sir?" the doorman asked, his voice a low, deep drawl that suggested, like most of the people in town, he was an implant from somewhere else—the South, in this case.

"A few weeks ago, I called to speak to the talent manager here. We arranged for me to do a showcase for my comedy. I know you have a vacant slot for an opener on Tuesdays. Hoping I could fill that." Pat spoke with a confidence he wasn't sure he actually had.

"Okay, okay. Stay here. I need to call him down from his office, if that's okay with you. Just a moment, sir—I appreciate your patience." The man hobbled over toward what Pat assumed to be the phones.

He closed his eyes, taking in the moment. His heart was throbbing; he could feel the blood in his veins pushing its way up into his skull and back out again, a weightlessness that he could remember from half-forgotten dreams. Everything around him faded: the doorman's footsteps, the small talk from the nearby card tables, the clink of coins and the clack of chips. There was nothing but a faint whistling, like the whipping wind as his car sped along the newly minted highways of Eisenhower.

"Is he down here with us? Or is he up in the clouds?" The voice had a faint German accent.

The road cut short as Pat opened his eyes. A short, stout man stood before him, arms folded, tweed blazer creasing at the elbows, foot tapping impatiently.

Pat looked down at him and grinned. His mother used to say the best impression was always a first impression. If this guy was who he was auditioning for, he wanted to come out firing.

"Roswell's nearby," he said. "Just wanted to make sure the skies were clear. Never know when the flying saucers might come back. All clear, think I scared them away." Pat came out firing.

The German man raised a brow before letting out a light chuckle. "So, you're one of those monologists? I can't say I've heard that one before. That bodes well for you. If you don't mind, I'd like to see you do your set *off* the casino floor."

The doorman walked ahead of them before opening the door to the theater. The German man followed suit, leaving Pat to bring up the rear.

As they filed in, Pat couldn't help but notice the stage light. It shone onto a bright silver microphone attached to a stand, even in the off hours. His Excalibur beckoned him, his golden opportunity. There were other casinos he had lined up, but nothing was quite like the first. As he made his way to his stage, he looked down at the German man seated in the first row.

"Let's see what you got." His hands folded as though he was praying up toward Pat on the stage, a sort of patron saint of comedy.

St. Patrick, that's right, Pat mused. *I drove the snake from the desert, from this island of the dunes. Pray to me. This is my stage, my sermon.*

A smug smile crossed Pat's lips as he gripped the microphone stand. The energy was electric. He felt a jolt in him as he spoke.

"So, I was talking to my mother the other day...."

6.

The rest of the auditions went well—at least as far as Pat was concerned. Nobody told him it was a done deal on the spot, but he was never sure if that's how it went. It was a new world to him, yet the warmth of their smiles provided his small-town sensibilities a semblance of hope. By the time he returned to the Slippery Slope, he'd tried out at all six casinos with openings for monologists.

Lars, the first Lederhosen Latino, was back to work, Gunther evidently rotating shifts with him. Fresh off the high of his possible success, Pat let his curiosity get the better of him.

"Say," he said, strolling up to the front desk. "I don't mean to pry, but is your name really Lars? There was another gentleman of the same persuasion with the name Gunther. Now, I'm not astute regarding ethnic names, but I'm not so sure Lars is commonplace."

It was an attempt at humor, but Lars didn't laugh. He didn't even smile, just shot him a malcontented gaze, which suggested this was very much a transitionary job.

"Wow, I didn't realize Sherlock Holmes was a potato eater," Lars said, rolling his eyes. "No, my name isn't Lars. They didn't think Juancho was very...immersive."

Pat's cheeks burned, and he immediately regretted asking. It was a dumb idea, and it brought him back down from cloud nine, an earth-shattering lesson in not being invasive.

"Now, now, get it right," he playfully chided, though his tone didn't match the shame he felt inside. "I'm a whiskey drinker, not a potato eater. Clearly, I'm a city boy, not a farmer's lad."

The expression on Juancho's face eased. "I'm only teasing you; don't worry." As he started cleaning up around the desk, he said, "Hardly seen your car in the lot. You getting up to trouble?" When Pat cocked his head to the side, Juancho shrugged. "Not that it's any of my business, but I like to keep tabs on our patrons. There's a lot of shady dealings that go on in this city."

Pat raised a brow. Juancho brought up a good point. He'd heard rumblings of Vegas' seedy underbelly, how it was more pronounced than at first glance, and the car he'd seen on the way in only hammered that home.

"Thanks for that," he said, "but I'm not one to get involved in those kinds of things. I just tell jokes and sip martinis. A marginal existence all around."

Juancho considered him for a moment, then said, "In a city like this, even the best laid plans go astray. Just...watch yourself. That's all. And if you need anything, you know where to find me."

Pat left Lars/Juancho to his work. Looking at his watch, he realized it was nearly five o'clock. He needed to call Tommy and keep him updated on the auditions. It was good to hear a familiar voice, someone who he didn't need to keep the mask on with. The phone rang as he eagerly awaited hearing from the man on the other side of the country.

"Hello? Brunwell residence."

The voice cut through the static as if he were in the room with Tommy, cutting up a steak while they chatted over a beer. With closed eyes, Pat could picture it now, another dream of a summer where the hot air stuck to skin, unlike this dry place, where he forced himself to slosh down water after water because dehydration crept in like a snake on the side of a desert road.

"It's me. Pat."

"Thought it might be." There was a smile in the man's voice. "How are you?"

"I think the auditions went well. They told me they'd be in touch, so I gave them the name of the hotel I was at. Think I may even hear back tomorrow."

"Hey, that's great."

"How are you, Tommy? I can't imagine much has changed over there."

There was a pause on the other end of the line, then, "Nothing for you to worry about, kid, just the usual sniffing around. Denise went off and blamed the department for it. They have some grudge from when they both played baseball for the Gaels back in high school." Pat tried to get a word in edgewise, but Tommy barreled on. "It's nonsense, of course. We know what happened. Doesn't matter. Fewer eyes on us, the better."

"Yeah," Pat said, filling the brief silence that followed.

"Glad you're doing okay, Patty," Tommy said gently, though his tone turned a little scolding as he added, "I will say, though, don't make these late-night conversations a habit. Whole city is out there, just within your grasp. Take advantage of your youth. No reason to be locked up inside chasing ghosts. You know?"

Pat looked at the corner of his room. The curtain rippled as though someone had touched it. He shook his head before responding.

"Me? Chasing Ghosts? Ain't no such thing, Tommy. Just wanted to let you know how I did."

" I am glad you got out of Clinton. It's a beautiful little town, but you belong in the hubbub. Say, did you meet Dean Martin while you were out and about?"

"I auditioned at his casino, can't say I'll get it."

"If you do, make sure you tell him Tommy Brunwell of Clinton, Mass named a sandwich after him at his delicatessen."

They both laughed, then Pat promised, "If they let me in, I'll be sure to give him and the whole Rat Pack a wheel of cheese."

With that, Pat hung up, feeling little need to exchange goodbyes. He was always more of a 'See you later' type of personality, anyway. He made his way to his window. In the future, he could imagine this would be a high rise, like the ones he saw in New York when he visited as a child. However, that dream was far away. Instead, he looked out at a strip of road on ground level, cars passing by in a blur, only the trails of red lights fading in the distance until the next bullet whizzed by.

***

The neon glow of hotel signs advertising hotels lined both sides of the road. The red lights of the Slippery Slope's sign coated Pat's skin in its cotton candy glow, only the shadows of surrounding cacti breaking the illusionary transformation of his flesh.

"You always stare at the sky like that?" someone asked. "So forlornly?"

Pat blinked, just noticing Lorenzo standing outside his car, leaning against the hood. The red of the neon lit his olive skin up, too, making him look decidedly sinister with the grin playing on his lips.

"I guess I never noticed the stars like that," Pat said. "You can see them back home easily enough, but the trees hide the full view. Out here? Nothing. Nothing in the way. It's hypnotic, a sea of stars, and we're just floating in it. Wonder what that Yuri guy saw when he looked down back at Earth."

"The Soviet?" Lorenzo quirked an amused smile at him. "You really are a deep thinker. He probably saw red, just like that neon sign. That's all they see over there—red. You need a drink, carrying the world's burdens like that."

"You think so? I'm not convinced they're all that different from us. McCarthy be damned, I say. There's got to be more to life than all that. Floating out in an ocean of celestial blackness, and we're more worried about who can build a bigger bomb. Silly when you take a step back." He rambled on, but his mind was firmly thinking of Randy floating away at the bottom of the deep body of water. He wondered if maggots would take root in the water.

No, fish. They'd eat him up, an easy meal. I wish he was buried. Those eyes...I can't get them out of my head. He tried to erase the imagery from his mind, but it wouldn't entirely go away.

"Come on, now, no need to be dour. You did well today. I can tell," Lorenzo said, thankfully unable to read his mind. "And you're not wrong. In a country like this, coloreds can't even use the same bathrooms as the whites. Somehow, we can't solve that and are more worried about...bombs? Feels all upside down. I don't know the answers." Standing upright, Lorenzo gestured for Pat to follow him. "Shit, let's get a drink in. I'd rather have a gin or two in me before I get the moxie to talk about the big picture issues."

Pat soon found himself in Lorenzo's car, brushing his fingers along the dashboard, finding the upholstery therapeutic. Lorenzo turned the key, and the engine roared to life, the sickly red of the neon lightning washed out by the bright beams of his headlights. He pulled out onto the roadway, lighting a cigarette with his free hand.

"How do you feel?" Lorenzo asked. "Is it what you thought it would be? Is it what you hoped it would be? Are they both the same?"

Pat thought about it for a moment. "Not sure. Never thought this would happen, that I'd be here, chasing my dreams."

"You strike me as an idealist, Pat. Nothing wrong with it. Vegas leaves you feeling like the world is at your fingertips."

As kind as Lorenzo was, Pat knew he had his own angle for being so complimentary—namely, lust. Which was fine by him. And it didn't stop him from saying what was on his mind. If anything, it encouraged him. No reason to play hard to get when he wanted to be had.

"I didn't know what to expect," Pat admitted, watching the city out the window without really taking it in. "Lived my whole life before this, expecting and preparing for anything. Now? Now, I know it doesn't matter. What's going to happen is going to happen. You just do your best to not get caught up in the moment, low or high."

Pat could sense that Lorenzo was processing, but finally, he said, "Never thought about it like that, you know. Think I've always sort of lived in the moment. We're Depression babies, you and I, so already we had the deck stacked against us. But my cousin? She lived through the Dust Bowl. Her parents caught that dust pneumonia, and she had to move in with us when they died. Things were tight as it was with Arizona being in the desert and all. We got some food from California, but everything was running real light in stores. Back then, all we could do was get caught up in the moment."

They drove in silence a little longer, Pat not knowing how to respond to that.

Eventually, Lorenzo spoke again. "Taking a step back, is...it's scary. I'm just another man, just another soul. Nothing special, and that...that's terrifying." He laughed sheepishly. "Just wanted to catch a drink, but you have a way of coaxing the truth out of a man."

"Didn't mean to. Being here makes me look at everything. This is what I want. I want it more than anything. I'd do anything to get it. You know how that is, to want something, to yearn for it." Pat felt the car slow down as Lorenzo parked outside the same casino where they'd met the night prior.

Instead of getting out of the car, Lorenzo looked over at him, his expression somewhere between troubled and pleasantly surprised. "You know, I've seen a lot of men in my day, Pat. I don't think any ever made me think about it all quite like you. And only after knowing you for all, what, one day? It's different. New. I appreciate that. More than I used to." Before Pat could reply, Lorenzo popped open his door, saying simply, "Let's drink."

And so they did.

7.

Exhaustion was setting in. Given how late he and Lorenzo had been up the night before, Pat requested to be dropped off at home after a few hours of drinking. He was back in the neon red, Lorenzo giving him a hug and kiss on the neck goodbye.

"I have a late shift tomorrow," Lorenzo said. "Unexpected issues. So I won't be around tomorrow night. Will you be fine without your local guide? Will you be able to find your way to the tacos?" When Pat blushed, Lorenzo chuckled. "Speechless? That's a first, Pat."

Pat was all too aware of how his mouth never stopped moving. It was no different from his brain. "I think I'll be fine, but if that changes, you'll be the first to know."

Their lips turned upward in a shared smile, and Lorenzo said his goodbyes. Before long, he was nothing more than a speck down the road, with only the faintest hint of cologne clinging to the cool, dry air.

Pat made his way into the hotel. The lobby was empty, no Gunther or Lars that he could see. In fact, when he thought about it, he hadn't even seen any other guests since he had been dropped off. That didn't bother him much, but the hairs on his neck still stood up.

"Maybe the UFOs are real," he whispered to himself as he waddled toward his room.

When he was a kid, he'd be locked out of the house often, parents arguing, trying to keep the kids away from the nastiness of their economic woes. The result left little patterns of behavior. For Pat, he'd always tug subconsciously on a door, regardless of if he had known it was locked or not. He knew he locked it this morning and knew housekeeping hadn't been by, as that cost extra. Yet, when he pulled the knob, it gave way. A pit dropped in his stomach, and suddenly he could feel his heart pumping, a shiver running up his back as he stepped away.

A voice crept out from the opening underneath the door. "Go on, come in. If you were going to be harmed, it would've already happened."

Pat blinked, wishing he'd taken his gun inside with him. He shook his head, trying to figure out what to do next.

"I am not going to ask again, Patrick." The voice was deep, flat, and matter-of-fact. The lack of inflection made it all the more horrifying to him. "Like I said, if you were in danger, it'd have been over by now."

Pat tentatively opened the door and stepped inside, then turned toward where the voice was coming from.

The man resting on his bed was completely bald, with no eyebrows or hair. His brow jutted out, his eyes sinking back into his skull, brown orbs that portrayed no emotion, cold and detached. His black suit draped over his body. It looked too big for him, which was peculiar, as the man was not frail and, instead, almost inhumanly muscular.

Despite his fear—or, maybe, because of it—Pat did what he always did. "Can I help you? You don't appear to be room service, but who knows? Maybe the staff changed uniforms before I went out to drink."

The man didn't react to Pat's joke. Instead, he stood up, the bed making a loud creak as it was relieved of the task of bearing the mountain of a man's weight.

"I do not require your help, but I know someone who does." Pat gulped, holding on to every word as the man went on.

"He saw you in the desert, stopping on the side of the road. Dozens of cars drove past that burning wreckage. You were the only one who stopped. Why is that?"

The man shifted his weight. Only then did Pat notice the firearm resting in the man's waistband. Pat gazed at the glint of metal before replying.

"I wanted to help. That's what good people do."

He knew there was little he could do to avoid getting shot. He was firmly entrenched in the trap. Yet, he sensed that despite all the fear tactics, the man who'd broken in wanted something deeper.

The man closed his eyes, nodding as though replaying Pat's answer repeatedly, as though he were analyzing each word. After half a minute, he seemed satisfied because his eyes opened, and he continued enigmatically, "Pure of heart? No, no, there are skeletons in your closet. Secrets you've buried. Regardless, I have come to you with a proposition, an offer."

Pat stared into the hairless man's stone gaze, trying to understand what exactly he was dealing with. If this guy knew about the car, was he the one who'd left that matchbook? "You're with Louie's Lounge? What is this? Extortion?"

"Extortion? No, no, we want our secrets kept. You want to be a monologist, a comedian. It is a natural fit. We give you the stage you clamor for, and the loose ends are tied. It needn't be difficult."

"That sounds lovely, but I already have opportunities." Pat kept his eyes on the man and, specifically, his gun, as he cautiously worked his way over to the dresser and leaned up against it. "I auditioned today for several places. It went well—extremely well. I don't think I'll need your offer. But I won't say anything about what I saw out there. There's a code, right? I respect that code."

The man looked at him, squinting. He reached for his gun but stopped short, his lips turning into a forced smile. "Is that so? Well, I implore you to come down to Louie's Lounge. About eleven. When you get there, ask for Hyland. We will be waiting for you."

Pat didn't like his smile. It suggested he knew something Pat didn't. "Did you not hear me? I told you I already auditioned. Anytime now, I'll be getting offers."

The man stood up, looking down at Pat, his unnaturally tall height causing his head to scrape against the ceiling. "Well, this town has a way of giving people false hope. If it doesn't work out...you know where to find us. We will wait."

Before Pat could respond, the man walked out of the room, craning his neck as he squeezed to fit through the doorway and shutting the door behind him.

His jaw still agape and his skin turning a bright, flustered pink, Pat dashed out into the hall. There was no sign of the man he'd just encountered, even as he paced up and down the hall, peering into alcoves and doorways. His thoughts raced as he ran back into his hotel room. *What the hell? That ain't normal. I knew something was up with the lounge. Never ignore your gut, Pat. It knows, even if you don't.*

His first urge was to leave and check in somewhere else, anywhere else, or maybe just leave the city entirely. But he stood in the middle of his room, his body not cooperating with his scattered mind. "They'd just find me, anyway.

Ain't no escaping. I'm not running. I earned this. I deserve this." Hearing the words said out loud instead of thinking them gave him reassurance.

As he turned toward his nightstand, he noticed there was a new set of matches sitting by the phone, *Louie's Lounge* imprinted on them in bright red lettering. However, upon closer inspection, he also saw a glint of green behind the phone, and the specter of fear swelled in his chest and down his spine.

There was a finger, a gold ring resting above the knuckle, and a bright emerald-encrusted shamrock staring back at him, each gem serving as a pupil. He could see himself in the crystals, fear gazing back at him. It was then he noticed dust caked on the finger.

"Did they...did they dig him up?"

There were no answers from the room, not that it mattered. It wouldn't change what was in front of him. He could hear chatter in the hall and quickly realized his room door was still ajar. He ran to shut it. The last thing he needed was someone to see the ring and conflate him with the one who had done the deed.

Should I call Tommy? What could he even do? No, if they wanted to harm me, they'd have done it already. I'd already be gone. They want me. I don't know why, but they want me. I need to get to sleep. I can tell Lorenzo tomorrow. He'll know what to do.

Pat wasn't entirely convinced by his own words, but there was little recourse to be had in the immediate. Tomorrow, all he would need was one call. It would change everything.

He quickly opened his nightstand drawer and grabbed the finger. It was cold, but he noticed it had been cleaned, the flesh devoid of dried blood. He'd dispose of it tomorrow; he couldn't risk running into the tall man if he was waiting outside for him. Slipping the finger inside and shutting the drawer, he moved toward the curtains. He pushed them to the side, his view of the road unobstructed from his room.

That night when he went to turn the light off, he was struck with a terror he thought he'd left behind in his youth. A younger Patrick hated the dark. He was always afraid of it, always afraid of who could be there. It wasn't until his father was awoken in the middle of the night by his pre-adolescent wails that he got a grip on it. His father was an abrupt man of few words, but that night, despite the lack of sleep, he was the opposite. He sat with Patrick, the moon illuminating his childhood room, basking disregarded toys and hardwood floors with its glow.

"Nothing to be afraid of in the dark besides our imagination," his father had said. "The real monsters come out in the daytime, wear suits, and shake your hand. They smile at you and nod, but the warmth of their palms is absent. You're just another person, just another obstacle to them." As Patrick pondered this, his father had added, "The decent people? They're in the madhouse, they know, it's all a game, Pat. We play the game, but we constantly lose. We always lose. The good men? They're all gone. The monsters sleep at night, just like you and me."

Even at Patrick's young age, he'd known it wasn't about him. It was at that moment he realized the world was so much more than the shadows in the corner of the room. Nightmares meant little when reality settled in, and even if he didn't know what his dad meant, he knew his dad was trying to connect. He never understood his worldview. Nobody in his life had. His father would die soon after.

Even Patrick's mom knew little of what ailed Patrick, Senior, writing off his rants as a by-product of what he'd seen in France while serving in the war. Patrick never argued with her about it, but instead spent more time with his father's best friend, Tommy Brunwell, the owner of the local deli. The man acted as the only uncle Pat had ever known and stepped in to do his best to approximate a father figure.

Pat found himself smoking a cigarette now, watching the cars pass by in the desert night, each with their own story left unshared, unknown to either the occupants or the observers. The buildings didn't change the desolate landscape surrounding them, instead serving only as a distraction.

"I ain't in the madhouse, Dad. Guess that makes me a bad man. Guess that makes me one of the men in the suits. Does daytime change if the lights never go out? It's never dark here. Either it's light or bright. I wish you could see it. You and Mom." He took another puff as he stopped talking, opting to sit in silence as his mind wandered.

It didn't take long for his thoughts to drift toward Randy. The man floated at the bottom of the reservoir, a soulless husk, no different than he'd been in life, really, in Pat's approximation. He closed his eyes. The red of the neon sign outside glowed on him as he took in deep breaths. At that moment, he could feel every part of himself, a rare slice of nirvana for a man more concerned with the performative than the introspective.

"Just one call, all I need. Good man or bad man, everyone loves a redemption story."

He took another puff of his cigarette as he watched life go on in front of him, his windowpane serving as the theater screen of the gods, a tapestry showcasing the vibrancy of degeneracy that overtook Sin City. Little did they know St. Patrick was watching in silent judgment, taking in all their misdeeds, their conversations, the words not mattering all that much. Anything to distract from the growing pit in his stomach that whatever came tomorrow would define him for the rest of his days.

He was right.

8.

The phone rang multiple times, yet each time the voice on the other end started the conversation with the same guilt-ridden tone.

"You're great Pat, it's just...we don't know if you'd be a fit for us."

Some would offer to let him try again during the next audition cycle, others not so much. He felt dejected at first, but that quickly turned to rage.

Pat was a sincere man; his timid nature had oft been mistaken for weakness. But if Louie's Lounge had scared off his potential suitors, there would be hell to pay. He debated asking Lorenzo, but when he took a step back, he realized that, as much as he cared about the other man, he didn't really know him. It settled in for him. He didn't know *anyone* there. It was a strange, foreign place, where even the sturdiest of beasts could be left to die in the heat, alone and isolated.

The urge to call Tommy was immense, but he refrained. *Clean your own mess, Pat. He can't do anything else for you. Go down there. They know you'll be coming. It's not a trap. You wouldn't have woken up if they wanted you dead this morning.* While the thought was unsettling, there was a strange reassurance in the fact that he was still breathing. They wanted more from him. He intended to find out exactly what that was.

As Pat made his way into the lobby, he saw Lars at the desk, the ever-reliable Lederhosen looking particularly disheveled today, as though he had rolled out of bed and immediately made his way to the Slippery Slope.

Lars turned to him, his gaze hovering before he smiled. "Hello, Patrick. How are you doing today?"

"Doing swell. Have a few more comedy clubs to hit today." Pat's voice was coated with a sugary sweetness reminiscent of artificiality. "Say, you told me Louie's Lounge is the biggest spot in town. Where about is that in relation to here?"

Lars, the Lederhosen Latino, looked him up and down, his brow raised, then said, "Sure, when you pull out of the lot, take a left. Second stop sign, take the right. Should be three blocks down from there. Can't miss it. Black and red on the outside. Parking is across the way. It should be fine."

Pat rubbed his eyes as if to wipe away the stress and mentally stored the directions.

"Are you alright?" Lars asked. "Look like you didn't sleep much."

"Your rooms are the lap of luxury," Pat assured him. "The peak of relaxation. I'm so well rested, I look as though I am exhausted. It's called Horseshoe Theory, Lars; I suppose it's true after all."

The words were there, but the usual injection of levity was not. His voice was devoid of its typical joy, replaced with contemptuous scorn. He was a man on the warpath, hunting down answers.

Lars offered a smile. "Well, let me know if you have an issue. I don't want you getting caught up in anything." As he turned back to whatever he'd been doing, he added, "Take care, potato eater, be safe."

Pat made his way to his car in a bit of a huff. *Could've stopped that bastard from waiting for me in my room. That would've been a good start. Hell, a great start.*

His gun was under the passenger seat of his car. He lunged for it, then double-checked to make sure it was still loaded. After confirming this, he tucked it into his belt before backing out of his parking spot.

His car pushed itself down the sleepy road, the sun hovering above, but the people slept late into the day, recovering from another night of gluttony. Normally, he would be at his best, reality having not eroded his burgeoning optimism upon waking up. Last night, however, he'd barely slept, passing out only after his eyes could no longer hold the massive weight of their lids. Even then, it was merely a brief respite before morning came and he returned to Las Vegas, a place that was once a dream but rapidly becoming a nightmare.

He found Louie's Lounge, the trademark red and black exterior giving no clues as to what he could expect within its walls. It fancied itself to be something akin to a cathedral, perhaps the flair of the Italians inside. He had seen enough of their churches to know how theatrical their architectural displays could be. He rapidly pulled into the lot across the street from it.

No doorman, he noticed. *Not that I'd expect one this time of day. More likely to encounter migrant laborers than charlatans who fancy themselves to be royalty. We all have dreams, and this place is trying to take mine away. No, no, I will fix it. I will show them.*

Slamming his car door shut but paying the solid industrial thud no mind, he darted across the empty road toward the entrance.

Outside the lounge, numerous cigarette butts and trails of ash showed where boots stomped them out before moving about their day. In front of him was a large wooden door, brown with gold plating at the bottom, perhaps to avoid scuff marks from the constant flow of patrons. There was a mosaic on each side of the door, stained glass painting indiscernible shapes that took on a life of their own.

He didn't care to parse through the imagery of the red and orange stained glass. Instead, he rapped his knuckles on the door. When no one answered, he tried again, banging with more vigor and ignoring the mild pain arcing through his fingers. Then he took a step back from the door and waited a moment.

It wasn't long before somebody answered: a woman opened the door, also hairless, save for her long eyelashes, which shielded her bright blue eyes from the harsh sun. She squinted as though stepping foot outside was a heinous act in itself.

"Patrick Gallagher?"

He didn't question how she knew his name, just asked, "Where is Hyland? I was told to come here today to speak to someone by that name."

The bald woman squinted no longer and simply walked back inside, shutting the door and leaving Pat on the steps of Louie's Lounge. He could hear the shuffling of feet from the other side before a familiar sinister face opened the door.

The tall man from his room the night prior stood in the doorway, his sunken features twisting into an artificial smile. One performer to another, just catering to different crowds. "I knew you'd come but didn't know you'd be so early. Full of surprises, aren't you?"

"So, you're Hyland?" Pat flashed his own fake smile.

But the tall bald man shook his head. "No, I am not. My colleague, Rosaline, mentioned you were here. Thought a familiar face would soften your edge. But...even I am wrong sometimes. Please, come in."

Pat's mind hovered over the idea of pulling out his firearm and showing how rough the edge had become. The impulse, however, went nowhere. No reason to harm the pawn when he had yet to meet the person moving the pieces on the chessboard. He was going for the king.

Pat stepped inside, and Rosaline shut the door behind them. *So, this is Las Vegas' premier club, huh?* It wasn't hard for him to see why; the outside had led him to believe it was unimpressive, but the interior was anything but. The central corridor of the club was below ground level. A staircase descended toward a dance pit. Railings circled around the ring of the hole, creating a second level with bars and seating on the outskirts, forming a two-level bar that felt alien to Pat. The stool seats a bright red leather, while the steel backs were a dark black with the faintest traces of metallic shine bouncing off the edison bulbs overlaid above their heads. He had never seen anything like it. It reminded him of the Springfield Armory he had visited as a kid, its industrial bones repurposed for entertainment. The metalwork along the railings formed shapes of animals that only existed in the pages of a fable.

"Down into the pit," the tall, hairless man said. "The offices are down there."

He pointed at a second staircase that descended into the dance pit. Pat nodded and made his way down. Neon-red lighting covered the entire floor, which was pristine. Even after a long night of clubbing, there was little sign of mess.

Pat made his way across the lit glass floor, dulled by the trickles of sunlight coming from the windows above, a reminder that even in the dark hellish pit, there was still light just waiting to burst in. The tall man closed the gap between him and his esteemed guest.

"To the right, another staircase to the offices."

Pat caught sight of the glint of a lit cigarette behind the dancing-level bar to his left. A man in a silver suit puffed on a cigar, only traces of his stubble-scruffed face visible with each pulsating light change. Pat blinked, and next, he saw a noseless man staring at him, a familiar blonde mop obstructing his eyes. With a second blink, it was gone, replaced with the smoking man, as though he had imagined it altogether.

Pat's guide clasped his shoulder now, causing him to nearly jump out of his skin. *Just an illusion, Pat,* he assured himself. *Ain't nothing more than shaky nerves.*

"Let's keep moving," the tall man said. "Plenty of time to take it in later."

"Yeah, sorry." Pat grimaced. "It's just a lot to take in. Never seen a place like it."

Within moments, they had left the central artery and entered a much more mundane subterranean floor. It resembled the parlor of a funeral home, seemingly full of warmth on the surface but, with further inspection, devoid of authentic personality. The tall, hairless man knocked on the door of an office that said "Hyland" on a bronze nameplate across the front.

The door opened instantly, as though Hyland had been waiting behind it the entire time. Pat eyed the staircase, trying to calculate the distance he needed to run in case things went badly. His eyes made their way back to the door, getting his first glimpse of the man he was here to see.

Hyland had long hair, a ponytail neatly braided to his hip, but no beard, mustache, or eyebrows. He was a man of some stature. That much was clear.

"Mr. Gallagher. Name's Hyland." His voice came out deep, rolling, and regal. "I'm the talent manager here at Louie's Lounge. Please, come in."

As the tall, hairless man left, Pat stepped into an office that felt more of its time. Hyland sat across from him at his desk, straightening his black tie, then wiped off the shoulders of his blazer before folding his hands, his ring-laden fingers clinking as gold rings brushed against each other, diamonds glinting in the low light of his lamp.

"So, you know what we are, what we are capable of. Are you willing to talk business?"

Pat kept his voice level. "You killed a man. Right hand to God, I won't say anything to anybody else, but I know what I saw. I stopped on my way in to make sure he was okay. He wasn't, and that ain't no fault of mine. Do you think you can make an example of molesting me? That I'm going to cave to your harassment?" He folded his arms, a smug look on his face.

Hyland raised his eyebrows, almost in amusement. "Haven't you? You're here, aren't you? Like my colleague Samuel said, you fit what we need, Pat. We need a monologist. You won't get a gig anywhere else in town. This is it; this is your shot. You should take it."

"Or else what?" Pat snorted. "You're going to bury me? No, you'd sooner leave the vultures to pick off the leftovers. I knew the Mob was sketchy, that you did some underhanded things. But aren't you also men of God? Don't you have any faith? Any humanity?"

Hyland chuckled at this, slinking back into his seat and eyeing Pat's waist. "Pat, do men of God come to a meeting with a revolver tucked into their belt? Hypocrite. You come in here playing the tough guy, but you're too earnest for that. But sure, you got some moxie; you got some edge. Did you think you were going to come in here and kill me?" He smirked. "No, I don't think even *you* believe that. You've been made to live a lie. It's natural to be guarded in your position."

"Why me? Why not any of the other comedians in town? I don't deserve this; I don't deserve blackmail or extortion."

"There's more to you than meets the eye, Pat. There are some secrets left in you." When Pat flinched, Hyland waved a dismissive hand. "I'm not talking about you being a homosexual. That doesn't bother us. It doesn't bother me. But the people here...well, they won't hire you—self-indulgent zealotry, as it were. Why do you think they called you back so soon? It's not because of your talent. You have it, kid. This town will hire Nazis and war criminals before it'll hire a queer. So, tell me, who is the good man here? Tell me, who is the righteous one?"

As Hyland went on, Pat felt his heart swell with fear, which was quickly replaced with rage. He could sense Hyland was telling the truth, even if it was angled for his own benefit.

Sighing, Pat said, "So, you want me to do stand-up at your club? In trade, for what? Keeping your secrets? What's the catch? Because if that was it, you wouldn't have gone through the hoops you did. You'd have just called me up, just spoke to me man-to-man."

"Louie has a flair for theatrics," Hyland explained, though it didn't really explain anything. "I suppose he wanted to see what you would do. Bringing a gun...well, that's bold. He must see something in you beyond doing a little jig and hollerin' on stage. Must see those secrets you think are so well hidden behind that innocent mask you put on. No stranger to getting your hands dirty?"

"I know you mobsters love to hide in ambiguity. Stop dancing around it. What exactly do you want me to do?"

Pat shifted in his seat, and he realized how clammy he felt. He was nervously sweating, unsure how much they knew. He was locked in a high-stakes poker game without understanding what his own hand was. Hyland shook his head; Pat had decided there was something different about him. The others tried to exert their will by fear. Hyland did not seem to embrace this notion.

Hyland spread his hands in front of him. "Everything has a price. It's not always apparent at first, but everything has a price. Call it debt collection, call it muscle, whichever lets you sleep at night. Assuming you still sleep at night, knowing what you did."

Pat's heart skipped a beat, his mind drifting back to Randy, his floating corpse becoming increasingly bloated in his vision, almost impossibly engorged. Had he been any more swollen, he'd have floated to the top of the reservoir.

Does he know? There's no way. Unless...maybe they bugged my phone. I heard Hoover does that to Reds. If he can do it, the Mob can't be far behind.

Pat looked into Hyland's eyes. There was a man behind them. They didn't feel lifeless. They didn't glaze over like those of a serpent. He wasn't sure why snakes came to mind, but he couldn't help but feel like he was in the viper pit. "So, the price for my opportunity, the price for my dream, is becoming your muscle?"

"Isn't that what you want most? To see your dream come true? If I were you, I'd take the trade-off. Being in debt? That's a far worse fate, one I've seen many, many times. Look, we'll give you an opportunity for a year, you do a few jobs, you keep your mouth shut unless there's a silver microphone staring back at you on a stage. We all leave better for it." Hyland spoke as though Pat had already decided. There wasn't much of a choice, really: success or obscurity.

Pat mulled in the silence. He hadn't risked giving failure more than a passing thought. He'd do anything to avoid that and make Tommy and his mother proud.

"A trade," he said finally. "It's a trade. Fair work for fair pay. And I don't have much of a choice."

Pat offered his hand out to Hyland. The man's face snarled into a sinister smile as he gripped the Irishman's hand. A mix of regret and the prospect of the future stirred in Pat's stomach as he locked eyes with Hyland, taking in his face more clearly. He was Native American, a rarity in the underworld, unheard of in Boston as far Pat knew.

"Sounding like a commie, are we?" Hyland's smile was no less unnerving. "Don't worry, I won't hold it against you. When can you start? We have an open slot tonight, even. No time like the present. What's done is done."

Pat let go of Hyland's hand as he shifted to stand-up. "Tomorrow? Can I do it tomorrow? I haven't—last night was hardly a proper night's sleep. Your friend left me quite restless." Pat feigned a smile, a convergence of conflicting emotions playing on his face.

Hyland stood up now as well, lighting a cigarette as he did so. "What's a day between friends? Go get some rest, Pat. Tomorrow, your dreams become a reality."

With that, Hyland opened the door to his dungeon office. Pat turned to make his way out without saying another word. As he ascended to the dance pit, he noticed some signs of life, revelers starting to spill in for the day. To his right was a doorway, and the flashing lights suggested this was where the casino portion of the establishment was. To his left was the same man in the silver suit. The cigar had been replaced with a drink. He sat at a table, stone-faced, but his gaze was fixated upon the redheaded comedian.

You've gambled enough today, Pat thought. *They want you to think you've won. But I don't know. It sure feels like a loss.*

His feet clamored forward until he found himself outside, never so grateful in his life to feel the sun kiss his flesh. He wasn't sure how long he had been inside, but the city had undoubtedly become livelier in that time. The streets were bustling, conversing, and smoke filled the air alongside the rumbling of passing engines from the roadway.

Las Vegas had been a beacon of hope just a few days prior. But as he started his car, he couldn't help but feel it was nothing more than a mirage now, a pitiful place where dreams went to die. Where *his* dreams went to die.

Yet, the other side of his brain argued the opposite. *You're going to do it. It might not be how you hoped, but it's happening. You'll have the stage, Pat. Isn't this what you always wanted? Respect? You'll have it both ways. Nobody crosses the Mob. Nobody crosses you.*

He drove back toward his hotel, not far from Louie's Lounge. The engine purred, but that wasn't why he felt powerful. "There are worse places to be than looking in from the other side of the glass. They don't care I am a homosexual; they don't care who I sleep with, who I love. Maybe they're not on the up and up, but they'll give me an opportunity. Nobody will be fixing to speak any type of way to me. I'm protected now." Pat was speaking to himself out loud, convincing himself, like many others, that somehow, he was making the only choice that made sense.

His car pulled into the Slippery Slope as he looked up at the neon sign, only the slightest hints of pink showing in the daylight as it neutered the otherwise overwhelming spectacle of light. "Damned if I do, damned if I don't. I'll give them a year. That's all I need, just one year, and I'll be free. I'll be so big, I'll be undeniable. Won't need no backroom wheelin' and dealin' then."

With that, the growing doubt had been stifled. A decision was made, and for the first time in his life, he had agency.

9.

His first month went better than Pat could've imagined. He and Lorenzo had become more serious, and Pat found himself splitting the time between the Slippery Slope and his lover's place. It wasn't that Pat couldn't have afforded more, but the Slope had become his home. He'd even convinced the staff at the hotel to turn out to a show of his.

Hyland was seldom seen besides dispersing a paycheck, a reminder of the literal backroom deal Pat had verbally signed up for. He waited for the day they'd task him with a job, anything related to their organization, but it hadn't yet come. Weeks passed, and there wasn't even a hint of the sinister side of Louie's Lounge nor a trace of what they were capable of.

"You're a natural, kid," Hyland told him after his third show. "Never had a doubt in my mind. Told you we have an eye for talent. The year will fly by in absolutely no time."

Pat's jitters were still on full display, but the crowd seemed to guffaw at his distress, though it was all part of the act. Pat had done this tap dance for most of his life, playing off his awkwardness as intentional charm. What was fifteen more minutes in front of a paying crowd?

One night, Lorenzo and Pat found themselves in a crowded bar, watching a few men in suits playing pool. "Summer's nearly over. Still amazed you did so well in the heat. I would've figured you'd have had at least one sunburn. That fair skin is deceptive," Lorenzo said, trying his hand at humor as he sipped his Manhattan slowly.

Pat smiled. "They don't tell you that Dublin was built in a desert. We only made it green through hard work and ingenuity. Arizona could take a lesson or two from us."

The retort left a mirthfully graceful smirk on Lorenzo's face. Pat returned to observing the room, a poker game happening on the other side of the bar.

"I will pass that on to the folks," Lorenzo joked. "I've been meaning to ask you. Why are you still at that hotel? It isn't bad. It's a good place to crash while you get settled in, but don't you want a house, somewhere to call your own? I don't mind cooking for you, but I'm starting to worry you can't work a stove." Humor was always coated with a bit of the truth.

With a shrug, Pat said, "Truthfully, I'm comfortable there. My whole life, it was the same faces and places. There? My neighbors change if I don't like them. They'll burn through their cash and return home by the week's end." Upon arriving, Vegas had thrown him a few curveballs, but the Slippery Slope was his rock. It was his oasis, a constant he could rely on.

His other constant, Lorenzo, now whiffed his drink before taking another sip. "That lounge, though," he pressed. "They're paying you a pretty penny. I know a few other entertainers. They aren't making the bread you are. A few more months of that may even buy a house outright." He looked thoughtful for a moment, then said, "I can't figure out how they did it. That place was nothing a year ago. Now? It's the hottest club in the whole city. Heard rumors Elvis was there last week. Elvis! Just incredible luck."

It's the Mob, Lorenzo, Pat thought. *They don't need luck. They've got cash to burn. Need to spend money to make money. Ain't that how it goes?*

Outwardly, Pat shrugged before chuckling weakly. "Everyone comes here thinking they're lucky. If I had a nickel every time someone told me I had the luck of the Irish...let's just say I'd be in Hollywood, taking in the limelight like Jerry Lewis, only better. I don't have luck. I have hard work. That's all I've ever had. I'm sure Louie's Lounge works hard, too. They have good talent, like me."

Lorenzo looked down at his glass. It was clear he had something he wanted to say, but he just smirked instead. "Just the start for you, I can tell. You know, we should probably get going. I have a shift tomorrow, early. You have your show in the evening. Got to get your practice in. I'll be there, always." Lorenzo rubbed Pat's back as he stood up, throwing a ten-dollar bill at the bartender before making his way to the door. Pat stood to follow him but took a moment, admiring his stride and rear end.

"There's more to him," someone said. "Not my business what homosexuals do, but Lorenzo, he's got himself a reputation."

Pat turned to the voice that had spoken; it was the bartender. He grimaced, hearing the label out loud. They were no different from any other couple that came to the casino to drink. That unto itself should've sufficed to stifle meddling, but there was always that asterisk at the end of every proclamation, nothing new to him, even if an unjust burden.

"Yeah? I'd tread carefully. Otherwise you'll find yourself with a reputation. What did you want to say about him?"

Pat scanned his eyes, his buzz gone, crashing back to the reality of sobriety in a graceless fashion. He stood tall and squared, his body language suggesting he was ready for confrontation. Mild-mannered Patrick had taken a step back for Pat, the Vegas monologist, who took lightly to very little.

"Ask yourself, all the times you've been to his house, you ever see anything that leads you to think he's a rubbish man? Does he come off to you like a man who handles trash?" He was flustered, his words rapidly coming out all at once. "I'm not trying to start trouble with you, but there's more to him than meets the eye. Figured you, of all people, should know."

Pat shook his head, but the truth was, he *had* thought about it. Lorenzo seemed to have a lot of money for someone in waste management. His house was almost *too* big. That didn't change anything, though. He still had affection for Pat. They spent damn near every night together.

Pat scoffed. "So? Don't all of us have things others shouldn't know? We all have our rights to secrets; he's no different."

"Just keep your eyes open. This city has a way of blinding people, even when the truth is right in front of them."

Pat laughed at that one. Even a few weeks ago, he would've shared that thought. Not anymore. "People are blinded by their own choices," he said. "You see what you want to until it's undeniable. Then you blame the situation. You blame the town or everyone else. But deep down? You know, you saw it coming. You just didn't care. I think we're going to find a new bar."

Lorenzo was waiting for Pat outside, lighting up a cigarette. "What did the Bartender want? I saw him call you over when we were heading out." Lorenzo rested against the exterior wall of the casino, allowing people to walk past him on the sidewalk.

"Told me you're hiding something." Pat puffed his own cigarette, leaning back into the wall next to Lorenzo, watching the people funnel in and out of various casinos around them. "Who isn't? Truth be told, Lorenzo, I'd rather not know. Unless it'll come back to bite me in the ass."

"I told you I'm in waste management."

So, he was doubling down on the lies? In a past life, Pat would've cared. He'd have demanded the truth, demanded to be in the know. The older he got, he realized there was ignorance in bliss. Not knowing, not carrying that burden, was liberating.

"I didn't say I believe him," Pat assured him. "Just that I don't want to know. I like you, but we just met. Let the good times roll, love. We'll have plenty of time later to languish in regret about past misgivings. We're still young and still have some hair on our chests. I will say, though, probably time to find a new bar. Don't you think?"

Lorenzo squinted, like he was trying to make sense of Pat. "You've been changing lately. I didn't know you well a month ago, but I ain't ever been a poor judge of character. You're different. I don't know how. I don't know why. Ever since you got that deal, you've changed."

"Isn't this where people come to shed their old skins?" Pat gestured around with his cigarette. "Isn't that why you came here? At least that's what you told me. I am not any different from you. A fresh start was what I wanted."

Looking at Lorenzo, he saw someone different, a ghost of his past. He saw Randy. His blonde hair looked soaking wet in the otherwise bone-dry backdrop. Water dripped down his khaki pants onto the dusty sidewalk. His nose was gone. In its place, blood dripped around the frame of his lips and to the point of his chin.

"What's wrong, Pat? You look like you've seen a ghost." Pat shook his head, stepping back as Randy reached out, a claw gripping Pat's wrist, pulling him closer. Pat yelped loudly, and the mindless drones passing by stopped, turning toward their interaction. As he blinked, he realized the claw belonged to Lorenzo. Pat shook his head in disbelief.

"I'm sorry; I'm sorry. I'm exhausted and in a bad mood. It's not you, Lorenzo. I think I just need to get some rest. Yeah, a good night's rest would do me good." He was babbling a mile a minute as Lorenzo recoiled his grip, his eyes full of genuine hurt. Pat shook his head like a dog drying off after a jaunt in the rain.

"Get some sleep, Pat. Maybe you just had too much to drink. We'll talk tomorrow when you're feeling clearer-headed." Pat opened his mouth to speak, but Lorenzo put his finger on his lips to silence him. "Don't. It's okay. I should be more sensitive. I don't know you yet. I know some things, but there's hurt there. I can see it. When you're ready, we can talk."

Pat wanted to hug him, but he didn't. Lorenzo turned, melding back into the crowd, and Pat stared after him in disbelief. How had he mistaken him for Randy? He'd never seen something that real before. It was always just an image in his brain, a man floating, never tangible. Was he going insane with guilt?

No, no, you did what you had to, he thought as he hurriedly made his way down the street. *It was you or him, Pat, you or him. Don't let that doubt fester anymore. You've already had plenty of sleepless nights.*

* * *

The Slippery Slope wasn't as close on foot. Lorenzo had neglected to call Pat a cab, and while he'd have done so for himself normally, the fresh air did a lot to flush the doubt out of his mind. The walk helped tamp down the rampant anxiety.

To everyone else passing by, Pat was just another face in the crowd. It was a humble feeling to be one of many, and it grounded him in reality. Randy was nothing more than a mirage of stress, a manifestation of doubt creeping in, abruptly slashing at his happiness. Self-sabotage and nothing more.

He stood now in the Slippery Slope's lounge, where Gunther greeted him. *Oh yeah, it's Wednesday, Lars' day off. Gunther's fine.* His thoughts hid behind an emotionless grin, the performative mask doing its best to not let the inner dichotomy spill. He doubted Gunther cared terribly which lobby man he preferred, but Pat did. Optics were everything.

"Hey, Gunther, doing anything fun this weekend?" Pat's voice pushed out of him with a calculated charm that was alarming, giving no hint of the dread he had experienced all night. "Heard a new steakhouse opened up down on Fremont. It might be worth trying it out. Vegas bovine is oh so divine."

Gunther raised his eyebrows and nodded approvingly. "You don't say? I've been meaning to get into something new. When's the next show? Lars told me all about it and said his guts hurt the next day from keeling over. Knew you were funny but had no idea you were so talented."

"I'll have to thank him. Let me know if you ever want to come to a show. They've got me on the stage next Saturday even. Could get you some good seats." Then he gave the man a weary smile. "If you don't mind, I'm pretty beat, may want to head to my room."

When Gunther gave him a curt nod, Pat trudged down the familiar hallway to his room. He slowly prodded the door, a habit he'd developed ever since the incident that'd preceded his ascent into the comedy circles of Las Vegas. Today, nobody waited for him on the other side, just darkness and the faintest hints of tobacco. Home Sweet Home.

He flicked the light on, and in the mirror, he saw Samuel's tall frame brooding in the doorway behind him. "How long have you been following me?" Pat asked as he turned around, watching the tall, hairless man creep through his doorway. He'd have been terrified a few weeks prior, but now he had become desensitized.

"I was waiting outside. We have no reason to follow you. You haven't done anything—yet." The way Samuel held on to that last word did a bit to shake Pat's stonewalling façade of confidence.

Pat shook his head, looking up at the behemoth before him, who was shutting the door, leaving the two to have a more private conversation.

"That's changing, isn't it?"

"How long will you need to get ready? We have a bit of a drive ahead of us."

Pat's heart sank. He'd known this moment would come, but he'd hoped it wouldn't. In the doldrums of day-to-day activities, it wasn't hard to convince himself that things would stay that way forever, to ignore the dark pact he'd made, hopeful his time would pass without incident.

Pat sighed. "I can be ready in about ten minutes. Does that work for you?"

Samuel nodded before making his way to the unmade bed and sitting down, the springs inside creaking in agony at the sudden displacement. He folded his hands neatly and watched Pat, saying only, "Sure."

Pat considered asking for privacy but knew better than to stir the pot. This was a situation of his own making, and he'd have to live with whatever came of it, for better or worse. "Sure, let me just go wash up."

Samuel cracked his knuckles, neatly folding his hands as though he were praying.

Once in his bathroom, Pat closed the door and found himself resting against the wall, looking into his reflection. He didn't appear any different, his clothing retaining his trademark tackiness and slight flair that could either pass as coincidental or purposeful.

It's big time, Pat. They need you. A bit surprised it took a month, but it's here. The Mob always collects its debts. You weren't anything different. Even if you'd like to think you were. Just another favor they can call in.

He turned the sink on, his hands cupped to grab the cold water as the pipes shook from inside the walls. On the lip of the sink rested the ring, its green gems glinting in the light, demanding his full focus. He had long since disposed of the finger and initially threw the ring out with it, though he quickly reversed course. After rummaging through the rubbish for the clover ring, he left it on his nightstand, but even that had become too much, a reminder of how fate had thrust him into a situation beyond understanding.

He moved it to the bathroom, unable to truly part with it. It almost seemed tailor-made for him. While he had yet to let it grace his flesh, he'd sized it up many times. It looked like a perfect fit, as though it was home, where it always belonged.

Tonight, his gaze fixated on it once more. He knew where it had been, where he had first seen it. *Don't put that thing on. Clover is ironic. That ring ain't nothing but bad luck, Pat. Look what happened to the last guy who owned it.* The reasonable portion of his brain made a plea for sanity, for morality.

He grimaced, looking into the mirror, sighing, unsure what to do. *I'm a showman, and that ring, dirty or not, completes my image. What is life but a stage, but a performance? Put it on, Patty. You'll like how it fits; I guarantee it.* His hand moved towards it, then he pulled it back like he'd been burned. But still, the performer in him cajoled, *C'mon! You want to do it. Besides, the last guy? He ain't you. He ain't got the wits about him. It's a dog-eat-dog world, Patty, and you're a rottweiler. Rottweilers get the ring. And it fits perfectly. You know it does. You can tell just by looking at it. Don't be so coy; don't pretend. Ain't nobody to pretend for.*

Pat flung his bathroom door open, the decision having been made. Samuel waited for him on the other side, standing now.

"You're all set then, I take it? Ready to go?" he asked, his hands falling to his side as though he were standing at attention.

"Sure thing. You driving, or am I?"

"Your car's personality is a bit too loud." Samuel's deep voice rolled out slow but assured. "I think it may serve us better to ride in something more inconspicuous. Follow me, Patrick."

"Lead the way."

He opened the door and waited for Samuel to step out, which he obliged, before shutting it behind him. They both stood in the hall, their contrasting appearances massacring any hope the pair had of remaining inconspicuous.

"We will make a stop for coffee," Samuel said, beginning to trod down the hall. "It's shaping up to be a long night."

Pat looked back at his room, locking the door before glancing again at his bedazzled hand.

He was right. It fit perfectly.

10.

Pat was again reminded of how desolate the desert became once the neon lights and empty promises of Vegas were in the distance. The gas station they found themselves at had coffee, but it wasn't very good. Pat recoiled after his first sip, unsure if the caffeine had been replaced with a fuel more befitting of a car.

He nursed the tar in his cup, staring out into the black night, only the faintest glints of stars filling the void with dazzling yet distant constellations. He often wondered what was in those stars, but those thoughts rarely went far. Reality had a way of siphoning a man's curiosity once he matured into adulthood. Seldom few got to dream of the stars, to dream of more than toiling away for faceless benefactors and filling other people's coffers before they filled a coffin. Such was the cycle.

Pat, however, was living his dream. Perhaps it wasn't how he envisioned it, but that was a universal truth. Dreams were dreams. You could make some of them a reality, but there was a price to pay. And driving along this dusty freeway, waiting for Samuel to guide him, tell him what to expect? That was his price.

"Where are we heading? Can't be that much further."

"Lake Mead. Some others have done you the generosity of acquiring your task ahead of time. You have the gift of the gab, not the gift of the jab." Samuel dryly chuckled at his own joke.

Pat shuddered. He had a past with reservoirs. Randy had even visited him in the guise of Lorenzo. While he'd tried to brush it off as exhaustion, a projection, he now suspected a different truth. Pat was a man of faith. Even though it was a paradox, he still believed in evil and good, heaven and hell. He didn't know if Randy had made it to either or if he had unfinished business.

"Lake Mead, huh?" Pat hoped his voice sounded calm, unbothered. "You know, I'd have preferred to visit it in the daytime. I've heard it's a beautiful place—an oceanic oasis in the desert." When Samuel didn't respond, Pat shifted uncomfortably in his seat, rubbing a hand over the back of his neck.

"So, you want me to talk to someone? Hurl some jokes? Doesn't feel like the typical wheelhouse of the Mob, but sure beats killing a guy."

"We aren't too far now," Samuel said. "Enjoy the silence. You will wish it stayed that way soon enough."

Pat shuddered at the thought as he looked over the dashboard of Samuel's car, its black hood reflecting the moonlight above. As they rode along, their car light was the only sign of life, the road as barren as it had been before humanity. Pat saw the sign for Lake Mead, with an *8* next to it. It wouldn't be all that much longer at all.

Anxiety rippled through his chest, and he started babbling to fight it off. "Silence is beautiful, too, but man, I was born to talk, and talk I do. It's my thing. I have mine. You have yours: being freakishly tall and breaking into people's hotel rooms. We all have our skills."

"Amongst other things," Samuel responded as he looked out the window. Nothing much to see besides the overwhelming blackness.

You'd think he'd lighten up. This guy doesn't know how to quit. Still, it's probably good to get a job under my belt. Well, depends on the job. Taking me out to the reservoir. Why are they doing that? Maybe they know about Randy. Perhaps they know about what we did—what I *did.*

The last half-mile came quickly, and Samuel nearly missed the turn, but at the last second, he course was corrected.

"Scatterbrained? You made me pay for your coffee. C'mon!"

Samuel rolled his eyes as they chugged along. Pat desperately wished to be free from the car. He'd take his chances with the task that was forced upon them.

"We're on the right path," Samuel grumbled in a rare show of emotion. "I'll get us there in one piece." As they got closer, he slowed the car down, until they were practically inching along, explaining even though Pat hadn't asked, "We want to approach slowly. Don't want them to mistake us for someone else. In the dark, mistaken identity is commonplace."

Samuel's sullen stare was replaced with a sinister smile, as though recalling other instances of mistaken identity. A light chuckle escaped his throat, and Pat kept his focus out the window, where he saw the moon reflecting on the water. The outline of a pier and the hum of a boat's engine weren't much further. He could also see the ship's lights, but they were fainter, discretion clearly a priority.

Samuel came to a halt, his headlights illuminating the entryway to the pier as he slunk out of the car before Pat even noticed. Alone for a moment, he closed his eyes, taking in the oddly gratifying pleasure from solitude. When he opened them again, he felt like he had napped, even if only seconds had passed—a mental reboot. Then he reached for his revolver, which he'd strapped to his waist before putting on the ring.

Stepping out of Samuel's car, he heard the crash of his trunk, followed by soft footfalls approaching him.

"Good call on the gun, Patrick. Who's to say when you will need to use it?" Samuel had clocked it because, of course, he had.

"Well, I'd like to think you have a pretty good sense of which way the wind is blowing tonight. But I'm in the dark about what's going on, so I figure, prepare for the worst and hope for the best." Pat looked toward the faint lights at the end of the pier. He realized from this close-up now the boat was small, too small to carry more than a handful of people. "How many are waiting on the boat?"

"The Ferryman brings us to the *Underworld*, the big ship," Samuel explained. "But only if you pay him. Otherwise, you have to wait out here on the shore."

Pat rolled his eyes. Wasn't the Mob Italian? Yet Samuel spoke of old Greek myths as though they were literal.

"How poetic. I didn't pack my coin purse. Suffice it to say, I'll pay you back once we cross back from the river of souls." Pat flashed a grin, almost forgetting how grim his reality had become.

Samuel nodded, handing him a coin. It was dark out, but even Pat could see this wasn't American currency. He wasn't sure it belonged to any nation; the language written on it was unfamiliar but evoked the imagery of *Lawrence of Arabia*, the land where civilization began. He caressed it with his fingers as he followed Samuel.

"What language is this?" Pat asked. When Samuel didn't respond, he added, "You guys are really committed to the aesthetic. I can't help but admire the depths to which you're willing to go."

They had made it to the boat. There was, in fact, a man standing inside of it. He stepped out, his scraggly beard more akin to one of a man who lived on the edge as opposed to the opulence and well-groomed nature of Las Vegas that Pat had grown accustomed to.

"Ye have yer coins? I ain't fixin' to ferry no one without their coins." He sounded like a pirate, a man of an era that no longer existed. Pat handed his coin over, as did Samuel, who did not speak. "Okay, get yerselves comfortable. Shan't be long on the ship together."

Pat obliged but raised a brow as he did so. Samuel sat next to him in silence. Only the moon saved him from being a faceless entity basking in the darkness.

Pat tried to fill the void of silence, not wanting to be consumed by the darkness. "You sound like Blackbeard. Well, what I'd imagine Blackbeard sounded like. My point is you're not from around here. What did you leave to be the Ferryman?"

The man turned to him. The yellows of his eyes were unwavering as he replied, "Always spent life by the sea. Ain't so different here. Just a sea made by man. Lot happens in the water when the sun sets. You lot are just too busy sleeping to see it. Samuel has been here 'fore and will be here again. Ye? Remains to be seen, ain't it so?"

Pat ignored the cryptic questioning, indulging in the man's rich voice. "You know, part of me feels nostalgic hearing your accent. Reminds me of back home. In the summer, we'd go to Gloucester for a weekend getaway. You sound just like the seamen. Incredible how I can recall those days perfectly, just by the sound of your voice."

The man Pat was calling Blackbeard in his head didn't respond to that beyond a barely perceptible nod and a quizzical look at Samuel.

"Pat will be here at least a year," Samuel said, answering his unspoken question. "Takes a while to build a reputation. Perhaps more, but no less. I don't know if you two will have the fortune of meeting again after tonight, but he will remain." His voice rolled like the waves they had left behind. If Pat hadn't known who it belonged to, he'd have found it hypnotic, soothing even.

"After that, who knows?" Pat said, staring into the dark night. "Maybe I'll see Rome, sell out the Coliseum. Paris? Just don't give me too much wine during the set. The world is mine." He could see a ship in the distance, lights from cabins below deck, making it clear that there was indeed life aboard.

"An entertainer, eh?" the old man said. "Be careful, starin' at the world like it's yer oyster. Not everythin' that shines is a pearl. I know that well, aye."

Pat glanced back at him before focusing on the ship again, dismissing the old man's ramblings. More troubling things were afoot, like whatever awaited him on that ship.

"I suppose that means this is where we depart, Ferryman?" Pat asked, pointing upward to the ship.

"That'd be correct, son. Samuel, I trust you can help him aboard?"

The old man slowed their smaller vessel down as it circled toward the back of the large boat, which was significantly larger. It was akin to the size of a river cruise. As he made his way to the back, Pat noticed a staircase obstructed by a door. Behind it stood two figures, one with a lit cigarette.

"Thank you again for the safe passage," Samuel said. "While the gabber here doesn't realize it, the water's calm surface can mask the turbulence beneath the waves. You have led us across the river once more."

As Samuel stood, the door on the larger boat flung open. One of the figures stepped forward, offering their hand to Samuel, who took it as he departed the ship. Pat followed suit, Samuel helping him out. The Ferryman looked up at them and gave a curt nod before departing. Pat went up the stairs after Samuel, noting that he didn't greet anybody. The nostalgic mood was gone as Pat shifted his focus to what lay before him—his first task in their agreement.

Samuel beckoned him toward the front of the boat. There, he saw several people of various races and genders. The only commonality was their lack of hair, much like Samuel.

Oh great, there's more of him, he groaned inwardly. *Just when I thought I was settling in.*

There was another stairwell that led into the interior of the ship, and Samuel waved him towards it, saying, "Come, Patrick, your first task awaits. We have until daylight to complete it."

Samuel made his way down. Pat couldn't help but feel the anxiety creep up his spine and into his throat, where his heart pounded. The warm glow from each side of the stairwell pushed upward, illuminating the staircase and almost beckoning Pat to descend.

And so he did.

11.

Below deck, the heart of the boat pumped oil through its arteries as though it were ichor, and the clang of piping filled Pat's eardrums as it passed through the veins.

"To the left." Samuel seemed to know where he was going, moving through its halls with familiarity.

Then, in the noise of the machinery, a new sound emerged—human voices, one even sounding distraught. Pat felt a lump in his throat, almost certain whatever they'd ask him to do would haunt him, just like Randy.

Samuel stopped in front of a door, the conversation beyond still indiscernible, but the voices undeniable. "This one. After you, don't be coy." Samuel propped the door open, bowing lightly.

Pat turned toward the door, a warm light pouring out into the hallway. As he entered the room, he realized the light came from candles. The room looked as though it were a makeshift chapel. Chairs were lined up in rows, leading up to what Pat imagined as an altar. There was a man in one of the chairs, taped to it, his wrists bound to the wooden armrests on either side.

He was talking. "I gave you everything you wanted. Let me go. There's no reason it needs to play out like this, fellas." The man tried to sound confident, but notes of fear still escaped, betraying his real feelings.

Several hairless people of varying genders sat in the aisles, watching him, their black suits reflecting the flame of the candles to the left and right of the man. The way the sparks danced, felt almost alive. Pat sensed something otherworldly was afoot.

"No debt goes unpaid." The voice belonged to the woman who had let Pat into Louie's Lounge the day he made his pact. She was the only one of the Black Suits that stood, walking toward the bound man, Rosaline. "Information is of value, but it will not save you. Much like money, you simply do not have enough. Lies reveal the picture of a man, and my, what a portrait you've painted."

As she finished speaking, she crouched over, her forefinger and thumb pushing up his chin to make eye contact. Pat noticed the man was beaten; his nose was broken and blood dripped from his nostrils. His eyes were swollen, nearly shut.

"Where is it?" she asked the man. "Where is what we are owed? Where is your proof?" The flames flickered to the cadence of her voice.

Samuel made his way to his seat, leaving Pat alone to stand, confused. *Do they want me to interrogate him? They really misjudged me, then; I can't do that. I won't get anything useful out of him. Did he also make a deal with them like mine? Am I next?*

Pat looked back at the door, locked from the outside in. They were all prisoners in here, even him.

To Samuel, he whispered, "What is it you wanted me to do? I don't want to be abrasive, but the journey here was theatrical. Crossing a river of souls, a man tied up in a makeshift chapel. It's all so performative. Am I supposed to just watch?"

He thought he was being quiet enough, but Pat's voice must've carried because she turned to him, almost like she was becoming aware for the first time that she was not alone with the prisoner. "Samuel? Is this the monologist? I am not very amused." Her voice boomed.

Samuel's eyes hovered over Pat's slight figure. He took one long blink as he sniffed the air, his lips turning to a gnarled smile as he did so. "Yes, he's here to fulfill his own deal. Perhaps this will serve as a reminder of what failure brings."

Pat stared at Samuel as his eyes closed, face wrought with ecstasy. He was enjoying the situation, coming to life at the prospect of torture and agony.

The man in the chair stifled a sob. "I told you all I don't know where it is. What do you want me to say? I won't lie. I'll cheat, steal, hurt, but I won't lie. I had it with me when we left." He was pleading, and Pat's heart sank.

Pat felt for him. He didn't know what kind of debt was owed, what sort of deal was made. However, his own dealings led him to believe it wasn't exactly an equitable arrangement.

The woman clucked her tongue. "Stop groveling. You know what we're owed. The exchange was simple. You only needed to return it to us as proof of your deeds. The consequences for such oversights are far beyond me. Not that I'd be much more generous."

She spoke with neither disgust nor joy. This was business to her. That much was clear. The guy was in over his head, unaware of the spider's web he had fallen into. Pat only hoped the venom wasn't worse than the bite.

"If you don't know the answers, does someone else?" Pat asked. "Did you work as a team with someone?" He wasn't trying to help the Black Suits. He was asking because he couldn't bear to be in this situation any longer. He almost wished they'd just asked him to kill someone. This was torture. The way the crowd watched only affirmed he was nothing like them, not even close.

Samuel opened his eyes, watching on with a smoldering intensity, clearly taken aback by Pat's boldness. Rosaline even took her finger off the captive's chin, turning to the comedian, seemingly in awe of what she was seeing.

"Look, you know they don't like me," Pat said, keeping his eyes on the man instead of the others. "Didn't even leave me a seat. Ain't like they don't have the space for it. We're both outsiders." The captive seemed skeptical, even in his precarious predicament. "I'm not trying to convince you to help them," Pat continued. "But help yourself. These people? They don't seem keen on reason. You mentioned 'we' like you were a part of a team. Ain't no use in protecting someone else. You're here. They ain't coming to save you. What does that say about them?"

The crowd didn't speak, their silence saying far more than any words could. Pat tried to make eye contact with the bound man, whose pupils could barely be seen in the swollen mass of his face.

The woman stood up now, walking toward Pat. "Your show, since you have all the answers." Her words were laced with contempt, as though Pat shouldn't be here.

Samuel was the only one in the crowd who stood, watching with fascination.

Pat made his way up to the man, who was mumbling a response to his words. "I ain't work alone, but what we did was for them. I have no way of knowing where he is. Crossed me the second we got out of there. Saved him from burning rubble, then we split back at the motel. Ain't seen him since." He coughed pink-hued spittle up as he spoke.

"What do you owe them?" Pat asked. "What do they want you to give them? I'm not much for cryptic chatter, so tell me plain: what do they want you to bring back to them?"

The man blinked. Even in this delirious state, he regarded Pat with confusion, seeing a man who was inarguably out of place. Finally, he said, "Rosary beads, they wanted the priest's rosary beads. Burned down the church, we did. That was what they wanted, wanted the priest to burn alive, his prayer beads taken from him in a burning chapel. Ain't that something? You make a deal with them too, then? Ain't hairless, ain't wearing black like they do."

They wanted him to burn down a church. Isn't the Mob religious? He bit his lip, thinking. *I don't know. Something ain't right about this.*

Pat's hand briefly brushed against his hip, feeling his gun tucked under his shirt in the waistline of his pants. He debated pulling it out, making quick work of Samuel and the woman—Rosaline, he remembered now. But the others would turn him into Swiss cheese. The gravity of his situation was settling in. He was no less a prisoner than the man in the chair. He wasn't bound by tape but by the threat of a swift demise, which hung in the air like an offensive perfume—all-consuming and inescapable.

"I made a deal, too, yeah," Pat admitted. "But on my lonesome. Nobody to double-cross me. Probably for the best. Sounds like your man let you down. You might not know where he is, but if they find him, your debt will be paid, and you can leave here. They're cruel, but they're fair. Right guys?"

Pat turned to the crowd and was met with silence at first. He knew he was being performative, but he had at least hoped there would be feigned reassurance.

"They don't care," the bound man said. "Listen, take it from me. I got in with this crowd, took their deals, and listened to their words. Hasn't a day passed where they don't remind me of my folly, my promise. I failed them. Don't matter if I sell him out. He'll just join me. No use in killing the both of us."

Pat didn't know if the man spoke figuratively or literally. He knew what the Mob could do—his ring finger was a grim reminder. He just didn't think they'd do it here, not like this, not with him watching.

"You don't realize it," Rosaline said, "but the fast talker is your best hope. If you wish to spurn his advice, do so." She spoke with a lack of energy, suggesting she was tired of the event.

Pat was still confused about why he'd been brought here, why this was the job they had chosen him for. Surely it was a daily event in the Mob to interrogate someone. This was run-of-the-mill. Not a single person in the crowd even seemed interested in what was happening.

"You're going to kill me," the prisoner said. "I know how it goes. Nothing you can do to coax me. Even if you send that unwilling errand boy to talk up a storm—" He nodded at Pat. "—I'm a dead man. No reason to help you put me in the ground quicker."

Do they want me to lie? he wondered. *Of course, they're going to kill him. Of course, he's a goner. These guys kill for a lot less. But they might make him suffer, they might make it painful, or they could make it quick, painless. Blackness before he even knows what happened to him.* His thoughts were starting to race. *How do I know it's blackness? What if there's more? Gosh, I need to calm down. I need to relax before they pick up on it.*

Pat looked at the man. He opened his mouth and closed it again, hesitating. *He deserves to die with hope, with dignity. If he doesn't spill his beans, I'm next. Of course, I'm next. He failed his job, and I'll have failed mine.* Irrational thoughts spiraled, and he realized what he must do—speak of empty promises in his ear, coaxing him into giving them what they wanted.

"They might kill you," he said gently. "But they might not. Seems like they want the deserter a lot more than they want you. Rosary beads or not, you still burned the church down. That counts for something. You made a bad deal, but that doesn't mean you're done. You showed them you're capable."

He was trying to convince *everyone* in this room: himself, the captive man, and the crowd. They wouldn't let him know how they felt—they never did—but there was common sense in his words. They only needed to see it.

The bound man snorted. "Yeah? You ain't one of them, but that doesn't make you one of me. You exist in the in-between, just an outsider looking in. Your voice, it's practiced. Everything about you, it's all a dance. I've lived a life of lies for far too long. I can tell when someone's wearing a mask. Can't fool me."

Pat felt his ego rise, then it pulled itself back. The anger in his eyes was supplanted with a smirk on his face. "You're not as profound as you think you are. I'm trying to help you. I'm not in such a different position as you. A few punches and some rope, and I'm right next to you. The only difference is they probably won't kill me. That guy left you to die, and here you are, letting him live. How gracious. A shame they won't bury you. We're on a boat for a reason."

The implication hung in the air like a pervasive summer humidity. Pat's facade of empathy was running out. Whether his own life was on the line was immaterial. All that mattered was his perception of it.

Samuel watched, his arms folded, the wrinkles on his forehead furrowed as Pat waited for a response.

"Getting me riled up?" the man in the chair scoffed. "Maybe you're not so different from the monsters in the suits. Sounds like a lot more than tape and bad luck separates us."

Pat grimaced as his father's words burned in his head like the flicker of a flame, a reminder of light in the darkness. He didn't fear the dark. That was all in a person's imagination. In the light, however, there was no mixing, no deniability. Everything about oneself was laid bare. *And the* real *monsters sleep at night like the rest of us...*

"If you want to be riled up, get riled up," Pat said, shrugging. "Makes no difference to me. I'm just stating the truth. He left you to die—alone. They might still kill you, but at least you know he won't be far behind. At least you know he'll get what he deserves." Pat had gotten closer to him, almost face to face with the man, his eyes studying his expression, hoping to find any trace of what was happening in his mind. "What does he want with rosary beads, anyway? Can't sell them. It's a trophy to him. It's your life to them. Ain't much to protect there."

"I doubt they could catch him," the man replied. "Probably deep in the Sierra Madre now. The guy was always shifty, always ahead of everyone else."

He was playing it loose. Pat saw the opening and attempted to pry it wide open like an oyster with a pearl.

"He fled across the border to California?" Pat asked. "Left you here to die over what? A useless trophy—rosary beads. Sounds like a stand-up fellow.

But hey, you keep guarding secrets for him. I'm sure he'll pray for your soul. Good thing he's got those beads, eh?"

Even to Pat, those words rang especially cruel. Yet he didn't want to die. Especially not for a stranger, not one who burned down churches, even if it was because he'd been made to.

Despite his beaten state, the man was not as dull as Pat assumed. "You're afraid. Even though you're playing like you're a tough guy, you're afraid. You need me. I'm here because I failed a job for them. Where do you think you'll end up? The difference is you won't have anything to trade. You need me. I'm a dead man either way."

Pat squinted at him. He was right, of course. Pat doubted they'd let this man live regardless of what he said. With that thought, an idea struck him, a sinister one that he tried to push away as quickly as it had come.

But he couldn't.

"There are many ways to die. Some are less painful than others. Do you really want to die painfully hiding his secrets?"

The words came out before Pat could contain them. Whoever was speaking was not the man he was. It was someone new, someone darker than he could've imagined. His ring glinted in the dimly lit room as the crowd was finally interested, Rosaline most of all. She observed with deep fascination, scanning both faces.

"You're not a killer," the man told Pat. "You're a talker. Those hands? Soft, no calluses. You're not built for this. They can see that—they want you dead. Don't you get it? You fail, and it's over. If you succeed, they'll keep making you dig the hole until you can't see the sunlight. Until it doesn't matter how clear the mirror is, the person looking back ain't the real you, just a husk. Is that what you want? Is that what you—"

He was interrupted by a gunshot. He screamed in pain as Pat looked on in shock, revolver in hand, the faintest hints of smoke coming from the barrel as the casing dropped to the ground. The hole in the man's left knee gazed back at Pat accusingly. A few in the crowd jumped up, hands at their waistbands. Rosaline raised her hand to stop anyone from moving.

Pat froze in place as the man screamed at him, "Oh god, it *fucking* hurts! I did what was asked of me! I burned the damn church down with the priest inside!" His voice was shrill now, the fresh layer of pain returning him to reality. Even if this man proclaimed he didn't fear death, the pain that came on the precipice shattered that illusion. "He took the beads. I did my part. It's just a trophy, right? Oh my *fucking* god, I'm going to bleed out."

"Tell them what they want to know," Pat demanded, "or I'll shoot your other knee. Where's the fucker who ran away with beads? You said the Sierra Madre, yeah? Where?" Pat didn't know who spoke now. It was his voice, his mouth, and yet he'd stooped far lower than he could've imagined. "You think I am a fucking joke? Just because I am a comedian?"

"How do I know?" the man spat out, then hissed in pain. "Guy has tons of hideouts and jumps from motel to motel in Eldorado. He's from Tahoe. That's all I know. That's all I know! Guy wasn't going to let me tag along. I didn't even know he'd left until it was too late. Just please make it stop. It hurts so much. It hurts so much."

"Hush," Rosaline said. "I thought the monologist talked too much. The priest didn't die. You both spared him. You warned him before you lit the church on fire, didn't you?" When he didn't deny it, Rosaline pressed, "We found your friend. He was nearly past Reno and told us everything. Samuel cleaned up your mistakes for you. Isn't that right, Samuel?"

Pat turned, and the bald man pulled rosary beads from his coat pocket, handing them to Rosaline as he let out a mirthful chuckle.

They had already caught the guy. They already knew. They were going to kill him, anyway. Or was it a test? If he was honest, would they have let him live? Pat tucked his gun back into his waistband, stepping back and watching in horror.

"Am I good to leave now?" he asked Rosaline, who had now stepped forward, placing the rosary beads around the neck of the man taped to the chair. "I did my part, yeah?"

"Not yet," she said. "Not until it is finished. Only then may you leave. Bring the canister, Samuel."

Samuel reached under the chair he was sitting in and pulled out something Pat hadn't noticed before: a red aluminum gasoline canister. He glided across the room toward the man, who started screeching, praying to anyone—anything—that would listen when he realized what was coming. There was no God, not in this wretched place, that much Pat was sure of. The others in the crowd stood, almost aroused at the prospect of what came next.

The man in the chair was begging for his life. "Please! No! No! I did what you asked! *I did what you fucking asked!*"

He was nothing more than a rabbit in a trap designed for true predators. The smell of gasoline filled Pat's nostrils, and he wrinkled his nose in disgust. The splash of the fluid hit the ground, and it doused the man in the chair. His screams became slightly more muted as the shock of his gunshot wound set in.

"C'mon, kill him first," Pat said, the last goodness within him desperately trying to undo the course he'd set them on. "If you're going to kill him, kill him first. Nobody deserves this. This is madness."

But on top of that, another voice in his head tried to absolve him. *They were going to kill you. Failure ain't an option. You wanted this career more than anything. Besides, this ain't the first time you've been here. Sure, there were better reasons for Randy, and it wasn't like this, but it ain't your first rodeo cowboy. Saddle up, ride the bull, or get the horns. Easy choice, mi amigo.*

Samuel gripped Pat's shoulder as he put the canister beside their feet. "He shall pay for his failure, and you need to see it out and reap the fruits of your labor. Besides, you were the one who pulled the gun and added your—ahem—natural theatrics to it."

They were standing roughly ten feet away from the makeshift altar. Rosaline had lit a cigarette and took a puff as she looked on. The candles flickered, all their flames in unison pointing toward the direction of the altar. The hairs on Pat's neck stood at full attention.

"The priest who was to burn in hell was given a quick death," she said casually. "Samuel shot him in the temple, a mercy killing for what he'd been accused of. So you shall burn in his place. The smell of your body cooking shall be your reminder that no good deed goes unpunished, and those who wish to judge as though they were God shall be set on the path to meet Him. Sweet dreams."

She flicked her cigarette after taking another inhale, then took a step back and watched as the flame erupted. The man was far from unconscious, and his screams renewed as the smell of burned hair filled the air.

"Oh God! Please! Please, Lord! Forgive me! Forgive me!"

The figures in the chapel sat in ominous silence, passive observers watching the fire grow. At first, his screams outpaced the growl of the flame, but it didn't take long for that to change. Soon enough, there was nothing but the crackle of flames, almost mocking the fuel that had given them life in the first place. Yet they did not spread past the burning mass of flesh that was once a human.

The smell was rancid. Pat felt sick and barely noticed Samuel grip his shoulder tighter as he watched. Pat was sure he would throw up, yet his stomach held on. Perhaps he wasn't as good of a man as he thought.

"It is the way of things," Samuel said. "What is a man without his word, Patrick? Do not look away. Take it in. Understand the pact you've made. You've done well, but understand what happens to the duplicitous, understand what comes of failure. It is not a pretty sight, but the unsavory motivates us. Lest we become another burned at the stake."

Pat couldn't process what he was seeing: a man cooked alive, a man he had shot. He hoped the shock from his wound did something to nullify the anguish of turning into ash while still alive.

Within minutes, the flame dissolved, the altar seemingly made of a material that did not transfer the flame. The smoke also cleared, but instead of going upward like physics would suggest, it was somehow sucked in from below them, leaving a thin amount around their ankles.

There was little doubt the man had passed. Pat stared at the man. He couldn't stare back—his eyes were no longer in their sockets—but he stared into them anyway.

"It is done," Rosaline said, her tone unreadable. Pat couldn't tell how she felt about the whole mess, but he doubted she would lose much sleep over it. "Dispose of the body once it has cooled, and throw him into the lake along with the priest before you head back into town. May they slumber together."

As the door opened and most of the crowd shuffled out with Rosaline, Pat stood in front of the dead man, still unable to tear his gaze away.

"Why?" he asked. "If you knew, why? He burned the church, isn't that the important part? Why do this?"

Samuel still stood beside him, swaying in silence. He cleared his throat before speaking. "You think he was alone? That he was the only one to make a deal with things he couldn't comprehend? Do you think it was just you two? I am no different. I learned a valuable lesson in this life, Patrick, one you'd do well to pick up on."

"What's that, exactly?"

"Those who fly too close to the sun get burned. It is a world of deep injustice, but to think you are absolved of its cruelty is foolhardy." Samuel closed his eyes, a pained grimace on his face. "Accept your limitations, Pat, before that's all you're remembered for." With that, Samuel left Pat alone to process his thoughts.

Pat was certain of two things in that moment. These guys weren't just the Mob. This was excessive. It was cruel and inhuman. Despite its unsavoriness, the Mob had a strict code, and while Pat wasn't a member, he knew it wasn't this. The other certainty was even more grim: his father was right; the men in the suits, the ones who shook your hands and offered you a deal? Those were far more frightening than any boogeyman the brain could conceive of.

He would never forget that smell, the look of a face that had been cooked alive. As he closed his eyes for a reprieve, he found no solace in his mind. Instead, Randy swam to the surface, bony half-eaten arms stroking upward as he ascended toward the waterline of the reservoir of Pat's drowning mind.

"Tell me a joke, Patty," Randy demanded, *"And God help you, it better be funny, you stupid fuckin' homosexual. You eye-fuckin' me? Look away. I said, look away!"*

Pat winced as the specter disappeared from his mind. He heard those words every night, and yet he never got used to hearing them. The guilt swallowed him every single time until he felt like he was the one drowning. As his eyes lingered once more on the burnt man, he knew there would be a new specter joining Randy in his nightmares.

12.

It was the peak of the summer. July in Central Massachusetts never ceased to amaze with its simultaneously overbearing humidity and jaw-dropping scenery. The summer of 1963 was no different. Patrick looked out over the Wachusett Reservoir and gasped. This time he was gasping for air, as he had run up a large flight of stone steps to reach the top of the dam. Other times he would gasp at the sunset, the water reflecting the sun's image in a manner befitting a landscape in an art museum. Here, though, it hung in Mother Nature's gallery, and he considered it one of her finest pieces.

"Ain't it just spectacular, even in this humidity?" Tommy Brunwell said. "Sure beats Boston. I tell ya, all the smoke and grime in the air there ain't good for you." He was standing next to Pat, puffing smoke into the air without the slightest hint of self-awareness.

"Yeah, I don't know about the humidity though. I can do hot, but the way it sticks? And the mosquitoes? I am a fan of gin, but I don't know if any amount of tonic can stop these bugs in their tracks." He leaned against the railing, musing, "Vegas is dry. That's what I keep hearing. No bugs, unless you count fruit flies and scorpions."

Patrick wiped the sweat off his brow as he looked across the water's surface. Bright green hills of pine and birch towered over in the distance. Behind them was a long stone staircase leading down to a grass field. In the middle of it was a large water fountain that gave way to a small dip, which fed into a long river snaking its way out of sight. They were roughly two hundred feet above the mouth of the river.

"If this thing collapsed," Patrick said, turning away from the man-made lake and looking at the fountain below them, "how high do you think the water would rise before it leveled out?"

"Can't say." Tommy had moved toward Pat, looking down the long dam. "My uncle helped build this thing back in the day. Did it by hand, he says. I don't know much about the machines of the day, but that sounds right. My guess, though? Maybe forty, thirty feet? Would drown out all those kids playing hide-n-seek, that's for sure."

Patrick let out a low whistle. "Still can't believe Johnny jumped a few years back. That's a long drop."

"Sure is." Tommy shook his head. "They tried to spruce it up, but the other side is just so much prettier. Something about a big body of water that gets ol' Tommy up in the morning." He puffed his cigarette, and Patrick shook his head laughing.

"Crazy how fifty years can pass by and the same stories, the same questions come to mind," Patrick said. "Still, if I told people back then this existed here now, they'd never believe it."

They stood there quietly for a while, Tommy finishing one cigarette and lighting another. Finally, he said, "Vegas, huh?"

"Yep. I'm fixin' to take a tour of Lake Mead when I get out there. Maybe even see the Hoover Dam. Think this thing looks pretty? It's nothing compared to there."

Tommy snorted. "Well, they don't got pines like we do. It's going to be large stretches of water and Wile E Coyote. Far cry from this place. But hey, kid, you deserve it. Chase your dreams. Clinton will be here when you get back—dam and all. Assuming you ever decide to come back, that is."

Tommy closed his eyes as a breeze rolled through. Patrick did the same, letting the wind caress his hair. Being elevated had its perks on a hot summer day, and nothing brought reprieve like a cool gust of air shooing away the humidity, even if only for a moment.

"Of course I will. Thinking I'll do a charity show and keep the deli in business. Once I'm gone, nobody will want to come by anymore. You thought they came for the roast beef? No, Tommy, they're all hankering to hear a good old Patrick Gallagher joke."

"Really?" Tommy grinned and waggled his eyebrows. "Few people told me once you beat town, they planned on coming back. They've been *avoiding* the old Patrick Gallagher jokes." Tommy must've seen him blushing because he added, "Sun's awfully bright today. That's surely the reason you're bright red, right, Patrick?"

"Yeah, should've brought my hat with me." Eager to duck out of any more ribbing, he asked, "Say, shouldn't you be opening shop soon? I gotta go home and get ready, but I can meet you there."

Tommy nodded, then made his way toward where he'd parked his car, walking off the dam and back toward the road with Patrick trailing after him. The lot was mostly empty, and the two of them sat on the hood of Tommy's car. Tommy stared out at the speeding cars, another sleepy summer morning in Clinton, Massachusetts, the only home either man had ever known. Despite Tommy's rants about how bad the pollution in Boston was, he had no memories of living there, having only been there as an infant, least as far as Patrick knew.

"Going to miss you, kid," Tommy said. "Only a few weeks now, and you'll be off in the desert. I just hope it's everything you want it to be."

Patrick didn't say anything, nor did he have to. Tommy always seemed to know what was on his mind. The man said nothing as he got in his car and pulled away, leaving Patrick alone in his thoughts. It was only then he spoke.

"Going to miss you, too." He sighed. "Going to miss you, too."

***

Patrick jogged the entire way home. The sleepy downtown slowly opened. Brick building after brick building lined Main Street, making way for a bright green grassy common with an elevated white gazebo, a format commonplace to the urban planning of all towns in this region. Patrick had seen the mill town slowly quiet down, a post-war America transitioning into a new era. He didn't know what its future brought, but he was sure it wouldn't involve him. He had brighter lights in his sights.

Also within view was his childhood home, with his and his mother's cars parked in the driveway. It was a small house, cozy and warm, with graying white shutters and a roof in need of patching. The door was painted green, but that was fading, much like the brown-painted wood siding of the home.

He fished out the key, giving a lazy wave to the man next door before turning it in the lock. Opening the door into the front hall revealed a lovingly decorated, if clearly a bit worn, house. A long, narrow, matted rag pointed from the doorway down the entrance into the kitchen. Patrick saw his mother inside, smoking a cigarette as she read the paper.

"Nasser said he's going to bomb Israel," she said as Patrick walked in. "Wonder what the Soviets think. Kennedy won't get us involved. He knows better than to get into the Brits and their mess." Sipping her tea, she gave her son a curt nod, her Irish accent slipping in occasionally as she talked further. "Hope you're going to the deli. We don't need the money much, but you do. You're a charming enough lad, Pat, real charming-like, but living at home with your mum isn't going to get you any women."

Pat's eyes lurked around awkwardly. He suspected she knew the truth, but it had never been said outwardly. His mother was of a different time, another place. While he doubted there would be much conflict between them, he never saw a reason to confide in her. It would just evoke more questions. Besides, he had tried in Clinton before, and outside of summer flings or one-off momentary lust-riddled affairs, nobody had taken enough shine to his post to tie themselves down.

"Ma, I told you I am going to Vegas in two weeks. I have money saved. Tommy makes good roast beef. Maybe he charges too much, but he doesn't skimp on wages. I'm taken care of. I'll have plenty."

Patrick wasn't wrong, it didn't take much time to save, and Tommy paid him more than he needed to, a by-product of their kinship.

His mother snorted. "Yeah, right. Do you want to tell jokes for a living? Back in Cork, those fellas? They ended up poor, begging for change. They were on the streets. Mum always made sure to leave 'em a penny. I felt bad for those fellas, I did. But maybe things will be different there. Maybe the roads will be paved with gold. Just make sure you take care of your mum like she took care of you. I did my best, I did; ye know it wasn't easy-like."

Patrick smiled at her, offering his hand to her, the other hand on her back, caressing it in loving, if patronizing circles.

"Of course, Ma, you built us a castle. What else is a queen to do?"

He looked around the house, aged and decidedly ramshackle, but growing up? It didn't matter. The stone fortress was all he ever knew. Childhood friends sitting around the Round Kitchen Table of Arthur deciding which grassy lot in the town carried Excalibur. He could see them now, running past his thighs, the specters of a past where success wasn't a carrot on a stick. Success was nothing more than getting a nickel to go to the corner store and buy penny candies until his stomach ran sour with their syrupy sweetness.

"Aren't you supposed to be workin' now?" his mother asked. "Fixin' to lose that job on the way out? Brunwell has been good to you, Pat, and good to us both. Oh boy, he and yer dad, the headaches those two lads left me."

He could sense a rant about his father coming. She missed him, and Patrick certainly missed the idea of him. Their moments were special, but he had been dead for over half of Patrick's life. Those memories faded with time, the good fading more than the bad at first, but eventually, all would be forgotten, save the tinges of nostalgia that jerked at the corner of his eyes in the shape of tears.

"You aren't wrong. Need to shower and freshen up before I head out to the deli. I love you, Ma. Enjoy yah paper. I will be sure to leave you some ham in the fridge when I get back. Sorry, I forgot to get it last shift."

Patrick was already running up the stairs as he heard the crinkle of her reshaping her paper to get the last words of the paragraph. When he looked back, his mom was gazing up the staircase at him, her reading glasses magnifying her eyes. Patrick stopped on the last stair that wouldn't obstruct his vision of her.

"I love ye, Patrick," she said. "I love ye, son."

"Right back at yah, Ma. Right back at yah." With that, he scurried up the remaining stairs.

As he went to his room, he grabbed his clothes for the day, putting them on his bed before rushing to the bathroom. As the steam from the shower filled the room and fogged the mirror, Patrick sat on the lip of the tub, water splashing on his back from the tub's floor. His eyes were closed now, and he could feel the warm moist air fill his lungs. He took a deep inhale.

"Just two more weeks, and you'll be rolling on out, Pat. Just two more weeks." He stood up, stepping into the shower, letting the hot water boil his skin with its unrelenting yet soothing crusade. He didn't know it yet, but he would have to leave town prematurely.

13.

The Brunwell Deli was a family-run business. Before Tommy, there was Thomas. It was confusing at first, so for a while, Tommy Brunwell was known as Junior. To some of the older crowd, he still was. But the fresh faces and the younger folks called him Tommy.

The deli was in the middle of downtown, a brick façade with a black and white tiled interior. The walls were painted white and adorned with photographs of Clinton before the war and family photographs throughout the years. Patrick even saw one with his father in his uniform, a young Patrick smiling as he munched a peanut butter and jelly sandwich by his side.

"You said half a pound of the turkey, Mrs. Powell?" Patrick was inspecting the meat, trying to find the one the customer had ordered. "I got a bit distracted when you mentioned Hubie. Can't believe he's growing up that quickly. Next thing you know, he'll be playing for the Gaels."

Mrs. Powell, like many patrons of the Brunwell Deli, had been a regular for as long as she'd lived in town—which is to say, her entire life. Patrick had to admit there was something about the predictability he hated about Clinton when he was younger. He knew the older he got, the more comfortable he'd become with its cadence, its way of speaking, its way of breathing.

Anything but that, I can do anything but that. I never want to be predictable; I never want to be predictable.

"Of course, of course," Mrs. Powell said. "You should've always gone into sports, too, Patrick. Ryan mentioned to me you did baseball in high school for a year and quit. Your father was a star for that team. I remember the day they went to regionals. He would've gone pro if not for the War."

Patrick realized he'd stopped looking for her meat. As he unwrapped a new package, he said, "You know, I don't know if that passed down. All that sports stuff. My mother's family, though? They are *talkers,* boy, let me tell you. You think we talk up here, Mrs. Powell? You would sooner grab cotton and stuff it in your ears just to hear your own thoughts 'gain." He gave her a smile and a wink. "Tommy came with me into Boston one time to meet them when they visited the States. Never asks about them, so do with that what you will."

The twinkle in Pat's eye relayed just the right amount of charm. She was wooed. It didn't take much for the older crowds. Patrick just had a way with them.

"Oh, I'm sure they're charming people, Pat. You sure are." The older woman smiled as she placed two dollars down on the counter. "That's for you. Call it a parting gift. I know you plan on leaving town soon. That may fill your tank up on the way out."

Patrick stopped slicing the turkey long enough to say, "You don't have to do—"

"But I want to," she insisted. "You're not the only one doing a bit of traveling. We're going up to Maine. We have some family there. My daughter and her little bundle, Hubie, will be meeting them for the first time. Juneberg, have you heard of it?"

As Patrick sliced the turkey, he shook his head. "Can't say I have. Couldn't tell you the first thing about the state besides Old Orchard. I went there once. You think my *hair's* red?" He gave a low whistle. "Golly, Ma didn't let me hear the end of that. Even got a photo 'fore she offered to throw me back into the ocean with the other crustaceans. If I wasn't such a respectable young man, I'd have tossed it in the rubbish to save myself the embarrassment."

Patrick chuckled as he folded her meat into its paper, bundling it as he did so before wrapping the twine on the outside and tying it together.

"Oh, it's a strange place, way up there." Mrs. Powell collected her turkey before unfurling another dollar bill, this one with exact change inside. She was also precise. It didn't hurt that Tommy rarely fluctuated prices to reflect the cost. "If I don't see you before you go, I just want to let you know you're a good boy. Keep your nose down and work hard. I'm sure the city won't be ready for a man like you."

"Thanks, ma'am. And be safe up there. Long winding roads. I got a long journey ahead of myself, too. I hope I do see you again before I go, but you take care now. Give Hubie a hug for us."

He'd put on a bright, cheerful smile, the kind of expression only those in customer service could pull out on a whim. As she left, the wrinkles of his eyes relaxed back into their natural positions. The artifice was gone as he called out to the back room, "Hey, Tommy? We're running low on turkey up here. There any left in the fridge? Leroy did inventory last week; wasn't me this time."

The mundaneness of it never bothered him much. There was always the abstract promise of the future, but now it was quantified. He could feel it on the horizon, and it burned with an itch, not unlike a mosquito bite—always far more intense than you could've imagined, swelling up until you couldn't help but claw at your flesh, ignoring the pain in anticipation of the relief.

Tommy had appeared from the back, adorned with an apron that carried the pink hue most found in butcher shops. "Plenty. Did Mrs. Powell come in? She loves that stuff—nearly three pounds a week." With a shrug, he added, "Shift's almost over, son. Did you still want to go to the pub after?"

Patrick looked at him, feeling a wave of exhaustion hit him all at once. He wanted to decline and just go home. But then he saw Tommy's smile. He was also exhausted, that much was evident, yet he pushed on.

"Sure," he said. "Not for too long, though, Tommy. It's a Sunday, the Lord's Day."

He smirked, knowing full well neither of them had been to a Mass in years. His mother still went, but when he got the job at the deli, it worked as the perfect excuse to abstain. He was sure she knew that, but she never pushed back.

Tommy wiped his hands on a rag cloth as he took his apron off, hanging it up in the back room. "In Clinton, we celebrate his sacrifice with a nice tall glass of lager. It's what he'd have wanted."

Patrick looked down at his watch. Technically speaking, they had thirty minutes left. However, it seemed the esteemed Deli Man Tommy Brunwell had mentally clocked out, and it was only a matter of time until his physical counterpart followed suit.

"You're a noble man to spend the duration of your evening consuming liquor in his honor," Patrick joked as he went to the front, flipping the *Open* sign to *Closed*. "I'll join you, if only so I can take in the unparalleled devoutness you exude. All the research may get me into a parish if the comedy route doesn't take hold."

Tommy chuckled as he moved cold cuts into the refrigerated area of the deli. "Take notes. I don't know if they drink out there in Vegas. Show them a beer and you could very well become a pioneer. Ain't they Morons?"

"*Mormons,* Tommy, but that's the spirit." He laughed and helped Tommy clean up by hauling the cheeses to the fridge. "I'll be the one who helps them discover spirits."

After a few minutes of lugging various oblong foods, everything had been stored away. The Brunwell Deli had officially been closed for the evening.

As they stepped outside, the humidity still hung in the air, but the sun was starting to weaken, the peak of the day having passed by. It still wasn't an entirely comfortable experience for Pat, who didn't mind the heat but abhorred the humidity that hugged his skin.

Tommy locked the door behind them and took a deep inhale of the summer air. "Nothing like it. I hate the winter. This is so much nicer."

"I don't mind the snow," Patrick said, falling in step beside him, "but I love the warmth. I love seeing people out and about. Hell, I even love going to the beach, even if the beach doesn't share the love I have for it."

Patrick and Tommy walked down the street. Several people nodded and waved at them; the town was lively, as masses always drew enormous crowds into the downtown area.

Although he was used to it, Patrick still marveled, "You'd think the city was in Worcester proper when the crowds get going. Sheesh, Tommy, it's a full house."

Nearing the bar, they dodged the large crowds of people conversing amongst themselves. The occasional bump was followed by an apology. Patrick thought he could even hear music in the distance. Occasionally, in the summer, people would sit outside and play their guitars for the crowds passing by. Usually, these impromptu performers were people just passing through, trying to make enough change to catch the next train to the next place. It was a lifestyle Patrick was fascinated with.

"Maybe we're the next boom town," Tommy said, interrupting his thoughts. "Brunwell Deli is going to make it big. You sure you don't want to stick around? Could be the best roast beef slicer this side of the Mississippi."

Patrick shook his head, a shit-eating grin playing about his face. "Lofty goals for me, eh? I'll think about it. At least until it's my turn to buy."

Slipping past a few men outside smoking cigarettes, Patrick grabbed the brass knob of the door and pulled it open. Sunlight flooded into what looked at first blush to be a dark, moody bar. The inside was anything but, and despite the atmosphere, the bar patrons were having the time of their lives.

Patrick reached for an available stool by the bar and beckoned Tommy over. "You sit; I'll stand. Still got those young legs."

Tommy rolled his eyes as he sat down at the bar. A man passed by, slapping him on the shoulder and giving him a wave, to which Tommy responded in kind. Several other people tipped their hats or hollered a hello, and the bartender was already making his way over. Tommy Brunwell was a V.I.P. in this town. The deli had been a staple in the neighborhood, and he'd done even more community work than his father before him. That showed in the deference and respect people showed him.

"What'll it be?" the bartender asked. "The same as usual?"

"Two," Tommy told him. "Pat's joining me this evening. We're celebrating...uhh, we made a sale today. That's a cause for celebration, right?"

As the bartender rolled his eyes and went over to grab a couple lagers, Tommy nudged Patrick with his elbow. "So, you got auditions lined up? I don't know much about show business, but I know that you're not famous—not yet, anyway. You had a good routine when we went to Boston that one time, but I don't think they've heard of you in Vegas."

Patrick stared down at the bar, debating how to answer the question. The truth was, he had reached out to a few venues, but he was underprepared and idealistic. Despite being in his mid-twenties, he still had a childlike optimism that things would fall into place—talent was, after all, undeniable.

"I have a few options, but I think all of them will offer me something once I'm there." Tommy sipped his beer as he let the statement breathe, smiling even if his eyes said something different. Then he asked, "I am funny, ain't I?"

"Yeah, of course, you are!" Tommy thumped him on the back. "The world is your oyster, Pat. Knock 'em dead. Leave 'em coming back for more. Chase your dreams. Beats being here, at least for you. Small-town, small-minded." He took a few contemplative sips of his beer, and Patrick got the feeling he was holding something back. But all he said was, "I love the simplicity; I love its predictability. We crave what we didn't have, y'know? You want bright lights and a new lease. Can't fault you for that, son."

Patrick sipped his beer too, sensing something more was on Tommy's mind, but still far too self-absorbed to put the puzzle together. "If it doesn't work out, I'll be back slicing turkey for Mrs. Powell until she's in the ground. And then probably for Hubie and his kids until *I'm* in the ground. A beautiful cycle."

"Yeah, that's the spirit!" Tommy clinked glasses with him. "You know, I don't have any kids of my own, no one but you to leave the joint to. Ain't a bad place to keep going. Dad never could've imagined it would be a staple. Neither could I. Just goes to show what hard work does. Monologuing ain't no different, Patrick."

Patrick smiled, touched. "You've always been good to me. You've always been a father after I lost mine. I know it isn't easy. I know I am difficult. I wanted to say thank you—for everything. You've done so much for me."

"Well, your dad—we go way back, nothing more than kids. I wish I served like he did, but my leg. You know the story."

Patrick did know. The muscle on it was underdeveloped as the result of an accident that had permanently damaged the leg. He'd have been unfit for service. To Tommy, it was a point of shame and regret, but most others held deep sympathy for him due to the mishap.

"I do," Patrick said. "But you know, the war changed him. I think he couldn't deal with coming back to this. Not that Clinton's bad. It's not. It's great. I think it was just...too different for him. He wanted to fix the world. The burden of it all was on his shoulders."

Patrick could understand why the simplicity of it could drive a man mad, to see how disconnected they'd all become. The injustices of war had hung over his father like a cloud with an endless ability to produce a storm. Some clouds didn't clear up, and some overcasts never broke for the sun.

"I'd like to think I knew him," Tommy said. "Don't we all like to think we know someone we're that close with? But it's been a long time. Years have passed since I heard his dumb jokes ring through this pub."

The surrounding crowd chatted on as though there wasn't something profound happening right next to them: the pillar of the town and his surrogate son pouring their hearts out to each other, their deepest thoughts laid bare.

"He was different," Tommy continued. "War changes a man. He couldn't deal with the unfairness of it all. Pat, don't tell anybody I told you this, but your father..." He lowered his voice so much that Patrick had to lean over to hear him. "He was a Red. And I ain't talking about the hair on his head."

Patrick blinked at him, surprised by the revelation. It didn't change his judgment of the man; he cared little for the government. Being gay, Patrick was always one step away from being crushed under its boot. Whatever they said about the Reds, he doubted the sincerity. It wasn't long ago that Americans called Stalin "Uncle Joe," so he found the heel turn especially unbelievable. But the reality was he never gave it all that much thought, choosing instead to focus on himself. Society had never done anything for him, anyway. Why feed into it?

"It doesn't matter much now Stalin's gone," Tommy said. "Ain't nobody witch hunting like they used to, but back then? One slip, he'd wind up in prison. It didn't matter if he did anything wrong." He was twisting his nearly empty beer mug around on the counter. "He saw things over in France. Ain't say much, but you could tell. War changes a man. He came back and saw through what he called 'indoctrination.' People in suits were evil—the men who sold and sold, consumed and consumed. He couldn't do it."

"I know," Patrick said, calling for another round.

"But he loved you, I know that. I promised him I'd make your dreams come true. I can't make you the world's best monologist, but I won't stand in your way. I know your mom won't either, even if she doesn't get it."

After the bartender poured their drinks, he headed to the other end of the bar, leaving the two men to ruminate in their thoughts in the otherwise jovial pub.

"I love her," Patrick said, not yet touching his second beer. "And she misses him. I don't think she cared much about economics. She just wanted the man she married back. To think, she barely even knows her son. Sometimes I want to tell her. I don't think she'd care. I don't think she'd push back, but her family? That's a different story. She ain't happy about me leaving. I know that much."

"Getting out of here will be good for you," Tommy said, chugging some of his beer before wiping his lips with his arm and setting the mug down on the bar. "Can't spend your life worrying about everyone else. Sometimes being selfish is good. Realizing you can't save everyone is one of the hardest things anyone goes through. Doubly so when the person drowning is someone you love."

Patrick stayed quiet, nursing his beer, curious—and a little nervous—where this was going.

"So many people walk around resigned, defeated, with dead looks in their eyes," Tommy continued. "I wanted you to keep the deli going, but that's *my* dream, not yours. This town has nothing for you. It'll eat you up inside. You're still so full of life, Pat. Do it there, no matter what it costs. Do it."

This was a moment of clarity, an open stream of consciousness pushing forward. It was too much for Patrick. He couldn't process it. Tommy was never dishonest, but he was rarely this self-aware, rarely this introspective. Patrick needed air. He needed a moment to breathe, to be in the summer dusk, basking in the last moments of the sun before it settled in for the night.

"Thanks, Tommy," he said, voice a little choked. "You mean everything to me. I can't even—sorry, I'm just at a loss for words. I just—I'll be back. I think a smoke would do me good. Some fresh air and a cigarette, yeah. I will be right back."

Tommy looked like he was going to protest, but instead, he just nodded. Patrick stepped away, rushing outside. He found himself in the warm embrace of a swiftly approaching dusk. It was peculiar how rapidly time passed by in the confines of a bar. Inside, it felt as if only thirty minutes had passed, yet the pink-tinged hue filling the sky suggested it had been several hours.

He brought the cigarette to his lips and lit it. He inhaled the sweet tobacco smoke as he craned his neck back, the scalp of his head making contact with the brick.

"Mind if I bum one off you?" someone asked. "I can pay you back after. I have some change in my car."

Patrick turned to see a tall man staring back at him. His scruffy blonde hair draped his face, obstructing the entirety of his features. His accent gave him away as a local as the word car came out as "*cah*" and after came out as "*aftah*." Patrick nodded, pulling a loose one out of the pack. It was then he realized who it was: Randy Lofton. The guy was a bit of a bully around town but had never explicitly given Patrick issues prior.

"No problem, Randy. Just pay me after you finish it," Patrick told him. "Even then, you don't have to."

The blonde shifted uncomfortably as he smoked his cigarette gifted to him by Patrick. For a while, neither of them spoke, just watched as a young family meandered past them. Just as they were hitting the other side of the block, the small boy who'd been tugging his father along, tripped on his untied shoelaces and almost fell. But the man scooped him up in the nick of time, sitting him down on a nearby bench and kneeling in front of him to tie his shoes for him.

Pat's heart ached for the father he'd lost...and the one he was moving away from. To distract himself, he opened his mouth to ask how Randy's day was going, but what came out instead was, "Randy, you got a dad, right?" He cringed, but the question was out, so he hastened to add, "I forget your whole story. Lots of names to keep up with. Everyone has a story. Don't mean nothing by it."

"Yeah, sure do." Randy puffed his cigarette, his voice distant, as though he wasn't trying to engage in conversation. "I know your dad ain't 'round—nasty accident."

"Never knew him. Not really, anyway." Patrick shrugged. "Few memories here or there. Probably a few more years, and I won't even get those memories right." Blowing out a puff of smoke, he said, "Getting older sucks, Randy."

"Ain't you a comedian?" Randy sneered. "Ain't you supposed to see the funny things in life? Tell a joke." His voice held no humor or good nature. It sounded dead and dull. "C'mon, tell a joke."

Patrick eyed the taller man's figure. His skin was red, the skin of a man who worked outside but was not built for the sun. It protruded from his olive-colored shirt. Patrick took note of the tapping foot—anxious—but passed it off as a smoker craving his next fix and thought nothing of it.

"Sure thing, I got a good one." Patrick plastered a smile on. "Say, if you're American in the bathroom, and you're American outside the bathroom, what are you inside?"

Patrick smirked as he waited to see if Randy would guess the punchline. Randy looked at him. His eyes seemed soulless, devoid of anything but rage. Patrick knew the man had a bit of a reputation, but he also knew people rarely became like that for the sake of it. It was a reaction to something else—whether that was reasonable or not, he didn't yet know.

"I don't know, Patty," he spat out. "You tell me. You're the funny man and all of that."

Patrick didn't really enjoy his tone of voice, but that didn't matter. One joke and the joy would be back in him. It happened to others. He saw no reason why Randy would be any different.

It didn't register to him that the crowds outside had seemingly become non-existent, as though a cloud followed Randy, the surrounding storm scaring everybody back indoors. Even the young family had scampered off, having crossed the road immediately after the boy's shoelaces were secured. Despite the clear sky and the sunny weather, there was a primal instinct left in people that trouble was afoot.

Intoxication nullified these senses for Patrick.

"European. Hahaha! Get it?" Patrick let out a raucous guffaw which was met by a light chuckle from Randy. Patrick felt assured of that. "I told you; this is what I do. Tell jokes, bring joy. I wish there was more. The world could always use more joy, more love." Patrick went into his usual speech, but it wasn't met with affirmation this time.

All Randy said was, "Thanks for the smoke. C'mon, let's get to my car. I'll give you some change for it."

Patrick took one last drag of his cigarette. He paused, debating waving off the payment for one loosie. But hell, he needed every dollar he could get for his trip to Vegas, so he followed behind the blonde man.

Randy opened the driver's side and sighed. "I think I left my change in the back seat. I tell you, I'm a weird guy, but shit, do you mind since you're already at the door?" He spoke from inside the car, and Pat, despite his reservations, could see quarters glinting in the back seat. That would settle it. He just needed to get the coins and then get back inside.

"Sure, thanks again," Patrick said. "You don't have to give this much. Even a nickel would've been plenty."

Patrick opened the door and reached in. His fingers clasped a quarter, but he paused, realizing he felt Randy's aura behind him. The streets were empty, even across from the bar. Everyone was inside drinking or back home. Patrick felt the weight of his isolation.

Randy flashed a gun at Patrick. "Get in the back. I am not asking again."

A Colt .45 stared back at the comedian. He blinked, his life flashing before his eyes. Confusion consumed him, the rational part of his brain complying, begging him for survival by any means.

Randy slammed the door and moved to the driver's seat. He turned, looking at Pat. "You can try to run if you want. I'm not a jokester, but I *am* a marksman."

Patrick didn't understand why he was being singled out. He knew Randy was a character, a man feared since his more youthful days. But they had hardly ever interacted, so what could he have ever done to the other man.

"Why? I don't understand." Patrick pleaded as Randy pulled away from his parking spot.

The vacant streets watched on in silence. Only the light wisp of wind pushing through the trees filled the silence outside the car.

"You will," Randy promised, his voice low and menacing. "It'll all make sense soon enough. Now, sit on your hands, and so help me, God, if you move them, your brain will be all over my back window."

With that, they departed the town center, Patrick unsure if anyone had even seen them leave at all.

14.

Even if the days lasted long, the night descended rapidly when it was time. The sun did not linger. Patrick wished it had, though. Unlike in downtown Clinton, there were signs of life on the back roads, other drivers who could help if they only knew what was going on. But Patrick sat in the back in silence, afraid to move a muscle.

The only noise to be had was the static of the evening's radio news broadcast cutting in and out as Randy made his way to the outskirts of civilization. When the radio made mention of some conflict in Cuba, Randy smacked the radio, which did nothing but further agitate him.

"Stupid, fucking stupid, ain't no good going to come from that," he growled. "Castro's a slippery bastard. They ain't gonna stop him. Ain't no way. Didn't they learn from the Bay of Pigs?"

Patrick couldn't care less. He just wanted to be out of there. He wanted an explanation, anything to make it make sense.

The car stopped, and Randy looked back at him as though he weren't conversing with himself just moments prior.

"Get out. Slowly."

Patrick slowly removed his hands from under his ass, just in case Randy was looking for an excuse. He knew the man was troubled, but this was a whole new level. Once Patrick was satisfied moving wouldn't get him shot, he opened the car door and climbed outside. He faced Randy, who had already pointed his pistol toward Patrick from his window as he simultaneously opened the driver's side door.

"Listen, Randy, I don't know what I did to you. I didn't mean to offend you. Whatever I did, I'm sorry, Randy. It wasn't on purpose. Just think about this. Ain't worth it."

Patrick was choking up, the reality of his situation settling in. The reasons didn't matter much. Clarity would bring no catharsis if this was the end.

"Sodomite." Randy spit. "Yeah, I know. Do you think you can lie to me? Do you think you're smarter than me? No, you don't even know, do you? No, why would you? You've got a big, inflated ego. Well, I'm the fire, and you're the goddamn Hindenburg. So, you know what comes next."

Patrick was trying to put the pieces together. Randy knew he was gay, so what? Unless...? Patrick began to understand, his eyes widening. In the shadows, he could see the resemblance now. How silly he had been to overlook it. Patrick had slept with Randy's younger brother, no different than any other whirlwind summer affair.

"Yeah, I know about him." Randy gripped the gun tighter. "He was my brother. Tried to tell my parents he was a homosexual." He shook his head, finger tickling the trigger. "You made him think that, didn't you? You forced yourself on him, filling him with your horseshit. Your father was one, too, huh? Bet he touched you. That's why you are the way you are. Ain't it? Don't lie, Patty. Don't lie to me."

Patrick ignored the dig at his father. Randy was looking for an excuse to shoot, and Patrick wouldn't give it to him, no matter how much it hurt. He needed to bide his time until there was an opening. Randy was well-trained. He knew about the military, but his mind was clouded with emotion—with anger.

"You said he *was* your brother. What happened to him? What did you do?"

"He—he hung himself. Ma and Pa sent him away to a camp, and that was it. They refused to let him have a mass because he died a homosexual. That's your fault, Patrick, so you're going to join him. If he can't go to heaven. Neither can you."

Patrick was appalled. How was it *his* fault? Randy's voice wavered as he spoke. He was in the midst of a full-on breakdown.

"You kill me, and it's over for you, Randy. It's done. If you know we slept together, he must've told your parents, too. If I go missing, they will know you're behind it."

Patrick looked at him pleadingly, but Randy just smirked.

"Man, that's the first funny thing I heard come out of your goddamn mouth." Randy chuckled, but there was no mirth behind it, only malice. "You think I'd tell them? You think *he'd* tell them? No, my parents didn't give a damn who it was. They just wanted their son back. It's not Daniel's fault you corrupted him. That's yours. So no, he didn't tell them. They didn't want to know. But he told me. He told me *everything*."

Patrick didn't believe him. Randy was a sick man. He didn't trust a word that came out of his mouth other than he somehow knew about Daniel and Pat.

To Pat, it was nothing more than a fling, a one-night stand never to be repeated. Just two men who went their separate ways. He'd even seen Daniel around town afterward, and he was polite but gave no indication he desired an encore and, more importantly, no hint that anything was going wrong.

Patrick went to respond, but Randy was on him. He threw Patrick to the ground. "Get up. We aren't done yet. Not until I say so, Patty. But tell you what, the mood's getting dark. Crack a damn joke. Why are you so quiet? Normally, you can't shut the fuck up."

Patrick slowly picked himself up, refusing to bend to his abductor's will. There was no space for Patrick to joke, even if he wanted to. Even in the vacuum of silence, Randy filled the forest with his contemptuous aura. Nobody was around except the fireflies lighting the woodland path. Patrick could hear the reservoir's waves in the distance and crickets chirping like the laugh track to a perverse sitcom. He shook his head, realizing what Randy wanted him to do.

"Say something! You like to talk, don't you?"

Patrick was pushed forward again, and he tripped on a tree root protruding out of the cleared pathway. Dried pine needles stuck to his face as he splayed out on the ground, tears welling up and throat swelling with grief and fear.

Hold it in. Don't give him the satisfaction. He wants to break you. That's what this is. He's broken, so he wants to break you. He's been broken a long time, Pat. A very long time.

Patrick got up. His nose was bleeding, and his knees were scraped. He wiped the blood from his face with the cuff of his shirt as he turned around. Then Patrick laughed like a madman. He knew it would piss off Randy—anything to throw him off his game. And it worked. He threw Patrick to the ground a third time.

"Aren't you scared? Tell me a joke, Patty, and God help you, it better be funny, you stupid fuckin' homosexual." Randy's eyes narrowed. "You eye fucking me? Look away. I said, *look away*!"

Patrick gripped the dirt, willing himself not to look away. If he was going to die, he was going to be defiant to his last breath.

"This isn't how this was supposed to go," Randy said. "You were supposed to be scared. You were supposed to beg for forgiveness. You *ruined* Daniel. You *broke* him. And *you* killed him!" He started pacing in a small agitated circle. "It's your fault. You're a real special kinda evil, you know that? You feel nothing. He's dead, and you feel nothing?"

The logic didn't mesh with Pat, but it didn't matter. Randy was going to kill him no matter what he had actually done. That much was clear to Pat. If he was going to die, he wasn't going to die groveling, not for being gay. He'd refuse to give Randy anything.

Patrick knelt on the ground and held his arms out wide, daring Randy to do his worst. "You going to kill me? Then do it, Randy. Do it, you walking sob story. Go ahead. Right between the eyes." He inched a little closer, though his knees wobbled a bit. "But you won't scare me. I've been living scared my whole life. Besides, the real monsters are the men in suits. The men who shake your hands. You're not a monster. You're a pathetic bully. Daniel was better without you."

The words would haunt Randy. He knew it. He wanted to twist the knife in Randy's gut. It was all he had left at his disposal.

"It's all your fault he's gone!" Randy screamed, his voice ringing out among the trees. "It's all your fault!"

Randy had lost control. While there was satisfaction in that, there was also a smaller dose of fear. It just took Randy pulling the trigger for it to end. Still, as he wailed, Patrick slowly pushed himself backward, the palms of his hands pressing up against dirt as his legs slid over the ground.

"Yeah, yeah, we get it," Patrick jeered. "All my fault. The evil homosexual. But you know what? He loved it. He'd do it again. *I'd* do it again because what you think and say don't mean a damn thing."

As he taunted the delirious man, his hand struck something, a sizable rock that he threw. It didn't hit Randy, but it startled him. He discharged his firearm into the sky as a jerk reaction. In the momentary lapse of focus,

Patrick stood up and ran into the trees, the slosh of the reservoir's waves reminding him how close he was to the moon and the shore. He had to avoid it, as the moonlight would give him away, and no matter how much of a mess Randy was, he wasn't one to miss more than once.

"C'mon, Pat!" Randy yelled into the woods. "Why don't you want to tell me some more jokes? I got a good one about a ginger in the woods. It's a blast."

Randy's light flickered a small flame, providing light in the darkness. Patrick could see his shadows against the birch trees, their white bark giving hints of his form on their trunks as Randy made his way to where he thought Patrick was hiding.

Get him closer to the water and turn on the jets, Patrick thought. *He didn't park far down. It was only a few minutes of walking. Zig zag, he won't see that far. It's too dark. He'd be firing at random. No way he could pin you down. Plus, it's remote, but somebody will hear those gunshots. Police won't be far.*

He wasn't sure he believed any of that, but he didn't have a lot of options. His hands searched for something, anything he could find to throw, make a noise, and distract Randy away from the path out.

"Stop hiding," Randy taunted. "C'mon, Pat. Do you really think people don't know we're here? They just don't care. People are cowards, afraid of their own shadows. I'm not scared of the dark. I'm not scared someone will find out. I have nothing to hide. I did nothing wrong. You took my brother from me."

Patrick ducked behind the brush, still searching for a solution. His heart pounded in his chest, and the sound of Randy's taunts dulled, his brain having little time to process anything else but survival.

As he crawled in the brush toward the path they had walked in on, Patrick turned back, watching Randy wade toward the water. The man's blonde hair shone in the moonlight, the trees no longer blocking its rays. Randy's body convulsed with rage as he searched through the brush at the shoreline. Patrick could see that even from this far away.

Pat's fingers worked through the leaf- and needle-covered ground as Randy moved further away, searching the parallel side of the brush the path had sliced through. Then, he felt the rotted-out core of a large branch from one of the behemoth oaks that had blissfully obstructed the moon from revealing where he hid. While it felt a bit brittle in his hands, he knew it would make enough noise to get Randy's attention. From there, he would run as fast as his legs would carry him. He gripped the rotted-out branch, which was so heavy, he needed to use both hands. He grunted a bit, which caused Randy to turn.

"Found you, you rat bastard!"

Randy hadn't, but he was much closer, facing the proper direction finally. He rushed over to the other side of the brush as Patrick threw the hollowed-out branch. It went about ten feet before smacking another tree. Randy followed the sound as Patrick booked it the other way, the two noises happening at once, causing Randy to pause, probably trying to determine which was real and which was a distraction.

"Oh, you bastard! Not now."

Randy was not fooled for long, and he began to run after Patrick, who could feel the sweat stick to the nape of his neck as he pushed forward. Mosquitos buzzed past, some smacking him in the face. A sharp pain hit his ankle from a misstep. He could hear ragged breaths get closer to him as Randy closed the distance. Next came the footsteps, out of rhythm with his own—Randy was catching up.

Patrick heard the blast and immediately dropped to the ground.

Randy whooped and hollered. "Got you! Nailed him." He leaped past what he must've thought was Pat's body and came to a stop, putting his free hand against a tree for support. His gun hand resting above his knee, he bent over, sharply intaking air and gasping out, "That...was for...Daniel."

Thoughts rushed through Pat's brain, slicing through the fear as he desperately held onto the chance to live. *He missed! I'm not dead! But I don't have long until he figures that out or decides to shoot again for good measure.*

There really was nothing else to do. Randy only stood a few yards away now. Patrick almost wished he hadn't missed. The dread of knowing death could still be coming consumed him.

Randy was rationalizing his next steps while Patrick played dead. "Throw him in the lake. He'll float up eventually, but I'll be long gone, even if they thought it was me." His breath was becoming less ragged as his body stabilized. What didn't change was how unhinged he sounded. His voice suggested he was still mentally shattered. He'd found no closure in the murder of Patrick Gallagher.

"What the hell is going on in here?" another voice boomed in the distance.

Patrick couldn't make out who it was at first, but when they called out a second time, he flinched, recognizing the voice.

"Randy? Why are you out here firing your gun?"

It was Tommy Brunwell.

"Put your damn hands up," Tommy said. "I got my own gun, and I'm not taking any chances with you. I'll put one between your eyes before you can say your prayers, so help me, God."

Patrick slowly shifted upward, catching sight of Randy, who looked toward where Tommy's voice was coming from and sighed.

"Mind your business," Randy growled. "I don't need your permission to be out here, you old bastard."

Randy looked on as Tommy slowly stalked towards him. Neither of them dropped their guns, and Randy widened his stance, preparing for a fight. They had themselves a stand-off, and Patrick felt powerless to do anything to help.. Sitting up now, he looked for anything he could use to give Tommy the edge. In his heart, he knew there was no peaceful solution to this.

"Did you kill him, Randy?" Tommy asked. "I saw you take him. You've gone too far. They found...they found Daniel and your...They know it was you. It's over. Your rampage is over." He shook his head—in sadness, in disbelief, in anger. "Did you *really* think you could get away with it? Your parents? Your own brother? Did you plan on killing yourself, too?"

As Tommy spoke, he stepped closer, and Randy stepped back, his gun now facing the older man.

Patrick blinked. He couldn't process what he was hearing. There was too much going on all at once. He needed to get Tommy and himself out of this situation by any means. He scoured the earth for a rock. Randy didn't bother paying attention to the noise behind him, most likely because the threat in front of him seemed much worse.

"I didn't kill anybody. Patrick did. Whoever was left wasn't my brother. And my parents, they...they just couldn't deal. I did what any good brother—any good son—would do. What any *man of faith* would do." Even in the dim light, Patrick could see a shift in Randy's eyes, like something was dawning on him. "You know what," he said, head cocked to the side, "maybe Patrick wasn't always a homosexual. Maybe *you* made him that way. Took advantage of his absent father, you sick freak."

Patrick could practically *see* the delusion solidifying in the man's head. The more Randy said, the more he gained confidence in what he was convincing himself was true. Patrick found a pinecone under the shadowy canopy off the path. He crawled toward it as the other two stared each other down, tension rolling in thick. It was like a fog, one that suggested a torrential downpour of revelations was no longer just in the forecast but had made landfall.

"Put your gun down, Randy," Tommy said. "I won't ask again. Just give up. You had a good run."

The boiling point had been reached, and Patrick could see Randy gearing up to fire his gun. He didn't know if Tommy was seeing it, but he didn't care. He whipped the pinecone at the back of Randy's head and yelled, "Turns out you can't aim for shit after all. Want a do-over? Come on, aim and fire."

Randy spun violently, his face contorted with utter rage and confusion, a glimpse into the soul of a man Patrick wasn't sure had one left.

"*How!?*" Randy's eyes widened, the weight of his mistake visibly showing in the way his shoulders tightened.

Tommy obviously had zero intentions of wasting this moment of distraction. The last look in Randy's eyes was acceptance—a bitter acknowledgement of the reality that awaited him. Whether it was blackness, the pearly gates, or anything in between, he looked ready to embrace it as he was ushered into the nether by the slug of Tommy Brunwell's revolver, which pierced through the back of his head and pushed through his nasal cavity. At first, there was a gasp, the body not realizing it was over. After a brief twitch, he fell, nothing left of the man who had terrorized them.

Tommy stood over Pat, looking down at him. His hand trembled. Patrick could see that even in the shadows. "I told him to drop it..." he said, voice just as shaky. "Pat, you're okay."

Patrick ran to Tommy, his arms wide open. They embraced each other tightly, Patrick trembling into the older man's shoulder.

"I was dead," Patrick choked out. "I thought I was dead." Tears flowed down his cheeks. "I didn't know he had a brother. I didn't know. I promise I didn't."

Tommy looked at his surrogate son, his embrace warm despite the anxious sweats they had built up in the summer heat. "You didn't do anything wrong, Patrick. You didn't do a damn thing wrong. That boy snapped. What he did to his family..." He wearily rubbed his eyes. "I'm just happy I got here in time. I'm just happy I got you out of this."

Tommy let go of Patrick and approached Randy's corpse, a pool of blood growing at his feet. There was a mess to clean up and with two gunshots. People would know, people would suspect.

"You need to leave, Patrick," Tommy said. "Take my car." When Patrick didn't move, Tommy made him take the keys. "Go ahead, take it. I'll clean this up. Take my car, park it in my driveway, and run home. Pack your bags, then skip town. I'll take care of this. I'll fix this."

Patrick still didn't move. He wasn't sure Tommy was thinking clearly. "There were two shots, Tommy. They heard it. And they'll know it was me if I run. This is my fault." Patrick was spiraling. "It's over for me. It's over. They'll be looking for him. You said he killed his brother and his parents?" When Tommy nodded, Patrick said, "This is a small town. *Too* small. Even if no one knows about me yet, it won't take long for them to connect the dots."

Patrick began pacing, trying to figure out what future awaited him. The pain in his body paled in comparison to the internal torment he was putting himself through. The stages of Las Vegas never seemed more distant. The only spotlights he could imagine now were those on the courtyard at night as he looked out his cell window.

"Listen to me, Patrick," Tommy said, snagging his arm to stop him from pacing. "Do *not* repeat this. What Randy did to his brother, Daniel...they'll look the other way. He killed his parents, too. Especially if they can't find him. If there's no body, if there's nothing tangible, they won't look."

"Wait, what?"

"You don't understand." Tommy patted his shoulder soothingly. "You did nothing wrong. After what he did to his family, they'll think he's on the run. Just go. Go home, pack your bags, and go to Vegas. Hell, in my glove compartment, there's at least two-hundred dollars. Take it with you. It should get you through to Las Vegas easily enough. Get out of town, pull all the money you can, and head west. Don't look back."

Patrick opened his mouth to protest, but Tommy went on.

"Randy was a disturbed soul. But it's done. What's done is done. I made a promise to your father, so go. No matter what, don't let this ruin your dream because it's mine, too."

Tommy left for his car, Patrick watching him in its distant lights. For a moment or two, Patrick thought maybe he would just leave, that he'd changed his mind and was going to abandon Patrick to clean this up on his own. But he soon returned with a few old aprons from the deli and brought them to the body.

"I'm not asking, Patrick," Tommy said. "You need to leave. The police won't chase you if there isn't a body, but the town? Rumors? They'll eat you up. There's nothing left for you here but me and your ma. That's it. You're destined for more."

Tommy offered his gun to Patrick, who was frozen in shock. When he snapped out of it and gripped the cool steel, it felt alien, foreign in his hands.

He hoped he'd never have to use it.

Tommy was able to pull Randy's keys out of his pocket. The man's eyes were still frozen open in his noseless face, leaving him looking like he was in perpetual shock.

"Tommy, I didn't know," Patrick said, his voice a low, pained moan. "I'm sorry. I don't understand. If he's dead, and we killed him, it doesn't matter if he was a bad guy. It doesn't make a difference who he killed. Two wrongs don't make a right. They'll want justice. That's how it works."

"I wish it were, kid," the older man said sadly. "I really wish it were. God abandoned us a long time ago, but still, I pray. I pray every damn day." He jerked his head towards his car. "Go. The longer you linger, the more likely someone notices us here."

Patrick stuffed the gun in his pocket. He started to walk away but stopped after a few more steps. He turned around, looking at the shadowy figure of Tommy in the darkness.

"Thank you," he said. "You saved my life. And you're giving me a second chance. Maybe there is a God, just not in the way we think."

Tommy stood there in silence, letting the crash of the waves and the buzzing of nocturnal insects fill the air before responding. "I love you, Patrick. Go, son. Go. I'll be here when you come back."

Patrick nodded as he turned back around, getting into Tommy's car. He turned the ignition, and the engine sputtered to life. He looked back at Tommy. He could see a shadowy figure working to clean up the mess. Patrick's dad was right—the darkness was less scary than the light. In the darkness, you knew who everyone was—good—or bad.

Tommy was one of the good ones, the men in suits be damned.

15.

Pat felt the warmth of Lorenzo's breath upon his back but otherwise felt numb—cold. The events of the boat replayed through his head even though it had only been a week prior. Nevertheless, his moans with each thrust gave Lorenzo no impression of the inner turmoil that plagued Pat.

"Yeah, just like that," Lorenzo said, as though Pat was doing any of the work.

But he wasn't. He lied there passively, letting Lorenzo's lust take over. His head was empty as Lorenzo's primal instincts kicked in. A rapidly growing pace began to shake the bed and, by extension, Pat's world.

It was over not long after. Pat stared out the window. So strange how his bedtime had become the daytime. He had expected to grow darker in Las Vegas, but if he only went out at night, he'd go the opposite direction.

Lorenzo flicked his cigarette on the ashtray on his nightstand, his free hand lightly touching Pat's chest. "I really thought we were done after that fight, Pat. I'd hoped you'd reach out, but you never know. You looked like you saw a ghost."

Pat's eyes didn't leave the sun shaft stabbing through the window from between a small gap in the curtains. "I needed time. We don't know each other yet. At least not well."

"I know. It's been a whirlwind. I want to get to know you. Sometimes I forget, y'know? People come to Las Vegas to become a new man. I didn't want to prod. I know we all have our pasts."

Lorenzo put out his cigarette and moved to embrace Pat. The smell of tobacco, mixed with notes of leather, created a comfortable, familiar scent that brought Pat out of his head, which was firmly entrenched in the clouds. He shook off anxiety like a dog after a bath before turning to Lorenzo.

"What's yours?" Pat asked. "Your past? People have been warning me, telling me there's more to you. The more I linger over it, the less it makes sense. You just happened to be there twenty minutes into my first night. Charming, knowing just the right things to say. Who are you, Lorenzo?"

"I'm Lorenzo, Pat. I'm just me." He must've been able to tell that wasn't enough because he sighed and said, "Alright, fine. I only work in waste management on paper. I work for—shit, I'm sorry. I work for the Mob. Grunt work, just collecting taxes from businesses for protection."

Pat's eyes widened. Lorenzo had his hair, like Hyland. He wasn't bald like the others. Though, that didn't mean Lorenzo wasn't in on what happened on the boat.

"Why hide it? I don't understand, Lorenzo. Why lie?" Pat broke off their hug and sat up in the bed, his head pushing against the walnut headboard as he gripped the cotton throw blanket, ready to lunge out of bed if he was left unsatisfied with the answer.

"I like you. You weren't like the others. I could tell that the moment we locked eyes. Sometimes you just get a feeling; it can't be put into words, but your stomach churns, and you feel a tingle in your spine. I only ever had that feeling once before." Lorenzo reached for another cigarette and lit it, saying, "I didn't want you to be disappointed in me. I shouldn't have lied, but you were—you *are*—straight and narrow. I didn't think you'd want anything to do with me if you knew the truth."

Pat relaxed, not ready to leave bed yet. "You like me, but I haven't gotten to know the real you. Just who you wanted me to see. Do you see why that hurts? I knew people here had secrets, but Lorenzo, that's a doozy."

Pat shifted out of bed. Lorenzo did the same. Both men stood naked on opposite sides, Lorenzo with a cigarette in his mouth, Pat with a sun shaft warming the small of his back.

Lorenzo didn't answer him, just asked, "Pat, what happened that night? You've changed. You won't talk about it either. And that ring? Where did you even get the money for that?"

"Don't you care that you hurt me, Lorenzo?" Pat asked, a pang running from his chest into his gut. "Don't you care that you lied? Why is this about the secrets *I'm* keeping? Especially with the skeletons in your closet. What's next? You have no issue with lying. What is the truth? Seriously? How am I supposed to know?"

Lorenzo hung his head low, absorbing that but not saying anything for a moment. This was followed by a deep, resigned sigh. "I told you I wanted to protect you from the truth. Do you think I'm proud? Ain't much work around here for a Mexican. Don't matter that I was born here. They look at me and write me off before I even open my mouth. But the Mob? They don't even care that I'm a homosexual so long as I produce. And I produce, Pat. Is that what you want to hear? That I couldn't make it on the straight and narrow? Or that I'm not as smart as you? I'm not as talented as you?"

"I didn't—"

But Lorenzo was just getting started, and his voice rose, steam practically pouring out of his ears the more incensed he got. "And even if I was, they'd look at my skin and look the other way. It's even worse for the Blacks. Almost all of us coloreds here work for the Mob. They're the only ones who'll give us dignified work. But even then, they don't see people. They see dollar signs. Is that what it takes to treat me like a man, like a human?"

As Pat started gathering up his clothes, he said, "You're right. I'm being selfish. And I'm sorry, Lorenzo. I just don't know what reality is anymore. That night we fought, Louie's Lounge asked me to go out on a boat with them to Lake Mead. I saw..." He plopped down into the chair in the corner of Lorenzo's room, shaking his head. "It doesn't matter what I saw. What matters is I'm in a bad way. I made a deal with them to be their monologist. I wanted it more than anything. Now I want anything but that." He slipped into his socks, one at a time. "This town...I thought it was full of hope. I thought I'd chase my dreams. I thought I could be anything I wanted. Now I'm a comedian for the Mob. It was stupid. I'm nothing but a fool."

Lorenzo's eyes went wide, and his voice trembled, taking Pat by surprise. Lorenzo was a lot of things, but fearful wasn't one of them. "Pat, Louie's Lounge isn't run by the Mob. It's one of the few places that refuses to even pay taxes. What do you mean you made a deal with them?"

"Who runs them, Lorenzo? They don't have hair or eyebrows. The things they did..."

The image of the man in the chair ran through his mind, a needless display of horror and a chilling exertion of power—a reminder of Pat's selfish shortcomings, even if he knew deep down protesting would've just made him the next in line. Still, he'd chosen to shoot the man in the interrogation, an act he'd never thought himself capable of.

"I had no idea," Pat whispered. "I'd have never agreed to do it if I had. You know that."

"We don't know who they are," Lorenzo said, pulling some fresh clothes out of his dresser. "None of the guys know. They're popular—wildly so. But nobody knows anything about where they came from."

Pat had already put on his pants and was now buttoning his shirt. "What *do* you know?"

"Louie, the owner, seems to be from New York, but nobody claimed him. People don't recognize him. That's basically all I've heard." As he shrugged into a button-down, he asked, "Why would you make a deal with them? You're talented—way too talented to make backroom deals, Pat. Why didn't you just keep auditioning? I don't understand."

Fully dressed, he slouched down into the chair again. "I'm *not* smarter than you, Lorenzo. And *definitely* not straight and narrow. I have skeletons in my closet, just like you. I promised a friend of mine—Tommy—I'd do anything to make it. He gave me a second chance at life. All he wanted to do was see me reach my dreams.

"But the owners of these clubs? They wouldn't give me a chance. They wrote me off because I'm gay. I'm not the same as them, and they knew it." He looked over at Lorenzo, who was half dressed and peering at him intently. "I don't know what it's like to be colored. I can fit in with the good ol' boys. But I'm still not them. They remind me at every turn, I'm not in their club, not part of the Rat Pack. I'm just the rodent on the outside looking in, a pest that they'd throw away at the first opportunity."

Pat was facing the truth of his situation now. There was no point in lying to himself. He had made a mistake. But that didn't mean he was entirely stuck. He just...couldn't think of a way out yet.

Seeming to read his thoughts, Lorenzo said, "We both made mistakes. They don't understand what a talent you are. I only wish you'd asked. If I knew you were going to go into that, I'd have tried to warn you." Lorenzo's brain was working in overdrive. Pat could see that much. "We don't know who they are or where they came from. But if you're inside their circle, maybe we can find out. Do you know where any of them live?"

Is this how he thinks he can help? But after a moment's thought, he realized, *This* is *how he can help. If this is what he does, why not let him? He can't be more evil than them. They burned a man alive, Pat, right in front of you. Why? Because they're savages. They're not human—they're demons.*

Pat hurriedly laced his shoes up as he said, "I don't know where they live, but I can find out. What would you do? Kill them? There's a lot more of them than I probably even realize."

Lorenzo held his hands up. "Take a breather—eat before you go, Pat. You don't need to rush out. We need to plan this." Guiding Pat by the shoulders to the kitchen, he said, "The Mob keeps tabs on everyone in town, but we can't get into Louie's circle no matter how hard we try. "We can help. *I* can help. Are they all bald and bizarre? Do any of them seem more like you or me? Not that being bald makes you any less human, but the bald ones seem distant. Only seen a few at your shows, but they never even look at the stage; their gazes are always elsewhere. It's all so very strange in hindsight."

Lorenzo pulled out some pans, using one to gesture for Pat to sit down at the table. Pat watched him putter around the kitchen as he thought about what to say.

"Hyland, the man who signs my checks," he began. "He's got all his hair. And he feels more...normal. The others are stoic and statue-like. A few will talk, though they seldom say much. But Hyland is a gabber. He talks plenty." He smiled as Lorenzo started making coffee. "He's a long-haired man. Looks Native. I don't know where he lives, but if we can find out, maybe you can get what you need. Maybe there's a way out of this deal for me after all."

While the coffee brewed, Lorenzo started frying up some eggs.. "Okay, your next show," he said. "You'll see some of us there, but don't say anything. Just act natural. We'll have some guys tail him when he leaves." He seemed excited by the prospect of being the one to pull the rug out from under them. "Always knew Louie's Lounge was sinister. We just couldn't prove it. But everything comes to light, eventually. Everything."

Pat got up to pull out coffee mugs, tempted to come up behind Lorenzo and wrap his arms around him, sink into him in the middle of that warm, comforting kitchen. Instead, he set the mugs down and leaned into the mundanity of reality rather than the whimsical fantasy playing through his head. "All I ask, Lorenzo, is to be honest with me from now on. I don't want to be a means to an end. I'm exhausted, making backroom deals with devils in suits."

Flipping the eggs in the pan, Lorenzo turned around and smiled, opening his arms up, as if he could sense Pat wanted to hold him. Their lips met right there in front of the stove, the smells of coffee and breakfast enveloping them the way their arms embraced each other.

"I won't ever give you a reason to lie again," Pat promised when their lips had parted. "Just be you, beautiful or ugly. I can take it...among other things." He gave Lorenzo a wink and pulled him in for another kiss.

Lorenzo smirked, his upper lip curling upward. "Thought we were eating breakfast."

"It's...sort of breakfast? Irish mom would faint if she knew eggs and coffee would suffice as a full meal."

Pat fluttered his eyelashes at Lorenzo, almost pouting. Lorenzo replied by rubbing his mustache and stubble as he groaned, enthralled by the implication.

"Oh no baby, that's just one course."

Lorenzo pressed him up against a nearby wall, giving him a deep kiss, then Pat pushed him back towards the bedroom, though they didn't get far. As they made out in the hallway, entangled in an embrace, they laughed as though they hadn't been perilously close to ending it all that morning. Their courtship mimicked the dance they did now, intense and earnest in its hopes of reciprocation. Despite the scorching heat, they only felt each other. The warmth of a lover proved distinct, even in the unforgiving heat of a desert. Their passion for reconciliation burned with an intensity that even the sun would envy.

We'll be alright, Pat told himself. *We have each other, and that's all we need. That's all I need.*

16.

Hyland often wondered what he'd gotten himself into, but a job was a job. Despite the dreams and promises that a city full of gambling seemed to offer, in reality, Las Vegas was a city full of losers. All of them attempted varying degrees of mental gymnastics to convince themselves that they were, in fact, one of the winners. But in the end, they all left empty handed…if they ever left at all.

Hyland had seen it all before and was undoubtedly sure he'd see it again. He was one of the winners. Even if he wasn't a big winner, Hyland had come a long way, and without making the pact with Louie that the others had. He was the rare Lounge employee who hadn't needed to seal his deal with what he likened to collateral. Even now, in his office, his spine shivered as he recalled the turnstile of willing souls who had given everything for a taste of Louie's power.

He scribbled numbers in the margins of his books. Accounting had become a drab part of what was otherwise an exciting existence. Being the outward face of a nightclub with Louie's Lounge's reputation had come with perks a younger Hyland could've only dreamed of. Unlike most of his tribe, he wished to assimilate into the ways of the White Man. Each time he touched a dollar, he was reminded of the face of another oppressor. His betrayal of his ancestors, who had fought tooth and nail against the hordes of pillagers to ensure Hyland had a future, once weighed heavy on his mind. That meant little to Hyland now. His pride had long since left in the pursuit of the almighty dollar and the perceived status that came with it.

"Not a bad night, not a bad night at all, Hyland. Plus, Patrick's week off is done. Comedy nights bring all the crowds."

He kept up a personal running monologue as he continued to add the numbers. Not that profitability mattered to anyone besides Hyland. Ownership cared little for financial success regarding raw profits, just that people continued to come. With the crowds came desperation and, in Louie's eyes, the opportunity to recruit to his crusade. It didn't sit well with Hyland, but what was he to say? The only thing that separated him from the others was his office door. Civilization was always the precipice of calamity, balancing on a tightrope so beautifully that nobody questioned how close it was to collapse, how close it was to snapping and bringing subsequent tragedy.

There was a knock at Hyland's door as he scribbled away.

"Come in."

He knew who the knock belonged to. There was a rhythm to life that mirrored routine, and despite the lack of humanity, those in the suits were still creatures of habit. The door swung open with a low creak, and on the other side was Samuel, who stepped in. His tall bald head nearly scraped the office ceiling as he went to the chair opposite Hyland's desk.

"Pat is coming in shortly," Samuel said, watching Hyland jot numbers down, none of which probably carried any meaning to him. "We believe the theatrical display on the boat has shaken him up. His week away from the stage is over. Do you wish for us to retrieve him?"

"There will be no need," Hyland assured him. "He will return. Besides, he still owes Louie. The lounge was his reward. Morality is fickle, and he's shown before he's not shy about pushing it to the side if it means he gets what he wants."

"One last thing. Louie intends to come to the show. Perhaps your assessment of Pat being a wolf in sheep's clothing is not so far off after all. Louie wants to see him up close. Maybe he *is* fit to be one of us. One of the Chosen."

Hyland smirked at him and nodded as he shifted back into his seat. *Fit to be one of you? No. That's a curse, Samuel. You know it is, too. Who cares how long you live if you don't live for yourself? Would rather collect my check and keep it moving. Don't care if you think I'm fit enough or not.*

"When I called him a wolf, I didn't mean like you," Hyland said. "I mean, he shot that guy, didn't he? You didn't threaten his life. He just thought it was between him and the guy in the chair. A man who thinks his back is against the wall is likely to lash out. You'd do well to think about that, Samuel. I don't know if he's ever starved, but that kid's hungry, and he's reactionary. That's a bad mix when he doesn't have the full picture."

Hyland folded his hands, and his pen rolled across the desk toward Samuel, then fell. The lanky man caught it in mid-air and handed it back to Hyland. His inhuman reflexes never ceased to amaze Hyland.

"Do you doubt Louie's conviction? If he sees something in the man, then there's something there. His ignorance leaves him ill-prepared to push back, which is to our benefit—most of all *yours*. If he suspects you don't share our powers, *you* become the weak link. I need not tell you how Louie handles weak links."

Samuel blinked once before his eyes shifted around the room, gazing over the décor, which predated Hyland—a reminder that even he was replaceable, as Hyland himself had been brought in to replace another. The turnover at Louie's Lounge was high for those not in the "Chosen," and Hyland was aware of that. However, Samuel and the others didn't understand Hyland. He was a survivor.

Hyland's people had dealt with demons before. They came offering deals, brokering a peace they never intended to fulfill. Pacification was followed by indifference as more and more settlers pushed their way through the lands of his ancestors. Once-holy places became pits to store their fecal waste; hunting grounds became farmsteads in which many crimes against humanity were carried out under the unknowing sun—itself sustaining the conditions in which life came to be, and with it, the barbarity that came next. Even bystanders had their role to play. It was enough to make any man bitter.

Hyland knew of the world's perpetual injustices and constantly saw his people suffering at the hands of false men with false promises. Yet when the opportunity came, he'd spurned the traditional ways.

"There's no going back. The White Man will take us all and push us further and further into obscurity. Assimilation or damnation: those are our choices. I'm proud, but I'm not arrogant. I'm going into their lands, and I'm going to do their jobs better than them. I'm going to be undeniable."

His father hadn't liked that, but his response had been nothing—apathy. Choosing silence was a way to freeze Hyland out until he bent the knee. However, in the Las Vegas heat, such coldness had little effect.

"Are we sure *I'm* the weak link, Samuel? Many of your Chosen elect to leave their brains at home. You are no fool, nor is Rosaline, but there's a lot of you. And as we both have seen, being his elite doesn't absolve you of error." When Samuel said nothing, Hyland waved a dismissive hand. "Pat will come back, but keep an eye on him. Don't assume he'll cave. Fearful men rarely go quietly into the night. Now, if you don't mind, I have some paperwork to finish before the show."

This was a lie; the paperwork held no meaning, but Hyland had grown tired of this conversation. The Chosen were nothing if smug, bordering on a self-righteousness that made their partnership nigh unbearable, if not untenable.

"So be it, Hyland," Samuel said, unfolding himself from the chair. "He will watch tonight. As should you. If Pat's a desperate animal, his perception may not be reality. You certainly look like the weak link from the outside."

With that, Samuel silently slunk out of the room, leaving Hyland with his thoughts and paperwork again. The door shut from the outside, and Hyland sighed as he shifted back in his seat.

When Hyland went hunting with the rest of his family, he'd never been the weak link. They'd bash him constantly for taking shortcuts, cutting corners, but it mattered little. They still ate his trophy, and he still produced results. Traditions were made to be broken as far as Hyland was concerned. While they'd called him sacrilegious for his inability to adhere to the ways of his ancestors before him, Hyland likened it to no more than evolving.

Weak link? Hyland snorted in his otherwise empty office. *I didn't need to make no deal to gain my superpowers. This was all me—just hard work. Let's see them live my life. None of them would've made it past the reservation before somebody put one between their eyes. By the calluses on my hands and the sweat on my brow, I ain't ever need no deal to sweeten the pot.* He's *the weak link, bug-eyed bastard.*

While Hyland knew he stood out in comparison, he doubted Pat could exploit him. He had hunted his entire life—just to get by—just to eat. Sure, the prey had changed from the bison of his motherland to humans down on their luck, trying to eke out an existence in the margins, but he hadn't changed. Once a hunter, always a hunter, and with that came never underestimating the prey. Pat was far more formidable than any of them knew.

He looked at his watch and chuckled. The show was nearly at hand. He finished scribbling a few more numbers into boxes before shuffling out of his leather seat. He straightened out his bolo tie and unhunched his shoulders, shaking the arms of his tan blazer before making his way out of his office and into the hall.

After he closed the door, he stared at the brass nameplate on it. "Hyland" was stamped across it at eye level. He could see a monstrous reflection of himself staring back in the spaces between the letters. He smirked at it before looking down at his burned brown cowboy boots—the attire of the oppressor. No amount of assimilation would ever make that resentment go away.

He closed his eyes, and for a second, the sticky warmth of his subterranean office reminded him of the grassy bluffs he begrudgingly missed more and more with each passing year. A breeze passed through his hair as the imaginary day was nearly at its end. When he opened his eyes again, the daydream was gone, replaced by bland industrial arteries that ran through the organs of the underbelly of the club. Around the corner and up the stairs was a much livelier place: the lounge for which the club had been named.

We'll see if Louie comes, he thought as he made his way down the hall. *Either way, there's going to be fireworks. If there's one thing the White Man has mastered, it's the art of theater. I get to sit back and watch it all unfurl. I played my part. Now the chips will fall where they may.*

Hyland smirked as a waft of tobacco smoke and cheap booze filled his nostrils. He could also hear the chatter of people arguing at card tables on the floor above him as he made his way up the staircase. He flicked his wrist and glanced down again at his watch.

"It's showtime."

17.

A few hours prior, Pat waited outside The Crane, a bird-themed hotel decorated in bright, loud pinks. Pat had been to the casinos outside of Fremont Street only once since he had relocated to town. This was the second occasion, and his first in the daytime. As he waited in the passenger seat of Lorenzo's car, he watched the passersby. He swore he saw at least one or two actors, people he couldn't name but that he recalled seeing in films he watched back at The Strand Theater in downtown Clinton.

I thought Fremont was corrupt, Pat mused, noting how many people were shiftily making their way inside. *But shit, look at this. Actors, singers, and mobsters, all in one place.*

Pat shifted as Lorenzo barreled out of the hotel, his dress shoes smacking against the marble steps with a *click-clack* noise that echoed in Pat's eardrums.

"Good news, they're sending big guns out. Now, you're sure Hyland is going to be there tonight? Right?"

Pat nodded.

"Good." Lorenzo glanced over his shoulder, like he was checking for prying ears, then said, "They know about the bald one you said waited in your room for you that one night. Samuel? Don't know where he lives, but they're pretty sure there's no talking to him without having a big fight on their hands."

"Sounds about right," Pat said, suppressing a shudder. He was thinking about that night on the boat.

Lorenzo got in the car and started it up. Despite sitting right next to Pat, he dropped his voice, and Pat had to lean in to hear him. "They're afraid to start a war over this. I can't blame them. I wouldn't start one against an enemy I don't know. But you said Hyland seems more reasonable, like he'd be willing to talk...or could at least be intimidated into doing so."

The car began to speed off, and Pat looked out the window one more time before saying, "Going to be a war anyway, Lorenzo. These guys can't be reasoned with. They burned a man alive to prove a point. I don't think they're shy about blowing up the powder keg." After a moment's thought, he added, "But Hyland might flip. He doesn't seem as far gone. And he wasn't there on that boat either. Maybe he's a bastard, but he ain't no demon, not like the others.

Lorenzo sighed as he turned down the next street. "I hope you're right, Pat. If this backfires, it's going to get messy."

Pat looked out at the *Welcome to Fabulous Las Vegas* sign, where a tourist was talking with a photographer, apparently arguing over payment. He suppressed a grin, longing for the mundanity of such a dispute.

"So, what's the plan? You're going to drop me off at the Slippery Slope like nothing happened?"

"If they're watching you—which seems likely, seeing as you said Samuel likes to wait for you on your bed—we want this to seem as routine as possible. It's why I wasn't in there long." Lorenzo patted his pocket. "I have some cash they handed me. I'm going to stop at the bank and make it seem like I'm just running errands. I'm hardly ever in the loop with their plan. Better that way. The longer I was in there, the more suspicious anyone watching might get."

"Why haven't your guys gone after Louie's Lounge sooner? The hottest club in town not being run by the Mob feels like the kind of thing they'd want to rectify."

Lorenzo shrugged. "I don't make the decisions; I'm just a mid-level guy. But my guess? They thought it was owned by the government—they like to launder, too. Nobody's squeaky clean. When I told them about the ship, they realized it was open season. There are some people you can't touch. Doesn't matter how bad they are. But even the government won't cross that line unless you're a threat."

"What do you mean?"

"Burning down a church? That draws a lot of attention. I heard about it from people who used to attend mass there. Why? Why burn down a church? Whoever they are, they sure sound like nasty pieces of work."

"Yeah..." Pat stared out the window, not sure what else to say.

The sun was setting, and he hadn't even gotten to practice his set. Comedy had never seemed further from his mind, but he had his role to play, and he would indulge. Besides, the man who wore the mask never needed to look in the mirror. The reflection would just be skewed, a façade looking back.

The car merged onto the freeway above the city's skyline, which was to their right. He could see crowds conversing below in the dusk-kissed urban center.

"You look far away," Lorenzo said.

"I just don't know who I am," Pat admitted. "I thought I did and then it all came undone. Now I'm here—and I've never felt more lost."

Lorenzo swapped lanes as he sighed. "We all owe it to ourselves to know who we are, to find out what we could be. You never told me what happened back home, and you never have to. It would be selfish for me to pry, even if I think I want to know."

"You do?" Pat asked.

"Curiosity killed the cat and all that. I don't care if I have nine lives. I'm not going to use one up on that. There's one thing I know you are, though, Pat—one thing I've never been surer of in my life."

Pat looked on as the ramp fed into familiar roads. The Slippery Slope was within reach. "What's that?"

"You're a monologist through and through." Lorenzo smiled at him. "Do what you do best. The rest will come in time. You made a bad deal, but I work in waste management, right? It's time for me to take out the trash."

Pat's heart swooned as he reached over, gripping Lorenzo's outstretched hand in a tight squeeze. He inhaled a deep breath of air, feeling it balloon in his chest, and as he exhaled, it expunged the anxiety that had been festering in his heart.

"I'm scared," Pat admitted as Lorenzo pulled into the Slippery Slope and slowed the car. "I guess the world is a lot bigger than I thought it was. There are things I thought I could explain, things I thought I was prepared for. World has a way of humbling you, I guess."

"The world knows no humility. Thankfully, it doesn't have an ego, either. It's just...indifferent. Up to us to find the meaning of life."

Pat still gripped Lorenzo's hand, but he was looking out the window at nothing at all. "I guess..."

"Look, you drove all the way across the country and left everything behind to be here. And things could be better. I'm not denying that. But you trusted me in a way I didn't trust you. Let me reward that, Pat." Lorenzo cupped his chin and turned his head so they were looking at each other. "The

Mob is full of wicked men. Maybe I'm one of those bad guys. Or maybe I just work for them. But that doesn't mean we can't do some good. That doesn't mean *I* can't do some good."

"I guess people *can* change," Pat teased. "A few weeks ago, you told me you weren't a deep thinker. Now you sound like Plato. Just need to grow out the beard and ditch the pants."

"Nah, not my style. Face smooth like a baby's bottom, the way Mami intended." He rubbed his mustache as he chuckled. "Well, mostly like how Mami intended."

Pat gripped Lorenzo's thigh as he leaned in for a kiss. Lorenzo met his lips with his own. When they pulled apart, Lorenzo gave him a bright smile, his lips wrinkling at the corners as he glowed in the familiar red neon lights of the Slippery Slope.

"I'll see you at the show tonight," Lorenzo said. "And act natural on the way to your room. Don't know if they're watching us right now. You can do this. I know you can."

Pat rubbed Lorenzo's arm, then opened the car door and got out. He looked in through the passenger's side window, giving his lover a smile, though his thoughts were more troubled than he was letting on.

I'm still mad at him. How could I not be? Still, he's my hope—the only hope I have to get out of this mess.

He looked down at the shamrock ring. Despite his fear and the spiraling situation, despite knowing the fate of its last wearer, he still bore it on his finger. A tainted treasure was still a treasure so long as it maintained its luster.

The car peeled off, leaving Pat alone in the ocean of neon flickers, the fluorescent lights of all the adjacent hotels joining the clash of waves. His own flesh was bathed in blood-red lighting. Despite this, he felt at peace. There was a plan. He felt in control for the first time since Randy had devastated his life. He was no longer reacting, but rather, he was putting the machinations in place. To prevent what, he wasn't entirely sure of. The people he worked for had never made a direct threat toward him, yet the implication couldn't have rung clearer.

"Hey, Pat, long time no see. Haven't seen you these past few shifts."

Lars, the Lederhosen Latino, was running the desk, and it was then Pat realized he hadn't been back in days. He spent more time with Lorenzo than anywhere else to get his mind off of the boat.

"Your show is still up for tonight, yeah?" Lars asked. When Pat nodded, he said, "I'm bringing my lady with me. You did a stellar job last show. Sad you missed last week, but hey, it's October. The bug is going around."

Pat mindlessly fidgeted with his shamrock ring as though he was winding a watch. After a few twists, he snapped into action, like a puppet coming to life on a stage. "Oh, yeah, sorry, stomach bug." He smiled sheepishly. "Back in Boston, they don't have tacos, but I think they're really going to catch on. If this comedy show thing doesn't work out, may just take their secret formula and make millions touring New England."

Lars scanned his face, and Pat could tell the man didn't believe him. The thing about puppets was, they could only mimic so far. The words sounded good—human, even. But the face was wooden, the body lifeless. Lars was not a prying man, but his face said it all.

Thankfully, all Lars said was, "I'll be there if you decide to poke fun at the crowd, but don't go after me too hard. Don't want to get too embarrassed. I like this girl; I really do."

"I'll...I'll try not to make you look too bad," Pat said, his voice slow. The puppet was running out of life.

Lars gave him a customer service grin before returning to his work, and Pat gratefully made his way to his room. The hotel was full of unfamiliar faces, which wasn't a new experience in his transient lifestyle, but it did little to assuage his newfound anxiety.

He made it to his room without incident. Housekeeping had neatly made his bed with no imprints of any kind. There was no Samuel lurking in the corner. His drapes were open, he assumed, to allow the sun in, but daytime had passed into night, and all that filled his room were the bright lights of all the casinos and hotels that lined the roadway.

Pat left his light off as he sprung onto the bed, hitting the quilt on top like a ton of bricks. He felt the springs rebound and catch his momentum as he lay on his stomach, the smell of clean sheets filling his nostrils.

"Take a load off; don't worry about me. I'm just floating on by." Randy's voice filled the empty room.

Startling and sitting up, Pat looked around. In the room's corner next to the windows, he could see a bloated hand in a neon-tinted shaft.

"You didn't think I was gone, did you, Pat?" Randy menacingly taunted. *"No, I'm here to stay. And I ain't no apparition."*

The figure stepped out into the light, and despite his insistence that he wasn't a ghost, his translucence when illuminated illustrated a different portrait.

"Did you think you were Ebenezer Scrooge? No lessons to be learned here, I'm afraid. The other side is darkness—icy darkness—just like the reservoir he left me to float in." He gave a dark chuckle. *"He doesn't tell you, but I watch him, too. He thinks he's going insane. And maybe he is, The question is, are you too?"*

"And if I am? What does it matter? You thought you were so powerful. Now look at you." Pat lit a cigarette and took a drag as he looked out the window through the specter of the past. "The novelty has worn off. Who's really the haunted one?"

Randy didn't speak, nor did he move, and Pat found he didn't really care. He had more important—more immediate—things to worry about.

Huffing out smoke, he said, "If you're real, congratulations. You get to watch powerlessly as I live the life you tried to take from me. And if you're fake? Well, Catholic guilt consumes us all." He let that hang in the air a moment, like the tendrils of smoke curling up to the ceiling. "Am I supposed to feel bad you died? Least you had a fighting chance. Daniel didn't, and he was your brother."

That piece tore at him the more he mulled it over. Pat hadn't known the two were related, not that it would've changed what happened. The world was a spider web—it all connected in the center, eventually. You just needed to find and follow the right strand to discover the through line that bound any two people.

"You've changed. You're not the Patrick I know." The menace had been sapped out of his voice, replaced with confoundment. *"Even in my last moments, I could smell the fear on you. Who are you?"* Pat took another drag and held up his ring. The green gems glinted in the darkness, unbelievably bright.

"You know something? You killed me in the end, after all, Randy. Well, more of a mortal wound. The Patrick you thought you knew died of his wounds out in the desert." He let out a bitter chuckle. "I'm Pat, the monologist. I'm a man who'd kill another to save his own ass. I don't feel guilty about what happened to you, not anymore. I was drowning in senseless guilt, but those days are over. So go ahead. Haunt me. Scream at me." His eyes were hard and cold when he said, "I don't fear you, Randy. I pity you."

The spirit's face twisted in a snarl. Real or not, it seemed intimidation was the only reaction Randy was capable of. The mask contorted, and nostrils would've flared had there been any, but this Randy looked like the one who'd died by Tommy's hand, obliterated nose and all.

"*No, that Patrick isn't dead, Not yet. I can still sense him, the lingering doubt creeping in. That deal you made threatens to snuff you out in a blaze of glory, burn you to your bones like the man on the ship. Perhaps literally, perhaps not. Either way, I'm sure you'll have a crowd. We'll be in touch.*"

Within a blink of his eye, the man was gone, and Pat was unsure if he'd ever really been there at all.

Pat shook his head, and thought sadly, *He ain't wrong. He's a bastard, but he ain't wrong about that, Pat. Bury the old you. It might be the only way you can get out of this.*

The room's silence said more than anyone—living or dead—ever could. He stood and flipped his light switch on before reaching for his room phone. His finger hovered over the dialer, and he closed his eyes for a moment, trying to focus himself. When he opened them again, he sighed heavily, stubbed his smoke into an ashtray, then snatched up the receiver and dialed.

As the phone rang, he swallowed a heavy lump in his throat. He heard a voice on the other line and almost slammed the receiver back down. Instead, he took a deep breath before speaking.

"Hey, Ma, we need to talk. I know it's been a long time."

18.

The black exterior of the building gave no real hint to how layered the labyrinth of Louie's Lounge truly was. Pat gazed back at his car as he stood outside. It took all he had to leave his firearm in the car. He had to trust Lorenzo and his people. It was the only way. Pat had to play his part, and it wasn't playing cowboy.

At night, the doors remained open, Rosaline standing beside them to welcome people inside. She scanned Pat, her eyes unreadable, before giving him a dry smirk. "Welcome, Mr. Gallagher. Good luck on your set tonight."

Pat gave a terse nod and attempted a half-hearted smile before ducking inside.

Lights graced the dance floor in strobing patterns unlike any he'd seen at other clubs, though he could see it catching on at some point. Even the industrial interior was far ahead of its time. Metal tables lined the ground-level corridors, which sat parallel to walkways that hung over the dance floor, tied together with metal cables bolted into the ceiling. Factory-style stairs descended into the chaotic club below. The walkways were made of steel, and through small slits in the flooring, one could see the backs of the strobe lights, which alternated from a wave effect to a pulsating one.

On the ground floor, ironically above the actual club and casino, was an average bar reminiscent of east coast dives with pool tables and dart boards—the works. Pat had always found it confounding how both spaces existed simultaneously. Somehow, the crowd at the dive above the pit never seemed to mind being so close to the chaos. It didn't hurt that it was also always nearly empty—could he blame them? Who would want to be up there when there was so much more to do down below?

As he descended the stairs, he kept an eye on the second bar, which formed the pit's perimeter. Two separate stations stood across from each other on the left and right of the pit. In the front was a stage for concerts and other performances, the stage Pat himself had graced a few times and would do so again shortly. Curtains draped on either side, preventing the crowd from seeing the tunnel work that led up to it.

At the edges of the parallel bars were doorways feeding into two different casinos, each sprawling out like equally intricate behemoths. Pat knew some back entrance led people onto the casino floor, but he hadn't seen it himself. He always chose to go through the front. Up until recently, he'd never felt ashamed of his association with Louie's Lounge, having almost forgotten he'd been strong-armed into the deal.

As he made his way down into the pit, he looked at the stage and the dance floor, the lights still strobing, but it was mostly empty. In a few minutes, there would be no one here besides the staff putting out chairs for the patrons of Pat's show.

Hyland was sitting on the right side of the bar, but he turned to see Pat and gave him a nod. "There's our superstar," Hyland said as he sipped his liquor.

"Not yet. Give me some time, Hyland. Talk about pressure. I am not going to turn around and become Frank Sinatra overnight."

There were no outward signs of nervousness in his voice. The puppet was dancing, the strings nowhere to be seen.

Hyland seemed not to notice the performance. "You get paid the same, Pat, full crowds or not. No pressure from me."

Playing the role of the unsuspecting and dutiful employee, Pat sat down next to him and asked, "How are you? Doing okay?"

Hyland shrugged. "Doing alright. But how are you? I know you took that week off after your job. Samuel wouldn't tell me what you guys did—not that I pushed too hard. More curious than anything else. But I'm your boss, so the door is always open."

Hyland was prodding. Pat could see that much. He didn't take the bait, however.

"I needed to reset. I'm in transition here. I love playing these shows, and I didn't sign up for those jobs, but I knew they came as a package deal. I did what was asked of me. This is all new to me. I am just a kid from a small town in Massachusetts. It's a whole new world. I needed to remind myself there's growing pains."

He flashed his shamrock ring at Hyland. The man took another sip from his glass, swirling the ice inside, and put it back on the bar top. He twisted in his stool to face the dance floor, which had been cleared, watching the staff laying out chairs. His elbows rested on the bar top, his forearms dangled by either side, and his neck reclined backward.

"It's a whole new world here," Hyland said. "I came to this city with nothing in my pocket, save a few coins and a bag of clothes. That was fifteen years ago. Back then, people would still gamble, but our big draw? It was mushroom clouds and bomb tests. People would come far and wide just to see the destruction." He huffed an unamused laugh. "I'm not a scientist or a doctor. But anything that can do that? It can't be that good for you to be this close, to breathe that in, for years. Yet, people wanted to see, so we showed them. We did what we had to so we could survive. Now look at this city. Sure, the tests were still happening even a few years ago, but this place took on a life of its own."

The chairs had nearly all been laid out. Pat looked on in awe at the rapid pace at which the staff worked, asking, "What's your point, Hyland? I know Vegas is moving up in the world. It's the only reason I came here."

"You don't have to hold it all inside yourself," Hyland said, turning back to his drink. "Look, I know we pushed you into this role. It wasn't my call. I do my job, the same as you. Neither of us is those bald monsters Louie trusts in his inner circle."

"What's with that?" Pat asked. Even if it was just an angle to get Pat to reveal something, Hyland wanted to buddy up to him for now, and Pat was going to take advantage of that, get some answers that were a long time coming.

"They weren't always like that," Hyland explained. "They made their own deals. Beyond the scope of ours, the things they wanted were bigger. They required a lot of changes. Samuel used to be short. I don't know how Louie does it, but you can see he's a mountain of a man now. It's unnatural. There are unexplainable things that happen here. And you and me? We're both on the outside looking in."

Pat doubted his sincerity. Confiding in him came off as a calculated risk. Hyland was a shrewd man who had, until now, rarely spoken outside of the fateful day the deal had been struck. It was likely this moment of camaraderie was a ploy of some sort.

But what Pat wasn't so sure of is whether or not what Hyland was saying about the bald people was true. It made sense. They seemed almost inhuman—their black suits too neat, their bald heads flawless—and even how they spoke felt inorganic. Hyland was being at least partially truthful, even if he was using the information to leverage the situation.

Pat took a deep breath before responding. "I hear you. Maybe we can meet for a coffee soon. I'd love to chat more, but I probably should get a drink and clear my head." Pat tapped Hyland's shoulder and stood up, winking. "I get paid the same, but I'm sure Louie wants as much money as possible. I think one more good set, and I'll sell the next one out."

After ordering a drink, he cut across the dance floor, which had been converted into a makeshift concert hall. He drifted through the rows of seats, sipping his gin and tonic and acting as though he was checking audience vantage points. What he was really doing was thinking about everything and waiting until Hyland left. Though he never saw the other man slip out, at one point he stopped feeling eyes on him and turned to see Hyland had disappeared.

He doesn't know about Lorenzo and our plan, but he suspects something's afoot. Lord, I only hope I threw him off the scent. If this doesn't work, I'm done. They'll burn me alive—just like that poor bastard. Hell, who even knows what they did to the guy who had this ring? His car was on fire when I drove past, too. I really wish I didn't stop when I saw it. I really wish I had just kept driving. I could've avoided all this.

As the bartender refilled his drink, Pat debated sitting on a red leather cushioned stool but thought better of it. "Any word who they have opening for me tonight?" he asked, leaning against the bar. Before the other man could answer, Pat added, "God, I hope it isn't that fella from Milwaukee. If I have to hear one more story about cheese..." He rolled his eyes as he sipped the G&T, Which was dry with a citrusy bite, just how he liked it.

"It was a rough set, Mr. Gallagher," the bartender replied. "They gave him the main stage last week when you were out, and I don't think they were fans. He's not on tonight, so they may have had their share. Believe they got a Negro woman from Kansas City tonight."

Pat raised a brow. A lot of bad things happened at Louie's Lounge, but segregation wasn't commonplace there. Even the language most of the staff used felt more progressive than what he was used to hearing elsewhere. He didn't, however, have the courage to discuss why it made him uncomfortable.

"Well, we all can't be rock stars," he said. "Six months ago, I was staring out the window of a deli, watching the buds bloom. Now *I'm* the flower boy." He turned bright red when the bartender chuckled as he wiped down the top. "Wait, that didn't come out right. But you know what I meant." He took one last sip and threw a dollar on the counter. "Thanks for the drink. Don't have time to finish it."

Pat slipped out of the bar through a door leading to one of the casinos. If he thought the lighting in the dance club had been intense, it was a whole new level on the gambling floor. The light was softer but much brighter in the casino. Beautiful maroon and gold ottoman-style carpets covered every inch of the floor. Marble pillars rose and gave way to a ceiling befitting a Renaissance palace in the northern reaches of Italy. Walking through the massive subterranean hall gave no indication of where you were in time or space. After a few cocktails, you could've convinced yourself that you were on a steamboat on the Riviera, heading toward Monaco.

In the casino, a door led to the back of the stage, feeding back into the center room that functioned as a club. As he made his way towards the door, he couldn't help but notice a group of well-dressed men yelling loudly at each other at a poker table. With a start, he realized who they must be.

Lorenzo's people are here. Nobody could mistake those guys for anything else. I just hope they don't make too big a scene at the show, or Hyland will notice them.

Louie's lackeys guarded the perimeter of the casino, their black suits and bald heads somehow melding in with eggshell-colored walls. Thankfully, they seemed not to notice the boisterous mobsters.

Pat found the side door to the stage. Samuel hovered over it like a guard dog that had been promised a steak. "It's been a while, Pat," he said with almost a hint of a smile. "Welcome back to Louie's Lounge. We missed you. Last week's performance wasn't good. I don't think they'll be back."

Even Samuel's showing personality? Pat tried to keep the surprise off his face. *Maybe they're playing coy. It wouldn't be the first time.*

"I trust you're well?" Samuel asked. "Got your head on straight again?"

"I'm fine. I'm sure the first time you did a job like that, you needed a moment to take a break, yeah? I'm only human."

Pat didn't bother sharing the depths to which his mood had sunk, the crushing depression he was wading through. The night immediately after the incident on the boat, he'd woken up in the middle of the night, screams ringing in his ears and the scent of cooked flesh filling his nostrils. The odor was disturbingly similar to the steaks he'd take home from the Brunwell Deli. He didn't share, either, that he'd driven back out into the desert to find where they'd buried the body he'd seen when he arrived in the city. But perhaps they knew, as they had known about everything else. Regardless, Pat wouldn't give him the satisfaction of admitting it.

Samuel nodded. "So I did, so I did. You're back now, though. Going backstage early? Need some time to recenter?"

"Say, Samuel. I never got to thank you."

Samuel raised his brow, the wrinkles on his forehead smooshing together. The behemoth of a man looked confused, head tilted like a dog trying to decipher a language it could only understand the tone of. "Why is that Pat? What do you need to thank me for?"

Pat locked eyes with him. "I used to think the world was a place of good, with evil sprinkled in. You showed me the truth—that isn't reality. That's what we tell children because we hope that's what we can become. We hope and dream of a world where it's that easy. But it's not."

Samuel's face remained impassive, but Pat sensed he was pleased. It was melodramatic, sure, but it was what Samuel wanted to hear: Pat becoming cynical.

"I learned that lesson too late," Pat continued, hand still wrapped around the doorknob. "I learned more about myself on that boat than I had in the entirety of my life. I know who I am, and I've made peace with that."

For a long moment, the two of them stood there, staring at each other. Samuel's expression never wavered, but he still held that air of morbid contentment. He enjoyed seeing Pat succumb to the reality of his situation, to realize that he wasn't one of the good guys, that there *was* no morality. It had gone and died under a porch somewhere. Its scent wafted upward through old, bloodstained floorboards, reminding those who remained of that which was lost in the pursuit of the American Dream.

Pat's speech was a farce, of course. He still believed in good and evil. Tommy had shown him sacrifice. Lorenzo had shown him adoration and affection. Randy had shown him what happened when bigotry consumed a person. Rosaline and Samuel had shown him what came when someone abandoned compassion and replaced it with selfishness. It was a balancing act between right and wrong, though he worried that wrong was tipping the scales.

There *was* good in the world. He just didn't know how much of it remained.

Pat shrugged. "So...thanks. And wish me luck tonight. I'll have them keeling over."

Samuel's jaw slacked for just a moment, as if he was at a loss for words. But he soon composed himself, a twisted smile forming at the corners of his mouth. "You know something, Pat? The world has a way of flipping when you think you've figured it out. Break a leg out there."

We will see about that, Sam, he thought, finally turning the knob and opening the door. *I have a feeling your world is about to flip real soon. Hold on tight, you bald bastard.*

He paused before he spoke, an attempt to regain his composure. "You, too, Sam," he said without a trace of a smile. "You, too."

As he strolled backstage, a shiver thrilled up his spine, one that he usually only experienced when he was performing on stage.

Success.

19.

From backstage, Pat could hear the cheers and applause from the crowd. The opening act had just told another zinger. She was good, a natural even. She'd practiced her jokes with Pat for about forty minutes before going onstage, and, unlike the Tractor Man of Milwaukee, her jokes had far more layers than twenty different ways to refer to cheddar or milking a cow.

"So, long story short, that's why the best BBQ in town is at a gas station." Her voice boomed through the curtains. "Fill up your tank and fill up your gut. Only in Kansas City, ladies and gentlemen. Thank you so much. You've been wonderful. I hope to see you again."

Pat scurried over to her as she made her way to the back, genuinely excited when he said, "Wow, better than the cheese guy, that's for sure. First time in town?"

The woman smiled at him and nodded. She was wearing a green dress with a sheen that Pat wished his own wardrobe held. It contrasted with his warm tartan jacket and corduroy pants.

"Yes!" she said. "I moved here from Kansas City. Didn't have enough money to make it to Los Angeles. People told me you could perform here in Las Vegas, didn't matter if you were Black or white, so long as you were good. This place was the first one to give me a chance. I just can't believe it went so well."

Pat was entranced by their similarities—two outsiders who'd both found an opportunity at Louie's Lounge—and he offered her his hand as he said, "I heard your set from back here. It was fantastic. You said onstage your name was Meredith? Is that right?"

"Yes, Meredith Wicker." She shook his hand. "Nice to meet you, too. Pat Gallagher, I assume? They have your name hanging off the banners above the audience.

He grinned. "That's me."

"I can't wait to see your set."

"Well, I'm up in the next five minutes, Meredith, so you'll get a chance if you stick around." As they shook hands, he said, "But I'm so happy to have met you. I really hope they keep you over the guy from Milwaukee. Don't think I could do another set after him. Really have to work to keep that audience from walking out."

She gave him a wave goodbye, and he applauded her as she departed back through the doorway that fed into the casino from backstage.

There was chatter on the other side of the curtain, as was often the case in between sets. The man who announced the performers had also come backstage, sipping a beer he'd been handed by one of the bald men. His black and white tuxedo gave him a look of composed regality, but it was a farce, as was often the case in Las Vegas. Pat had gone drinking with him once. He had the mouth of a sailor and the face of a leading man, which made a good pairing for an orator at a nightclub.

"What a fun set. That woman had them keeling over," the man said. "No pressure, though, Pat. I heard Louie himself is finally coming out to watch the show. Haven't seen him down on the floor…in, well, it's been basically since we opened." He shrugged and took a swig of his beer. "You'd have thought he'd be more involved, what with him being the namesake and all. Suppose not."

Louie? Here, now? Maybe Hyland figured it out. Maybe he and Samuel are just toying with me. Fuck, do I warn Lorenzo? I don't even know who's with him, anyway.

The other man gave him a curious look. "Alright there, Pat?"

He nodded, giving a terse smile. "Fine."

Just play it cool, Pat, play it cool. This is your stage, your crowd. Who cares what name is on the outside? This is Pat Gallagher's theater, even if it's only for two hours on a Saturday. Wow them, make them laugh, make them forget their suspicions, their fears. Trust Lorenzo. Trust his guys will be on their toes. Have faith.

"Just a little taken aback that Louie himself will be here," he added. "Surprised he's got time. I'm sure he has all sorts of busy work, tons of paperwork, palms to grease. Stuff like that never ends when you're in charge. Wouldn't want to do that sort of job, no, sir. I just do my job, make them laugh, and get them back for more." His chuckle sounded forced. "Speaking of which, I think it's time for you to announce me."

Pat cracked his knuckles and looked up toward the rafters backstage. He heard the curtain move, and the crowd began to yell from the other side.

"The fun's just beginning at Louie's Lounge!" the announcer boomed. "What a set that was, huh? But it was just a warm-up. Ladies and gentlemen, I present to you our resident jester! The guffawing ginger! The king of the cackle himself! PAAAAAATRICK GAAALLAGHERRRRR!"

The lights shone brightly. A silver microphone stood in the middle of the stage above the applauding horde, resting up a similarly silver stand. The man in the suit stood to the left, hand out towards the crowd, as though they were an offering for Pat. Pat stepped out, his hand up, waving at the applauding fans. His rehearsed smile gave no indication of insincerity, a ruse developed by perceived necessity. You'd have thought people in a casino would notice a man with a poker face. Every poker face was different, of course. Some were stoic; others were intimidating. But the rarest poker face of them all was a disarming, shit-eating grin.

"Thank you! Thank you all! I took last week off because it turns out my local joke supplier was in the hospital. You know what's not funny? Medical bills."

Laughter rose from the crowd. It was going to be an easy night for him.

Despite the bright lights blocking out most of the crowd, one figure stood out above the rest. His silver suit looked out of place in the sea of black surrounding him, worn by bald people of various races and genders. The man in silver, however, had hair—black, slicked-back hair that formed a pompadour with a gray streak running under his temple on either side. Even from where Pat stood, he could see the glint of the man's many rings adorning his fingers.

This whole time, Pat hadn't missed a beat. He knew this set so well, he could do it in his sleep.

"So, long story short," he said, "I'm not welcome back there. Who knew alligator leather shoes could offend the otherwise warm people of Louisiana?"

Another wave of laughter from the audience crashed over him, but this time, Pat felt washed away by it rather than carried along.

His eyes were fixed on The-Man-In-The-Silver-Suit, who stood laughing. His eyes didn't blink, not once, and Pat was almost entirely sure they met his own. Had he not been on stage, he'd have shuddered. There was no warmth in Louie's gaze. What looked back at him from those eyes was no man.

Who was this guy, really? He was far more than a two-bit criminal or a club owner, that was for sure. Pat had his suspicions.

That's the Devil in disguise.

20.

Hyland had come up to watch the set. Despite his suspicions about Patrick, part of him still rooted for the kid. It wasn't long ago that he himself had been a man without a place to call his own. Even if the existence he had built was marred with internal strife, it was too late to go now. Plus, it would pass, as phases often did.

In Hyland's memory, Louie had rarely come down to shows, perhaps only twice before. He hadn't spoken to Louie about the suspicions he harbored about Patrick, but he assumed Samuel wasn't one to keep his thoughts close to his vest. The Chosen rarely did, instead electing to act like a hive-mind, only serving Louie. Hyland had seen the gifts they received in return, but despite his inclinations to embrace Western European virtues, some things were too far for him.

"You were right, Hyland," Louie said to the Native man, who snapped out of his trance. The set Pat was giving had proved to be hypnotizing. "This one's special. He's not like everyone else. He carries himself differently." Louie's head was cocked to the side, and he was staring up at the stage. "That face...it's so familiar, but I can't place it." Then he waved a dismissive hand. "Doesn't matter. Surprised no one else snatched him up."

Hyland folded his arms and shrugged. "You hired me to do the books and hire talent, Louie. That's what I do, and I'm damn good at it. I saw he was a natural. Other venues wouldn't touch him, being a homosexual with a father on the FBI's watch list of Reds, too. More afraid of a gay man or collectivization than bankruptcy, I guess. But not Louie's Lounge. We're always ahead of the curve"

The downtrodden were diamonds in the rough, only in name. Their talent shone brighter than any gem could muster, but dirt could cover even the shiniest of objects if there was enough of it. The world had tried to bury them repeatedly, but talent could only be suppressed for so long.

"That we are," Louie said. "You should join the Chosen, Hyland. Surely there's something more you want than money. You've seen the miracles I can make happen. Look at Rosaline. Look at Samuel."

He pointed to the woman on his right and Samuel, who sat ahead of him. Hyland looked at Louie, his body covered in tattoos that peeked over the top button of his dress shirt and the wrist cuffs of his blazer.

Hyland gave a half-smirk. "They're miracles, sure. You've given them the lives they always dreamed of, but I'm a man of simple desires. You've already given me all I could want, Louie. I don't need more. There will be others who can serve you and become your Chosen. For now, I'm happy to be your bookkeeper."

Louie sized Hyland up. He opened his mouth, and gold-capped teeth glinted back at Hyland. He was unsure where Louie had originally come from. He once thought the lounge's namesake was nothing more than an East Coast gangster with an eclectic wardrobe. But the more those types migrated to Las Vegas, the more he realized Louie was so much greater than he could've imagined.

"Well, do me a favor, Hyland, think about it." He gave a wink before he turned his attention back to the show.

But Hyland's attention was on the man in silver. *He knows something I don't*, he thought. *The guy's got eyes in the back of his head. He's not here to watch the show. Something else has him out here. I just don't know what—not yet, at least.*

Hyland shifted in his seat, his focus no longer the stage. His eyes were no longer focused on the show. They darted across the audience, looking for anything amiss, something—or some*one* that might be worthy of Louie's personal attendance. But nobody stood out to him; it was the typical crowd tonight, tourists and mobsters alike. He scanned the rafters above, where people were peering over the railings to watch the show. Any one of them could be packing a gun, but they were still too far away to do much of anything. No, whatever danger there may be wouldn't come from there. It was down in the pit where the real enemies would lurk.

When he finally admitted there was nothing to be seen, he asked, "Why did you come out, Louie? You never come to these things."

Louie had been chuckling lightly at Patrick's set, but now he looked down at his watch with a flick of his wrist. "You know somethin', Hyland? After all these years, all the places I've been and things I've seen, there's something I can't place. There's a feeling I get in my gut. Call it intuition or what have you. The word isn't important. What matters is there's something in the air, Hyland, and I'm just sitting back, waiting to see exactly what that something is. I'm a sucker for some theater. Love a good show."

Then he turned back toward the stage, smugness radiating off of him as he chuckled at Pat's next joke.

The comedian was pacing the stage with a composed swagger that Hyland wasn't sure he'd ever seen from him before. "Thank you, ladies and gentlemen. You've been a fantastic crowd tonight. One more time, give a round of applause to our guest of honor, Louie himself. He rarely comes down into our den of madness, so it's fantastic to see him here."

The spotlight from the crowd managed to find its way to Louie. He stood up, and the light bounced off the back of his scalp. Through the thin layer of Louie's tapered haircut, Hyland could see the Devil staring back at him. Its tongue stuck out, and its horns curved upward until hidden by the top layer of his haircut. It was a tattoo, the brand of the beast. Hyland cared not about Western religion, but it was an ominous reminder that Louie was no mobster. Not even they dared carry the Devil himself on their bodies.

Louie raised his hand to the crowd as it wildly applauded, the chorus of clapping hands drowning out anything Pat said from the stage. Hyland took the chance to scan the room once more. There wasn't a single soul in the building not applauding and cheering, which killed his theory that maybe someone was here to take Pat out. He frowned as Louie sat down, the spotlight moving back to the stage as Pat took a bow.

Maybe I'm losing my touch, Hyland thought sadly. *Perhaps I'm losing my ability to hunt.* Then he shook his head. *No. No, Samuel is wrong. I'm not the weak link. They are. I'll show them.*

Hyland shifted up out of his seat as Pat left the stage, and the crowd began to disperse.

Louie turned as well to make his way to the exit. He held his hand up and beckoned Hyland over. "Before you head out, Hyland, I need you to finish that quarterly for the third quarter earnings. I left most of the paperwork you need on your desk. It shouldn't take more than a few hours, but I need the numbers done. Today."

Hyland didn't believe him, especially since Louie wasn't smiling. There was a test somewhere in that statement.

"Of course, I can do that. Enjoy your night, Louie. Thanks for coming out."

Hyland offered his hand, which Louie took, though there was no warmth in his handshake. But neither was it cold. In fact, it bore no resemblance to flesh. But what else it could be, Hyland didn't dare to guess. He knew Louie was more than a man; that much had become apparent. But what he might be, Hyland couldn't say. Nor did it matter.

"Watch your back, Hyland," Louie said before departing and leaving Hyland alone in the dispersing crowd. "Never know what's coming."

Hyland watched him go, then stood there as the staff started clearing out the chairs to convert the space back to a dance floor. He made note of the bars on either side. Nobody in those crowds seemed noteworthy. Nor did anyone else.

He was on edge. There was no denial of that, but perhaps he was also being paranoid. Louie had insisted something was coming, but he hadn't specified when or where. it didn't have to be *now*. It didn't have to be at the lounge. Surely nobody would be so foolish to do anything in Louie's domain. Outside of it? Those were far murkier waters.

Louie's words had chilled him. He hadn't suspected until he'd been told to watch his back that the feeling Louie had gotten might be about *him*. Now, he checked over his shoulder even more than usual as he made his way downstairs to his office.

If someone or something is coming for me, it won't be in the lounge. It'll be once I'm out of here, once I don't think my back is against the wall. Finish his paperwork, then head straight home. Nobody can touch you here. Nobody can touch you there. You'll be fine, Hyland. You're the hunter, not the prey.

He wasn't entirely convinced of that himself, but he knew that regardless of who he was in the food chain, he wouldn't prove easy to catch.

He had come too far for that.

21.

Hours passed, but eventually Hyland finished the last piece of paperwork. It was obviously busy work, as he doubted Louie cared much for the fiscal state of the casino. Blank check after blank check without stipulations early in the lounge's history had affirmed that for him.

His watch told him it was the dead of night, but the bright lights in the subterranean club made him think it was the apex of the day. It was a trick often deployed by casinos. There was no reason to leave if the sun never set. But it was time for Hyland to leave.

When he got outside, he saw the lot was full. It didn't matter that it was nearly three in the morning. The potential to earn quick money and free drinks proved too enticing for many people. His car was in a lot across from the club, an inconspicuous vehicle by Las Vegas standards. When you were the bookkeeper for a wildly successful casino that wasn't in the hands of the Mob, you had to tread carefully.

The engine sputtered to life, and the newsman filled the radio with his static-riddled voice. "There's been tension in Cuba as of late. There have been rumblings that Fidel Castro has made backroom dealings with Khrushchev for a nuclear pact. Updates will be reported accordingly as soon as we know. In other news, rain will come into town tomorrow evening, as storms have been reported heading northward from Phoenix, Arizona, toward Nevada."

Hyland changed the radio to a jazz station, a saxophone solo pouring through the speakers as he made his way from the city center. He checked his back mirror—the roads were nearly barren. A truck was passing him on the opposite side, its taillights nothing more than two small red orbs that shrunk with each passing second as the truck disappeared into the night.

The further he pushed from the city center, the more relief washed over him. He'd feared that someone had been watching from the casino, just waiting for his departure. But he hadn't seen anyone following him, nor had he noticed any cars pulling out after his. If there was a plus to the vast empty spaces of the road, it was that they made it hard to hide from those who knew where to look.

It wasn't long before he made it back to his neighborhood. His home was entrenched in an area that was firmly middle class. The white picket fences and manicured lawns descended into cul-de-sacs that felt wholly out of place in the arid landscapes stretching for miles outside the city limits. This late at night, there wasn't a house in the neighborhood with its lights on.

Pulling into his driveway, Hyland gripped the steering wheel and closed his eyes. It was only then that he realized how heavy his eyelids were becoming. It was a universal sign that exhaustion and, by extension, sleep was in his immediate future. He shifted in his seat and took his key out of the ignition. The engine cut as the headlights of his car dulled.

Hyland looked out the windshield at his home. At night, its pink stucco clay exterior resembled Soviet concrete gray. A window in the front of the house exposed the living room. Hyland was a private man and obscured this voyeuristic view with two layers of curtains. One was sheer, and shapes could be made out from the outside if closely inspected. There was a second layer, this one made of kitschy wood shutters. He never left his home without both layers covering the window. So, he froze for a moment as he only saw the sheer layer in the window, the wood one having been pulled up.

Someone had broken into his home.

They were reckless, though. Each minor detail of this house was something Hyland had committed to memory, especially the curtains and how he'd configured them. While he could see no figures in the living room from where he stood, he knew them to still be there, as though they discharged an energy that jolted him awake and alert. They had suspected him to be prey, but like in the wild, this pack of wolves had severely overestimated their ability to subdue Hyland. He was no buck.

He was a bear. And now he was pissed.

There were no other outward signs of disruption. Perhaps they'd misperceived Hyland as an incautious man. That was a mistake. The Native man crept closer to the entrance of his home, which he knew to be a trap. His brain worked in overdrive as he thought about how to make them pounce, what he could do to draw them out.

I know, I know. Start the car. They'll peer through the window to get a look. Might wake up the neighbors, but that doesn't matter. They'll call the police.

Stepping back towards his car, he wondered, *Did Pat send them? No, he's not as dumb as he looks, but he's not connected. This is something else.*

Slipping back into the front seat, he reached behind him for his briefcase, then set it on the seat next to him. There was still no movement from behind the glass and the thin curtain. He looked around one last time to ensure there were no other cars he didn't recognize on the street. Once satisfied that his prey had no escape, he ducked down with the briefcase. He put the gas on, his engine revving loudly in the night's silence. As he sat up, he pushed the driver's door open, his outstretched hand switching the gears as the car lurched forward. The briefcase pressed hard against the gas as he lurched out, rolling to the ground, one hand trying to break his fall as the other reached into his waistband for his gun.

He faced away from the house as the behemoth of metal and oil pushed through glass and stucco. A loud pop filled the air, and Hyland turned to see one tire had caught on the glass of the window frame as the car slammed into it. The wheels kept spinning, and the uneven car climbed upward, smacking against the ceiling, its headlights piercing into the second floor through holes in the ceiling, causing one beam of light to pour out of the windows.

"What the hell? Where is he? Is he in the car? Fuckin' Indian is off his rocker!" a man with a New Yorker accent yelled from inside the house.

Bingo.

Hyland made his way to the door now. There were other voices, at least two. They didn't matter. Shock set in, and even if they were professional, which they weren't in his approximation, it wouldn't make a difference. He pushed through the awning, his pistol drawn. As the door swung open, one of the men inspecting the car faced away from Hyland. He turned to face him, hand in the back of his pants, reaching for a firearm. He crumpled halfway through his turn, landing with a dull thud on the ground. There was no scream, and there was no drawn-out death. Hyland knew where to shoot.

"Do you want to draw this out, or do you want to tell me who you work for?" Hyland didn't wait for an answer and instead ran for the staircase, the balusters providing at least a semblance of coverage in case the others decided to shoot.

It was only then that screaming filled his ears. He hadn't noticed before, but his car was dripping with blood. A man was being dragged out of his living room into the kitchen to the right of his staircase on the first floor. He heard the kitchen back door open, which fed into the backyard. He moved from the stairs into the living room, half filled with a car still moving.

As he looked upward, he chuckled to himself. The car had taken one of their arms clean off. Its elbow nudged itself into the grill of the car. "White man getting sloppy," Hyland said as he examined the room. He took a moment, knowing the man missing his arm couldn't move quickly, not that it mattered. Hyland would just follow the blood trail.

"I loved this living room—I loved this house. I loved my life."

Well, that one was a stretch. He was malcontent, but what human wasn't? The burgeoning appetite did not acknowledge how little time had passed since it had last been starving, only the overindulgent hunger, even though it had eaten well the day before and the day before that. Consumption had become the new norm—subsistence had been replaced with opulence. So, yes, Hyland loved this home, but only as a reminder of his hubris and how far his ego had taken him: from the grasslands of his ancestors to a vapid city of artificiality that shouldn't exist but did, despite Mother Nature deeming the location unfit for human life.

He turned now to his kitchen and the door that fed into the backyard. The sandstone-colored linoleum tiles were tainted with one long, thick streak of bright red blood trailing toward the door, where a bloody handprint was smeared on the doorknob.

"Sloppy." Hyland clicked his tongue, shaking his head. "Tremendously sloppy." He knew they weren't special forces, but he hadn't expected them to collapse as quickly as they did.

He peered out the kitchen window. The two mobsters were struggling over the fence into another yard. The one without one of his arms gripped the top of the fence. "Help me out! Don't leave me here."

But the second mobster, who hadn't been hurt by the barreling car, had apparently decided to look out for himself, leaving his misfortunate brother behind. There was no honor amongst thieves, and despite the lies they told themselves, that's all they were.

Perhaps they couldn't see the whites of their eyes, the havoc their empty promises of easy money had wreaked upon countless lives, or the damage of their vague threats if offerings weren't paid for protection. They didn't see these consequences, as they didn't look. They didn't *want* to. Bandits is all they were, the last thieves of the dying Wild West.

"He left you for dead," Hyland called out to the armless thug. "Guess that oath only goes so far."

He made his way outside, the screen snapping back into place behind him as he trod across the unnaturally verdant grass of his backyard. His hand stretched outward, a brown-handled .45 pointed at the mobster, who wore a gray suit covered in green grass stains and a growing pool of blood streaking down his right side. His white shirt shone in the moonlight, as did his face. The snot that covered it reflected what little light flickered in the night.

"And?" the thug challenged. "I would've too. Ain't disrespecting me. Somebody has to tell them. You're one smart Indian. Fooled us real good."

Hyland had expected the man to scream in pain or shrink back fearfully in the face of a firearm, but perhaps shock had taken hold—humanity's last respite consuming his brain, an utter refusal to allow agony to overwhelm. It would come to pass, and so, too, would the mobster. There was no recovery from those wounds. That window had closed.

"I'm not the worst of it. I'm the kind one, but kind doesn't mean weak. That's where you messed up. You picked the wrong weak link, and now you'll die." He shook his head in mock amazement. "Ain't that something? In a city with card games on every street corner, you chose to gamble with your own life instead. Shit...pshh, yeah, that's, well, that's bad luck."

He lowered his gun—no use wasting a bullet. Besides, it was over. His friend was long gone, and he was bleeding out.

"You can't win. Ain't no way you can win. Jesus is on our side. Jesus is on *my* side."

Hyland spied the crucifix on a chain that the man was pulling out from under his dress shirt. Blood had seeped under his fingernails like dirt, but his grubby hand held it out toward the Native American man.

Hyland stifled a chuckle as he looked up at the sky. "You know, I don't know if there's a higher spirit up there. I don't think there's a God, that's for sure. But, man, the Devil? Oh, I know there's one of him."

He made his way over to the man holding the crucifix in his hand, which trembled. His face was pale. His time was soon.

"Let me guess, you're the Devil? Mighty big ego there on you, Indian."

He gave a toothy grin. His eyes flickered in pain. Hyland shifted up. He hadn't realized he had been bent over, making himself eye level with the man. Now, however? He towered over the soon-to-be deceased mobster. He was in control.

"No, no. I'm not the Devil," he said softly as the other man collapsed to the ground. "No, but I've seen him. I know him. I wasn't so sure before, but I am now. I see him every single day. Even when his face isn't there, he haunts me. His name's in big bright letters, hanging overhead, inviting the poor and hungry to his dinner table." He knelt beside the man. "He's real. You're lucky you met me. The rest of you? Not so much."

With one last ragged breath, the man slipped away into the afterlife, leaving Hyland alone with his thoughts once more.

The silence of the night proved Hyland's theory. There were no sirens. There were no police coming to see the commotion, nor did his neighbors step outside. Surely, they'd been at home, sleeping before a long day at their desk jobs. There was something beyond comprehension at work. It was then that he realized Louie was everything he suspected and more.

He was the Devil. He was coming.

And God help those who he had in his sights.

<h1 style="text-align:center">22.</h1>

In time, Pat found the dreamless nights to be good ones. With no dreams, there was no Randy taunting him from the depths of the reservoir. There was no burning man pleading for his life despite knowing it was over the second he smelled gasoline. Those nights were the easiest. One second, he felt himself falling, and the next, the sun's rays pushed through the curtains of his hotel room, a reminder that he was, in fact, alive.

He shifted in his bed, his cream blanket pushed to the side. As his feet hit the carpeted floor, he rubbed the lingering sleep out of his eyes. Blinking to ensure it was gone, he got up and made his way to the red velvet drapes, then pulled them open. The daytime brightness dulled the neon signs, yet if he focused on them, he could tell they were still on, biding their time before they'd shine brightly, too.

Yawning, he padded across the room to his wardrobe. His collection of suits had grown in the last few weeks, some vibrant reds and pinks, others more subdued grays and browns. Today, he settled somewhere in the middle, a tartan print with hues of green and faded pink.

After a brief shower, Pat dressed and headed out to face another day. As he strolled towards the lobby, he found the corridors empty. Usually, there were at least people rushing to check out or in. He looked down at his watch to confirm the time. The face looked back at him, its hands ticking toward the end of the hour: 10:56 A.M.

That doesn't track. Check-out is in four minutes, and there's nobody in the hallways? Something's wrong.

He shuddered, his heart sinking into his stomach—the sense humans could not define beyond instincts, a gut feeling when all wasn't right with the world. Despite this, he continued onward. The cold steel of his firearm, which he'd tucked into his waistline, reminded him he wasn't entirely without recourse if the situation devolved.

As the lobby drew closer, he could hear the chatter of the office television, a sign that civilization still remained. He relaxed momentarily as he saw Gunther, the other receptionist, at the desk, typing away.

"Pat! Good to see you," the other man said. "I was worried you skipped town without saying goodbye like most of the other guests!"

Pat raised a brow. So that would explain why the place felt so empty. But he still didn't know *why* they had left. He peered over the desk to see the TV in the backroom of the reception desk. It was a news anchor repeating some sort of speech given by the president the night prior.

"Castro," Gunther said. "They found missiles on the island. If *we're* hearing about it, odds are it's been happening for weeks, months, even. People think Khrushchev's going to wipe Las Vegas off the face of the earth. Guess all those missile tests weren't so good after all."

Pat absorbed every word. In last night's chaos, he hadn't even seen the speech. No one at Louie's Lounge had mentioned it, and the place didn't have television sets playing all over because that would distract patrons from spending as much as possible.

Pat watched the news alongside Gunther, asking questions the whole time. "So, the Reds put them there? Castro doesn't seem like a dull man, but he does seem like a rather busy one. He didn't build those himself, not with us on his doorstep. Did he threaten to use them? What's got people spooked?"

Gunther shrugged. "What's anyone ever spooked about these days?" He made the sound of an explosion with his mouth, letting his hands blossom out in a pantomime of a mushroom cloud.

Pat could admit that spooked him as much as the next guy, but he was troubled by something else, as well—the feeling that maybe what he was watching unfold on the TV screen was somehow related to his own unfortunate predicament.

No, Pat, this is the work of man. Maybe Louie is the Devil, perhaps he isn't, but this isn't him. This is unrelated. C'mon, get your head straight, buddy. Things are moving now, can't be caught in a daze.

He shook off his thoughts like a dog that'd come in from the rain. Gunther seemed to not notice, focusing on the television in front of him instead, his stubbled jaw slightly agape. Kennedy gave his practiced grin through the grainy footage before it cut back to the local station.

"I bet there are still people in the casinos," Gunther said as he puffed on his cigarette. "Wonder if any of them know. Reckon by this time tomorrow, town will be a ghost town. Heard there are tons of those in Colorado and Wyoming, never seen one myself."

Pat turned toward the glass panels of the entryway and could see outside of it a nearly empty lot. Across the roadway stood another hotel with even fewer cars in its own respective lot.

"Well, if it's all the same to you, Gunther," Pat said, " I need to get out to the comedy club. I want to make sure they didn't up and leave town before signing my check."

Gunther nodded at him, and with that, Pat slunk out of the lobby and into the parking lot.

He had seen the city at its peak, having arrived in the middle of August. Now that it was October, there was a cool waft in the air that could be felt but not described. The city was winding down but still vibrant. But with the missile crisis, the surrounding chaos stood still. For just a moment, he wasn't Patrick Gallagher, St. Patrick, or even Pat the Monologist. He was just a person, of no name, of no origin, just a human enjoying the pleasantries of a cool breeze. Nothing else mattered. The threat of nuclear winter—or even pacts with the proverbial devil—was rendered meaningless.

It only lasted for a moment.

The most beautiful piece of humanity was its self-awareness. This stood as a paradox against its ugliest feature—which was *also* self-awareness. Simple issues became complex and complex issues became simple. A breeze, a graceful caress from the earth itself, only lasted so long, and Pat was reminded upon opening his eyes that reality was frightening. He didn't know what Lorenzo had done — he didn't know if Louie had figured out their plan. The unknown propelled him forward. Answers or no answers, he still had to keep moving. The human condition did poorly when faced with the ambiguous.

Pat was no different. Even as his body drove his car almost by instinct, his mind wandered elsewhere. Lorenzo hadn't said they'd call. Instead, he recommended Pat go through his typical day as though nothing was wrong. So that's what he did—plowing along the familiar commute to Louie's Lounge.

The roads were filled with substantially less traffic than the previous day. The city, which had felt seedy when vibrant with life, took on a sinister aura with the storefronts lining both sides of the road seemingly vacant. Despite his trepidation, he was almost glad when he parked in the familiar lot across from Louie's because he now desired to see other people.

Rosaline guarded the front entrance in the daytime. "Ahh, what a show last night, Pat," she said as he made his way through the entryway. "It was like watching fireworks." The only acknowledgment he gave her was a curt nod.

The bar on the ground floor was empty, except for bartenders measuring liquor bottles. The dance floor below was also bare, a stark reminder of the crisis engrossing the public. As he descended the familiar industrial metal staircase, he looked for anything abnormal besides the lack of crowds. Louie's Lounge was busy 24/7, yet all he could hear was light chatter coming from the two casino entryways on either side of the dance floor.

He looked up at the stage where he'd performed the night prior. The silver microphone on its stand stared back down at him despite the lack of eyes. His dreams had become a reality here, even if nightmares didn't lag far behind. A man of contradictions was laid bare. The paradoxes that had defined him pulled at him in a multitude of directions as he stared at each curve, each groove in the microphone. He couldn't see the details from afar, but his mind filled in the gaps, recalling the countless nights when his lips practically kissed the metal.

It's everything I ever wanted, he thought. *I knew the risks. Hell, I remember driving in. I remember seeing that car burn. I still looked. I still came here when the other places rejected me. Maybe I'm not so different.*

Was it a moment of honest reflection? The moment when he realized that the monsters in the suits were him, that, like them, his own inhibitions had supplanted his humanity. He hadn't objected when they burned the man alive. He didn't turn himself in when Randy's noseless face stared back at him with vacant eyes. He still wore the shamrock ring on his finger, night after night, even when he knew the previous owner had perished in ways that he couldn't fathom.

No, Pat, you messed up. Of course, you messed up. If you knew it would've been all of this, you'd have never done any of this. Tommy gave you this chance. It was you or Randy. It's truly that simple. The ring was theatrical, but you're allowed to mess up. You're a good man, you know that. Lorenzo knows that, too.

The dueling narratives pushed into his brain, warring so loudly that he almost didn't notice when someone tapped his shoulder.

Hyland stood before him. A freshly pressed suit jacket framed his shoulder blades as he fiddled with his bolo tie, and a leather boot tapped against the flooring as he waited for Pat to say something. When Pat didn't, he said, "Mr. Gallagher, I was getting worried you'd left town. You had a remarkable show last night, a fantastic one. Louie had wanted to see his brightest star in person. He was not disappointed, though he *was* surprised he didn't get to speak with you."

"I just didn't want to get caught up in logistical business. I should've stayed and met him. I owe him so much. I guess I'm a bit skittish still after that boat. Even after taking that time off, I still toss and turn at night, wondering why I was there, questioning if I...acted how I was supposed to."

"We are men, nothing more, nothing less. You did nothing wrong, not that I'm aware of yet." The way Hyland spoke bothered him. It was straight to the point. Indifferent. Then he gave a grimace of a smile and said, "Let's get your paycheck sorted out, Patrick. Come, follow me into my office."

"Of course. Lead the way."

Pat eyed the exits. There was a conspicuous lack of bald, black-suited people guarding the doorways. If it had been even a day prior, this would have relieved Pat, but today it only served to cause his neck and back to tense up even more. He was rapidly feeling trapped, like a cornered feral animal.

"Long night. Had some paperwork to do for Louie. Didn't get out 'til late. What did you do after you left? Normally you spend more time around here drinking with that tall Latin fella. Lonny? Lourie? Hell, if I know."

As they made their way down a second flight of stairs, Pat said, "We went out drinking at his favorite bar. I keep telling him to support this place. Sometimes he does, sometimes he doesn't." Pat's nerves jangled inside of him, and he started to ramble a bit. "Say, you know what tacos are? I didn't until he showed me. Now? I can't picture a life without them. He wanted to go to a place that served them. Squeeze a lime over them, and you're in heaven."

They turned down a hallway, now only one corridor away from Hyland's office.

"Yeah, didn't know much about those back on the Rez," Hyland said. "Out here? Seems to be everywhere. Told Louie to get them on the menu. But those New York guys? Hard to convince. We can leave it at that."

They had made it to Hyland's office. He stood outside it, his face stoic and unmoving. It made sense the man who ran the casino knew how to broadcast a poker face.

"Come in, Pat, let's talk. Get you paid and on your way *home*."

Pat paused, desperately hoping Hyland's stone face would give something, anything, away as to what to expect from the door behind him. There was, of course, no reprieve or way to know what awaited him on the other side.

It didn't matter. None of it really mattered to begin with. It was like when a dry breeze rolled through, and he'd discard his name, discard his purpose, and instead embrace everything in totality. He was just another living being, nothing more, nothing less. Everything else had just been icing on the cake. If a bullet awaited him in that office, what could be done? If things broke his way? What then? Accepting yourself candidly was never easy, but there was no time like the present. What was life without risk?

No nightlights. Nothing to hide from, Pat. Accept it.

"Sure, let's do this."

23.

Neither man could've predicted what awaited them on the other side when Hyland turned the doorknob.

"Hands up!" a voice bellowed the second Hyland let go of the doorknob. "Put them up!"

Pat blinked in shock. He took a step back, Hyland's hands held up in surrender.

The voice belonged to Lorenzo.

Pat had never seen him with a firearm before. He had never seen Lorenzo so much as ball his hand into a fist. Of course, he knew he was capable of it. How could he not know? He knew what "waste management" meant to his lover.

"You thought you pulled a fast one on us? No, no. Think again, you bastard. Now we're all going to sit down and wait." He gestured with his firearm to a chair opposite Hyland's desk. Pat knew its walnut armrests and red stitched leather upholstery well. It was, after all, in this very room that he'd sold his soul for his fifteen minutes.

"Waiting for what, exactly? Do you think you're in control here? Why, because you have a gun?" Hyland spoke with no fear, no concern in his voice, his initial shock having been absorbed. He was all business once more, confident he was in control regardless of the reality before him.

Pat ran over to Lorenzo, standing behind him. They both faced Hyland, whose serious face had turned into a smirk. Whether it was disbelief or confidence, Pat could not say. His own brain was still trying to process how rapidly everything had progressed.

Hyland cocked his head to the side. "I told them Pat wasn't weak. I told them he was resourceful. Yet, they ignored me, and here you are. Did you wait for them to leave? How long have you been watching?"

Hyland's hands remained raised in the face of Lorenzo's gun. Pat's eyes darted back and forth between the two men. Hyland was referring to the night prior—to his fake olive branches, his tales spun of kinship, as though the two were in the same boat.

Perhaps he was simply playing both sides. Pat couldn't say he wouldn't act differently in the man's shoes. Hyland was a survivor of hardships Pat couldn't conceive, and from the way he moved, he had seen much more than his lips would ever speak.

"You were right, Hyland, I'm not weak. You weren't there, but you know what they do. That man on the ship? He didn't deserve that. Nobody deserves that." He came down like a judge's gavel, even if the verdict was still in flux within his mind.

"Oh, we both know what they do. I am no more trapped than you, Pat. The difference is I don't lie to myself about my humanity." Hyland shook his head.

"You cashed those checks and cracked those jokes. You could've walked away. You could've turned around the day you saw that burning car, but no. You chose to wear that ring—you knew *exactly* what you signed up for."

There was a flicker in Lorenzo's eyes as his gaze flashed down briefly to Pat's ring finger on his left hand.

Hyland's grin widened. "So, you thought you'd just damn him, too? You mean Pat didn't tell you before he had you hide in my office? He had a choice. They always have a choice."

"Didn't need to tell me. He's not the one pointing the gun. I am. He didn't know I'd be here either."

Lorenzo straightened his grip, the pistol barrel pointing at Hyland's head. He flicked his wrist again toward the seat he wanted Hyland to sit in. This time there was no snark, only compliance.

"I knew there was muscle behind him," Hyland said. "I mean, look at Pat. You're here to save his life, and he can't even process it. Overwhelmed. Did you wait for the bald men and women in the suits to leave? Came for revenge after what happened to your Mafia friends last night?"

Pat had no idea what Hyland was talking about, though he could just barely read between the lines. Whatever Lorenzo's plan involved had made Hyland a target of the Mob, and it sounded like it hadn't gone well for Lorenzo's guys.

I knew they kept me out of the loop for my safety, but I could've warned them. They thought they knew better, thought they *were watching* him. *Didn't know they were going to go after him.*

Pat felt a tinge of regret for not being more involved. From the sounds of it, Hyland had killed those men, and Pat's inaction let them die, just like the man who burned on the boat. Guilt didn't need to be well-founded to be all-consuming.

Lorenzo shrugged. "They knew what they signed up for, the risks it involved. They took their lives into their own hands, and now yours is mine. So, let's sit and wait." He kept the gun steady, and his posture was relaxed. Pat was surprised at how unfazed his lover seemed. "You sent that guy, Samuel, off to Pat's hotel, didn't you? Why? You knew he was coming here anyway. You didn't want him, so what did you want?"

How long had they been watching Hyland? Pat had only informed Lorenzo about him a day prior. It was frightening to ponder the surveillance capabilities that the Mob had set up around town.

"You've been playing coy, Lorenzo," Hyland said, ignoring his question. "They took a lot of risk for you. Who are you really? You're no grunt. That much is clear. Answer me that, and I will answer you. Not that it matters. It's out of my hands."

Pat didn't like the sound of that. He took a surreptitious glance around to get the lay of the land. Lorenzo was sitting in the guest chair across from Hyland, who was behind his desk. The office was set up in such a way that it would be impossible for Hyland to make it to the door without passing Lorenzo or Pat, who was standing awkwardly behind him.

"What does it matter?" Lorenzo challenged. "Leadership or not, you pricks have been a thorn in our side since you opened shop. I could be a grunt in the know. I could be a leader. But you're not dumb, Hyland. This town's big, but not so big that I don't know who you were before Louie's Lounge. What did Samuel go to Pat's for?" Hyland's face looked unamused when his past was mentioned. It was just a flash before he shifted gears back into the air of arrogance that opulence had gifted him. "Louie wants an audience with him. You sent men to kill me or kidnap me, whichever. He's a smart...*man,* but he's not omniscient. He can't predict someone who acts like a caged animal. Samuel was sent to retrieve him after our meeting here."

"Pat's been loyal to you," Lorenzo said. "He came to me out of fear that it wouldn't be reciprocated. Burning that man alive was pure theater. Now you're talking about abduction. What did you want with him? What's your angle?"

Lorenzo's gun was still trained on Hyland, but his curiosity had obviously broken down his barrier, if only slightly. Hyland took note, Pat could see that, but he had his firearm tucked in his waistband. Even if Hyland got past Lorenzo, Pat wasn't afraid to use the tools he had.

"I didn't want anything besides money," Hyland said. "Louie—he's a different person. The things he wants? I'm not given those details. I didn't sacrifice myself to be one of his playthings. I'm here to earn a living, like any man. What do *you* do for work? How many people did you murder with that gun? With those hands?"

Hyland was playing all the right notes to a song he didn't know the ending of. Lorenzo's flair was gone, replaced with disgust, and Pat assumed his past was replaying in his head.

"Don't play so coy, Lorenzo," Hyland continued. "You thought us the same because we're both in this nasty underbelly? No, no, I never killed for Louie. I signed checks and booked shows. You? You're a murderer. Saving Patrick from whatever evil you think we are isn't going to change that, Lorenzo. Neither will killing me. You know that. Otherwise? I wouldn't have made it this far."

Pat watched on in silence. He'd never considered that he could be Lorenzo's redemption project. It was a lie, though—a farce told by a man who knew what buttons to press. Hyland was a smooth talker. Pat already knew that. But now, with a gun pointed at him, he was in control, and he wasn't shy about showing it.

"You're trying to guilt trip him, Hyland, seriously?" Pat scoffed. "After everything you've done, everyone you associate with, *you* want to guilt trip *him*? We all have skeletons in our closet, including you. Louie isn't a man, is he? What is he?" When Hyland didn't say anything, Pat said, "I don't know Lorenzo's plans, and I don't really care about them. I just want to get out of here, so if that means putting one between your eyes, so help me, God, I will do it."

"You're so naïve, Pat." Hyland's tone was almost sad. "You think *I* am in charge? Why? Because I sign those checks? No, no...we're both willing prisoners. I just don't have the desire to mask the truth. I know who I am and why I'm here. It sounds like you don't. Floating from place to place, trying to find 'your people.' They don't exist. You enter this world alone and die alone. None of us can escape that." Lorenzo was no longer mesmerized, no longer engrossed in the words. He saw them for what they were—a distraction.

"Quit distracting us. You're biding time, but for who? Samuel? The bald nut jobs in the suits?"

Hyland merely chuckled, his arrogance beginning to grate, as though he were trying to goad the two men into escalation. "Them? No, no, you haven't been listening. I'm no more important to them than you are. I'm not one of Louie's Chosen. I never made a deal with him. I didn't sell everything. I'm no fool. I'd never sell my whole self to anybody, no matter what promises he gave me. They won't come to help me."

"If not them, then who, Hyland? Who?" Pat demanded.

These theatrics, these impassioned speeches, were definitely a stalling tactic. But Pat wasn't so sure it was Samuel Hyland was hoping would come. The burning urge to get answers about Louie meant little if Hyland had a trick up his sleeve. Pat wouldn't be deterred, no matter how tempting the answers were, no matter how much his questions plagued him.

There was a knock at the door. Hyland closed his eyes. "Right on time. If one of you go answer it, she's not going to be leaving. She wants her paycheck. Helluva show last night—the two of you had a helluva show."

Pat's eyes widened as he understood: Meredith. She didn't know the game they had been playing. She didn't know the risk she had just undertaken. Wrong place, wrong time.

"Let her in," Pat said. "We can explain, Lorenzo. We can make her understand."

Lorenzo's eyes were full of skepticism. His cynicism overcame his affection, even if for a moment. With a blink, it was gone, in its place a begrudging acceptance, but behind it was doubt, stuffed down in the pursuit of faith.

"Yeah, okay," Lorenzo sighed. "Let her in, Pat. Just keep your eye out. Hyland could be lying. It could be someone else."

Pat nodded as he made his way to the door. He could feel Hyland's and Lorenzo's eyes on his back as he went.

"C'mon, open it up. Don't be scared, Patty. We'll be here. We got your back." Randy was back, whispering in his ear. The sharp intake of air through his exposed nasal cavities filled Pat's eardrums with a low growl, a bestial sound from beyond the grave.

The door opened slowly, and Pat looked through to the other side, his clammy hand in his back pocket, hoping he didn't need to pull out the gun but also hoping it wasn't Meredith. Nobody else needed to be caught in the whirlpool of his poor decisions.

24

Pat's heart was in his throat. He could feel every hair on his neck stand up as the person on the other side of the door spoke.

"Pat? Where's—oh no. What are you doing? What's going on? Should I call the police? I *should* call the police."

Meredith stood across from him. Her green manicured nails pressed over her mouth as her eyes widened with shock.

"No, no," Pat whispered. "Hyland is a dangerous man. They all are here at the lounge. There's no need for that, Meredith."

Her eyes scanned his own, and when she looked upon his face, Pat became acutely aware of his unkempt hair, his stubble-covered chin and cheeks. He looked less composed than usual and hoped his dishevelment wouldn't breed distrust.

After a brief scan of Lorenzo behind Pat, she noticed the gun, and her demeanor changed. "No, I really should be going, sorry. I didn't mean to interrupt. I don't want any problems." It was a rehearsed statement, composed but detached, like she'd practiced it in a mirror in case she'd ever need to say it. Pat knew it well. It was a voice, a tone he had grown accustomed to.

Randy was beside him now, lips pressed close to his ear. *"Go ahead,"* he cooed. *"You said you're different, Patrick. Show us. Show us how different you really are. C'mon, don't be coy. I know you can feel that gun, just itching. Wouldn't be the first time, now, would it? Betcha didn't tell Lorenzo about that one. Not poor, innocent, Pat."*

Randy's voice was high pitched, sing-songy, as though this were a Saturday morning cartoon, not real life, as though he spoke to a child, as though pulling a trigger on an innocent woman was as commonplace as playing catch in the front yard.

"Oh, she'll catch something, alright. Don't worry about her. She'll be gone before she knows what happened. I'm speaking from experience, Patty Cakes."

"You're not in danger," Pat promised her. "This place, it's *wrong*. I didn't know before I started here. I promise you, Meredith, we aren't the bad guys. Lorenzo, he's trying to save me from their plans. Please, trust me. They're not people. They're demons. I know, I know it sounds crazy, but just trust me." Pat was pleading, praying that his faith wasn't misplaced.

St. Patrick once pushed the snakes away from the Isle of Ireland. Now it was Pat's turn. Not only was Las Vegas full of snakes, it was also an island, a dot of civilization in the barren seas of sand dunes. Like every good showman, an encore was in order. The staff at Louie's Lounge had shown themselves to be serpents, and Pat was here to drive them out. This was his divine duty, to what God he couldn't say, but he felt it deep down in his bones.

It all made sense in his own head. It was so clear. But Meredith obviously didn't understand. In fact, the look she was giving him suggested she thought he was insane. They had hardly known each other. How could he be so foolish to believe she'd ignore her instincts?

"I need to go, Pat," she said, eyes wide with fear. "I need to go. Please, just let me go, and I won't speak a word of this. Hyland can keep my money."

"No, I need you to help me, Meredith," Hyland called out. "These men, they're no good. This guy? He's Pat's lover. They strong-armed us and threatened to kill us if we didn't give him stage time."

Lorenzo did not look amused. His brow creased as sweat trickled off his forehead and past his mustache.

"We told Pat we wouldn't cave in anymore. He brought this man down here with him to shake me down. I have a kid, a wife!"

It was bullshit. Of course, it was. Hyland knew what strings to pull. Who wouldn't sympathize with a kid, with a wife? Thick honey oozed from his hive of lies, and it looked like Meredith was eating it all up. Unfortunately for her, the closer she got, the likelier she'd be stung by the swarm—and Pat knew Hyland had every intention of striking her with his venom.

"If you're good men, let him go," Meredith said to Pat. "If you're good, nobody needs to die. Nobody needs to get hurt. You aren't better than him if you hurt him."

"*Oh, phooey, a peaceful resolution,*" Randy complained, blowing a raspberry. "*C'mon Pat. You know he's coming back. And worst of all, now he knows what you're up to. You're fucked. And so is Lorenzo. Look at him. Sticking up for you, even when you called him a liar. It's enough to make me sick...*"

"No, Pat," Lorenzo said. "We let him go, and he'll come at us with those bald-headed freaks. He killed two men last night—*two*. He has no remorse." Lorenzo turned toward the doorway. His hand was still steadfast with Hyland in his gun's sights. "Look at him—smug, like he's in control. Listen, I ain't a good man; I'll be the first to admit that. But I ain't—I ain't like them. Like *him*."

Meredith's eyes narrowed. The fear on her face had been replaced with disgust. "I don't know about your morals. I don't rightly care, either. If it's all the same to you, I'd like to leave. And if you're as decent as you say, you'll let Hyland do the same. Show me you ain't like them."

Pat considered this for a moment, his morality swinging around like a haphazard hammer in a china shop. It was only a matter of time before something shattered in a porcelain explosion.

He eyed the doorway, hopeful she'd move out of the way. He was willing to do what she asked. Pat and Lorenzo could outrun them all. They only needed each other, anyway. What they shared was perhaps the only genuine thing he had found in this city of façades and duplicity. Theirs was an unlikely romance, one that held no assurances of blossoming into its full potential. But what was life without a little risk?

Lorenzo had tried to help, and Pat appreciated that. Truly, he did. But this wasn't them. This wasn't how they won. He wasn't even sure if they *could*, but if there was a chance, it shouldn't come at the expense of what Pat stood for. It felt wrong, like trying to run with a shoe on the wrong foot.

"Let him go, Lorenzo," he said. "Let him go. She's right. We aren't this. We aren't them. We aren't evil men."

"*Same ol' Patrick.*" Randy clucked his tongue. "*Waiting for everyone else to carry his water. Tommy ain't here to save you. Not that it'd matter. They're going to kill you and her. And you know why? Because you're too weak, Pat. You can't do what needs to be done. People don't change. They just learn to hide it better.*"

No, Randy, they can *change,* Pat insisted. *I did. I've been selfish. I wanted success more than anything. I told myself it was for Tommy because he gave me a second chance, but I was lying. I held onto a dream even after I woke up. I was no better than the men in the suits, but I still could be. I won't have Hyland's blood on my hands. I won't kill him.*

Pat stepped out into the hall, pushing past Meredith. Lorenzo looked at him in disbelief, then began backing toward the doorway. Pat stood in the hall next to Meredith, whose jaw was agape. It was clear she hadn't believed they'd listen to her request, no matter how reasonable it was.

Lorenzo watched Hyland from the hallway, still aiming his firearm through the doorway at the man sitting at his desk. "Pat, take her and go. Get out of here. I'll be right behind you. I'm not turning my back, not with him here." There was fear in his voice. It was masked in standoffish masculinity, but it still seeped through.

Pat hadn't known about the incident at Hyland's home. He didn't know the man was a hunter, forgoing his rifle and traditions in pursuit of the almighty dollar and the comforts therein. That didn't mean Hyland couldn't go back, and that didn't mean he'd lost those skills—something Lorenzo and Pat were quickly finding out.

"Meredith, we need to leave. It's not safe here. I know you don't trust us, but we weren't kidding. Hyland's a bad guy."

Meredith looked bewildered. Despite their adherence to her request, she obviously remained unconvinced. Pat tried to find the words to convince her, but that was the thing about when people made their minds up—nothing could be said, nothing would change.

She turned and dashed away from them.

Lorenzo sighed as she made her way out of view, heading back upward toward the casino. "Well, there goes your good deed of the day. We still need to get out of here. He took out a squad of hitmen by himself, Pat."

They were roughly twenty feet away from the office now. Lorenzo's gun was still trained on the door as he walked backward. Pat looked briefly in his direction and then back to the one Meredith ran in.

"Doesn't matter. It was the right thing to do." Pat sighed. "Let's get out of here. You shouldn't have snuck in. If those bald guys come back, we're done for."

Even as he said it, though, Pat was more worried about Hyland. The look in his eyes had frightened him. Plus, that danger was tangible. He was still sitting in the office, possibly just waiting for an opportunity to strike. The others? They might not come back at all.

Almost as if reading Pat's mind, Hyland yelled from inside his office, "I'll give you twenty seconds! Run! Make it a challenge. You owe me that much."

"Pat, run, now!" Lorenzo shouted.

The two men fled down the corridor toward the casino and the club floor, heading for the ascending staircase trailing toward the left. There was a crash from behind them, but Pat glanced back only after making the stairwell. Hyland stood in the hall. His blazer was gone, and his salmon dress shirt was creased at the elbows as his arms swung upward, a large rifle in his hands. He pulled back the bolt of the gun and fired once, shooting from the hip and yet somehow nearly hitting Lorenzo. A loud crack filled the air. Bricks from the wall crumbled on impact, turning into dust that fell upon the steps.

"C'mon, I said make it a challenge!" Hyland shouted as he pulled the bolt once more.

Pat's mind jumped, the fight or flight instinct kicking in. Lorenzo was already at the top of the stairs, looking down at Pat.

"Pat. Run! You can't beat him. Not here, not in his dungeon."

Pat jumped as a second shot whizzed past him. This one was closer. Much closer.

He ran up the stairs, joining Lorenzo. The casino floor was on the other end of the hallway, and the door to it felt miles away. The bronze doorknob glinted in the darkened hall, teasing that liberation was only a wrist turn from reality.

"Go! Go, Pat! Come on!" Lorenzo cried.

Pat's breaths grew ragged trying to keep up with Lorenzo, who took long strides with the grace of a gazelle and the desperation of a water buffalo in the heat of the hunt. Prey or not, they weren't defenseless. They weren't hopeless. Not yet.

Lorenzo grabbed the knob, swinging the door open as Hyland's thundering steps behind them grew louder. The bright lights of the casino flooded the narrow, dim hallway. Lorenzo pulled Pat onto the floor, landing on the carpet with a thud as another shot whizzed past. Pat was dazed, in utter shock.

"Roll. Separately," Lorenzo ordered him. "We can meet in the middle of the floor. Blend with the crowds. He can't get us."

Before Pat could respond, Lorenzo had already rolled to the right. Pat rolled to the left and got up, dashing through the crowds toward the dance floor. Patrons screamed and stampeded away as a second shot filled the room. Hyland was on their tails.

"*Stop hiding!*" Hyland roared.

There was a third shot, but this time it was followed by a scream of pain. Hyland had struck an innocent bystander. Pat dared not look back. Instead, he lunged over a poker table, rolling to the other side as he broke into a sprint, nearly blinded by the strobe lights on the dance floor that doubled as a stage—*his* stage—during events.

Lorenzo had once again beaten him to the other side of the room. He looked back, his pistol cocked, as they saw the man with the rifle zigging and zagging across the floor, his rifle pointed outward.

"I got him," Lorenzo said, only slightly breathless. "I got a clean shot."

Pat put his hand up. "No, what if you hit someone? Let's keep running, Lorenzo. I don't want to kill someone on accident."

Pat hoped Meredith had escaped, even if he wasn't sure what his own fate was. It was stupid, letting her go almost assuredly damned him, but so what? He chose his fate, he made his choices, and he was ready to live with them, to deal with the consequences. Meredith shouldn't have to. He refused to let an innocent person die for his failures.

That was a step too far.

"Fuckin' Pat, bleedin' heart," Lorenzo scoffed. "You're making it tough to beat them. He's out of shots. He needs to reload. Those only got five rounds in them. We can push out of here. I can get help."

"No." There was a finality to Pat's tone, and Lorenzo lowered his gun.

Despite Lorenzo's protests, he relented, turning toward the central artery connecting all the rooms of Louie's Lounge. Pat followed him as the crowds of screaming people rushed past them. They climbed the industrial stairs, slowly but surely, nothing more than another body in the desperate crowd which pushed up toward the entrance.

Pat joined them in their chorus of chaos, initially pretending to be in hysterics to meld into the crowd, but soon it became genuine. It had been so long since he had screamed, so long he could be himself. Lorenzo caught on to his ploy and joined him in the screaming as they made their way for the stairwell, bodies pushing up against them in a sweaty mess.

The light of the day flooded through the sea of humans. Freedom was at hand. Pat looked back once, knowing Hyland was still in the crowd below, but he didn't care. All he saw was his stage, the silver microphone sitting alone in the middle, red velvet curtains behind it.

Only the night prior, it was all his, every person in the crowd focused on him—even Louie himself. Nothing else had mattered. Pat had given up everything, and Tommy had risked it all for just a few months of success, a speck of dirt in the vast landscapes of time where he otherwise felt insignificant.

Like all good things, it was unsustainable, if only because the human appetite was never satisfied, never satiated, always on to the next step of a journey that had no end. Pat had shaken the cold hands of men in suits despite the only lesson his late father had ever taught him was to avoid them. Pat had been cocky. He thought he could get the best of them, that he could come out on top. People rarely doubted their own competence.

Pat did now. Seeing the consequences of his actions had humbled him. Meredith hadn't died, but the person Hyland shot? They might not be so lucky. Deep in thought, he didn't notice that Lorenzo had dragged him to the side of the entrance, patrons still pouring out past them.

"Where did you park, Pat?" Lorenzo asked. "We need to get out of here before Samuel and those other nut jobs come to help him out."

He had parked in the lot across the street, but the lot was full of beeping cars, everyone desperate to get out. As if on cue, a car crashed through the chain link fence, which broke the windshield, but the driver paid no mind, speeding away. The piece of the fence fell to the side of the road as two cars collided with each other at low speed.

Another shot rang out from inside the lounge. Hyland had made his way up the stairs, and with him came chaos outside.

"Might need to take yours," Pat said. Where'd you park?"

Lorenzo grimaced, shaking his head and releasing a deep, primal stress growl. "Two streets over. God, I hope I have to never run again."

There was a second shot into the thinning crowd.

Pat thought for a second. "Behind or in front of us?"

"Behind, why?" Lorenzo asked, trying to find a way out of the calamity.

"There's an alley over here on the left," Pat said, pulling Lorenzo along with him. "It cuts along the side of the building and feeds out back. It's where they store the garbage. Some bartenders hide back there for smoke breaks."

"I did say I work in waste management," Lorenzo joked as Pat opened the door to a narrow alleyway lined with garbage cans and rubbish.

It was the first time that day Lorenzo smiled, his charming grin causing a swoon in Pat's heart. For a moment, nothing mattered, just him, just his smile.

"Well, let's put that to the test and get the hell out of here," Pat said.

He wrenched the shamrock ring of his finger and threw it to the ground before taking Lorenzo's hand into his own. They pushed through the alley of trash, leaving the chaos behind them.

His hands are warm, Pat thought. *There's nothing cold there at all, Dad. Suit be damned.*

25.

Hyland wanted the couple to get away, prepared for it, but this wasn't how he'd expected the couple to escape. The police were already in the Mafia's pocket, and it was only a matter of time before they arrived at Louie's Lounge. With the news of the Cuban Missile Crisis that morning, they would be on alert, looking for any suspicious acts reeking of insurgency. Marxists had activated their sleeper cells, Stalin's long-lost dream from beyond the grave had become a reality, and the world would be bathed in a Red tide.

At least that's how it would appear to the suburbanite sensationalists that would call the authorities about Louie's Lounge.

There were sirens in the distance. Most cars had left, save one, whose driver had tried to run over the man with the gun. Hyland sat on the hood, the horn blowing as a dead man's head rested on the steering wheel. He smoked a cigarette as he waited to see if the Chosen would come to save him. They wanted him there to stall Patrick until Samuel snuck into his room.

"I know you don't understand me. I know you think I speak in riddles." Louie's voice rang out as he recalled their conversation. *"But, Hyland, this is for the greater good. Patrick isn't ready. He's almost there, but he's not yet. Samuel will grab him, and they can talk and work together. Just stall him, do that last favor for me, and I'll send you wherever you want to go. I know you don't trust me, but I ain't ever crossed you. I ain't ever crossed my Chosen. Oath or not, you're one of us."*

Rosaline had picked him up from his home. She even offered to kill the straggler, but Hyland politely declined, assuming the man would embellish their capabilities and cause the Mob to act flustered. And it worked. Although he hadn't expected Lorenzo to be waiting for him at his desk. Hyland had only slipped out for fifteen minutes. He wondered how long Lorenzo had waited for his opportunity.

It was irrelevant now.

The surrounding chaos had subsided, and people had fled from the scene. A police cruiser pulled up before him, its sirens wailing in the otherwise silent broad daylight. A woman poured out of the car, her police uniform looking ill-fitted, clothing far too large for her body. A shoulder-length platinum blonde wig dropped to the ground as she strutted over to Hyland.

It was Rosaline, her face blank. She was Hyland's soft spot, the apple of his eye. He hadn't worked up the courage to court her, reasoning there was always tomorrow.

"You just couldn't keep them occupied, could you?" she asked. "Always with the showing off, Hyland. We get it; you're not a pushover. But you didn't need to cause a scene." Her words cut, but her voice was amused, detached from the carnage Hyland had caused outside the lounge.

"That kid," Hyland said, flicking his cigarette. "You thought he was different. You're right, but he isn't the tough kid you think. I don't think he's cut out for the life Louie wants for him. He has a heart, could've killed that comedian who opened last night, but he didn't. He let her go, even though he knew it would mean letting me go."

"Samuel knows," Rosaline said. "I told him when I stopped by the Slippery Slope. He's working on getting the Chosen together. It looks like the day of reckoning is here. They'll come for you. You're tough as nails, Hyland, but you're not superhuman."

"I make my own luck. Look how far I've come without his gifts. Just with my own damn hands."

Rosaline frowned as he said that, looking down at her shoes before meeting his eye. "Not all of us had things we could change without his help. Living in a body that felt alien even though it was your own."

Hyland immediately regretted his words. He'd been too harsh. He'd known her before she was a Chosen. She was still Rosaline but different. He remembered the way she was treated when she tried to join a cabaret troop: the slurs, the hurtful words, a reminder that, to them, she was no more a woman than Hyland. He would make them all pay. He'd burn it all to the ground.

"You're right." He got up off the hood, wanting to hold her, comfort her. But he didn't. "I'm sorry. Shouldn't have said that. Pat doesn't know anything. Not yet, anyway. I was worried when his boyfriend got into my office. Lorenzo? I was aiming for him. Louie only needs Pat. Lucky prick." He shook his head disbelievingly. "That kid keeps adapting."

Hyland made his way to the cruiser, getting in the passenger side, electing not to ask how she'd procured the vehicle. Some things were better left unsaid.

Rosaline shut the driver's side door, gazing out through the windshield. More sirens sounded in the distance. Despite Louie's power, which had defied logic, there were some things even he couldn't mask. A shooting this close to Fremont was too big an event to suppress. "So, you said he saved someone? The comedian from the night prior? I don't know about her."

Hyland took one look out his window back at Louie's Lounge. It jutted out into the otherwise cookie-cutter neighborhood.

"Meredith, the woman from Kansas City, opened for him," he explained. "She showed up to grab her paycheck. You wanted me to distract him. Well, improvisation isn't my strong suit. I just hope Louie understands. I wouldn't have hurt Pat."

He wouldn't have hurt Meredith, either. Honestly, the whole thing had gone pear-shaped, as far as he was concerned. Once Lorenzo entered the picture, he was out of his depth. Not that it mattered. Even if he sympathized with Louie, Hyland had his role and dared not move beyond that. That was playing with fire. It was bad enough he'd nearly killed Louie's prized possession.

"Do you ever wonder if Louie's right?" Rosaline asked. "He's saved so many of us from the brink. And yet, the world looks at him and his misfit toys with disdain. Sure, he can be militant, cruel. That church was excessive, but they deserved it after what they did." When Hyland didn't say anything, she turned down the next street, saying, "Pat's one of us. I didn't say a word to him. Didn't threaten him. He pushed that guy to give up his friend out of self-preservation, all on his own. There's some edge in him, even if he keeps trying to pretend there isn't. Louie can use that. He can channel that for good."

Hyland hadn't been there on the boat. He hadn't seen what desperation had pushed Pat to do, but he believed Rosaline. The threat of death lingered around every corner, but they kept Pat in the dark, though Hyland couldn't say why. When he'd chosen to abstain from their games, it'd come with the consequence of being ignorant.

"Kid's hiding something. I'm sure you'll find out what." He closed his eyes, his neck pressing against the headrest of his seat.

"Tonight, you'll see it all. I can't say more. You aren't one of the—"

"Yeah, I am not one of the Chosen. I get it. Think I'm doing okay without it." Taking a slow, deep breath, he said, "I'm not judging you, Rosaline, but I can't. I don't trust like that. The game I'm playing is different. I'm here for me, not some greater good. Maybe that makes me a lesser man, a lesser person than you. But it's my way, and I won't ever give that up, no matter how green the grass is."

He could hear her smile, though he couldn't see it. "I have faith. I've seen the vision. It's never too late, Hyland. It's never too late to join. In the meantime, it looks like the outside world will blow itself into dust."

Hyland opened his eyes. They were on the freeway, the streets barren. In the distance, he could see police cruisers making their way toward Louie's Lounge, with other higher-end cars tagging along behind—the Mob joining their pet pigs on a field trip. He was sure they'd burn it down. It was a war between another gang, a faceless organization, and perhaps even Communists. Who could say anything different?

Not them.

"The Missiles, Cuba, I thought it was Louie at first," Hyland said. "He's not a man. Not with what he did for you all. No, no. But when I thought about it, he doesn't care about political squabbles. Fidel, Khrushchev, Kennedy, no, they're plotters. Men in suits. Some are for more noble causes than others, but they want to be remembered at the end of the day. Louie? He wants to be forgotten. An unknown lurking in the shadows of dreams, shaping the world in his image." Hyland could admit to himself that he sympathized with that vision or at least his interpretation of it.

"I stopped trying to figure it out a while ago," Rosaline replied. "Sometimes a blessing can't be questioned, only felt. Whoever he is, wherever he came from, he changed my life. So, I will go wherever he asks."

One person's blessing was another's curse. Hyland wasn't sure which side of the fence he was on. His bank accounts suggested he, too, was blessed. But the dreams of home, the longing to return to being poor with his own again, gnawed at him. There was a beauty in simplicity, as though it was the way God intended.

The Devil had his own vision—a seemingly more equitable one.

He looked out toward the brown mountains standing in the distance as the car drove in isolation. "Where are we heading anyway, Rosaline? The city is in the opposite direction."

She turned to him, her grin growing as she stretched her hand out to him. He took her hand in his as they briefly locked eyes.

"We have a boat to catch."

26.

Lorenzo knew a place. He always seemed to know where to go, just the spot to avoid all the chaos. They were on the outskirts of town, where civilization had dissipated to nothing more than a few pockets of stucco buildings and the occasional abandoned ranch. There they found their motel. It stuck out if only because there was such little else around it.

Lorenzo was sitting in a rocking chair in their dingy motel room. It faced the window, tattered linen curtains obstructing outsiders from looking inside. "How did it all get so messy, Pat? Those guys aren't in the Mob. I don't know who they are, but they ain't got no ethics. Us? Even we have a damn code."

"How was I to know?" Pat asked. "You didn't know them, either, but you still told me to go down there and audition. You don't even like them, so why?"

"They hired queers," Lorenzo explained. "Mob barely even keeps me around. I earn far more than anybody else does, and even I am not a made guy. I knew Louie hired some suspect characters, but I didn't think being a monologist would put you in with that crowd. I had no idea what would happen."

Pat wanted to argue with him. Made guy or not, Lorenzo knew far more than he let on. Why let Pat join them at all? He couldn't understand. It didn't help that his head was throbbing, waves of overstimulation smacking his cranium as though it were high tide.

"I never thought things would go like this. They burned a man in front of me. That's something even *you* wouldn't do." The words hung in the air, the vague threat of them exploding into another cyclic argument clinging to the syllable.

Luckily for both of them, Lorenzo chose not to indulge. "I'm sorry. Really, I am. But we can't control that. We need to find a way out of here, go somewhere without them tailing us. Ain't no use going back into town, Pat. Ain't no use. Nothing but trouble there."

Somehow, Pat knew before Lorenzo explained that this wasn't just about Louie's anymore.

"Mob is scaling up for a war," Lorenzo continued. "They ain't fought a war like this since Prohibition. It'll be messy, and nobody will be there to stop it, not with that missile crisis. Every town in the country is having its own meltdown. See how quick Vegas cleared out?"

Pat watched the static-riddled television set, another replaying of John F. Kennedy's speech to the American people. The President couldn't even hide his own anxiety behind measured, flowery speeches. The world at large was on edge, and Pat would usually be right there with them, but his small corner of that world was crumbling. If it was all going to blow up, he wanted to be isolated with Lorenzo.

But his thoughts were still troubled.

He kept hiding stuff, but maybe that's why he's alive. Maybe that's how he survived. I shouldn't be so quick to judge. He doesn't know everything about me. He doesn't know about Randy. Not that it matters. We're in this together, for better or worse.

"Do we need to go back into town for anything?" Pat asked, turning away from the broadcast to look at Lorenzo. "Do you have everything you need? If we are going on the run, going to need a lot more than pocket change."

"Briefcase I brought in? About five thousand cash. It ain't going to be the lap of luxury, but we'll make do until we can settle in somewhere. There's more at my house, but I don't think that's a good idea. Best be on the road and up and on to better things. Come morning, the Mob and whoever runs Louie's Lounge will be far too busy with each other."

Pat didn't think the Mob would put up much of a fight. He remembered what Hyland had said about the bald ones. They were Louie's Chosen. While Pat didn't fully understand what that entailed, he knew it couldn't be good for anyone going up against them.

"You ever been to Alaska?" Pat asked, only half watching Walter Cronkite on the pixelated television try to calmly explain what was going on in Cuba. "I bet nobody could find us there. Drive up to Seattle and see if there's a boat or plane. Maybe a train. Doesn't matter. They won't find us there. I always wanted to see the mountains. True wilderness."

"Yeah." He didn't seem convinced at first, but then Lorenzo said with more conviction, "Yeah. This whole missile thing will die down by the time we get up there. It may do us good to be up north. Never seen a bear, and I heard there's no shortage of them in Alaska."

Pat could see the verdant pines now, standing tall with an air of regality, stretching as far as his mind's vision would allow. The smell of balsam filled his nostrils, cool air flowed over his skin, and with each breath he took, an icy fire filled his lungs as he marched through some nameless forest to their secluded cabin, just him and Lorenzo against the world.

Like most of the best things in life, it happened unexpectedly. They had met his first night in town, by chance, standing at the same bar. At first, he thought Lorenzo was a plant, leading him straight to Louie's. Those worries had grown after his first meeting with Hyland, but they no longer lingered. He knew now that their meeting was just luck: something true, something unexpected, something honest, even with its flaws. Nothing was perfect, but intention was everything, and it was clear to Pat, clear as day.

Lorenzo intended to be there for him.

"We'll leave tomorrow morning," Lorenzo said.

"Well, if we got until tomorrow morning, I can think of a way to pass the time," Pat said, turning off the TV and standing in front of it. His hip slightly jutted out as his legs spread into a wide stance.

Lorenzo looked up at him, the glint in his eyes suggesting he could read between the lines. "You always know just the right things to say, Pat. Always."

Pat moved toward him, falling into his lap, their eyes meeting. "It's the gift of the gab. It has its moments."

With that, he kissed him. Stress released each time their lips met, replaced with passion and lust. Disrobing was not far behind. Within moments, they were on each other, melding into one person in that hotel room for two.

The chaos of their lives outside the walls meant nothing in the face of their love. They were nothing more than ants in a snow globe, floating in the emptiness of space. It was a humbling thought, for sure, but it quickly passed, troubling neither man's mind as they became decidedly more primal. Everything else could wait. They had business to attend to.

* * *

Sleep had a strange ability to warp time. Sometimes you could've sworn you'd been sleeping for hours, yet only fifteen minutes had passed, while other times, the entirety of the day is gone in the flash of a brief dream. Then there was the dreaded purgatory. What was a dream? What was reality? Was there really even a difference? The swimming between consciousness and dreamscapes, the fixation on ideas or concepts that made total sense in one world and were wholly irrelevant in the other.

Then there was that breeze. Pat had been sure the dingy motel they were staying in didn't have a draft. Perhaps he misremembered. He was, after all, only half awake. That was until he turned over, his sleepy eyes opening to see the bed empty, his partner no longer there. With another blink, he realized the door was wide open.

"Oh, Patty Cakes, you are fucked. Slept right through. His goose is cooked. You're up next."

From over by the window, the specter of Randy sneered at Pat, who was still trying to shake off sleep. He sat up in the bed, only a familiar hiss beneath his feet causing him to pause. His mind became more alert. He could hear the rattling of snakes beneath him.

"Don't look at me." Randy shrugged. *"I'm just a ghost. I couldn't tell you, even if I wanted to."* Then he cackled. *"Heh, looks like the joke's on you. Ironic."*

Pat couldn't believe it—how had he slept through whatever had happened? How had he ended up in bed surrounded by snakes? And where was Lorenzo?

"Fuck...*fuck!*"

The rattling below him made his heart race. He closed his eyes. It was a test of some kind. Otherwise, he'd be dead. Louie's crew had seen their golden opportunity and taken it.

"Ohh, I get it," Pat said, trying not to shiver. *"I'm St. Patrick. I drove the snakes off the island. Hyland? Samuel? Louie? Maybe all three of them, Lorenzo said they'd be busy fighting a war, but they're not like us, so it must've been a quick fight. If I jump down, I'll get bitten almost instantly, right? No, no. They'll be afraid of me, won't they? It's a test, and I'm not scared of death. I don't fear them."*

"Don't give me that," Randy said. *"You're terrified. Still the same ol' Patty Cakes. Nose or not, I can smell that piss running down your leg when I had*

you." Randy was now pacing in front of the bed, wholly undisturbed by the snakes underfoot, who didn't even seem to notice he was there. *"Ohh, Tommy, Tommy, you old bastard, you ruined everything. Maybe my soul will finally be at peace when those snakes fill you with venom."*

Pat looked at the ghost, his features mercifully muted by the blackness of the hotel room. He was still unsure if Randy was doubt manifesting into a hallucination or a genuine malevolent spirit. It didn't matter. Pat had died inside a thousand times over from his inability to act, from fear of retribution, and from trying to please everyone but himself. This time, he would be selfish.

So, he leaped out of bed.

The snakes hissed, their rattling filling his ears. His body tensed in regret as his feet hit the ground. The snakes leapt at his ankles but stopped, their forked tongues kissing the surrounding air before recoiling.

He was right.

Dozens of snakes backed away from him, parting with each step he took to be away from the rattlers surrounding the bed. They pushed through the small opening of his hotel room door and back outside. He wasn't entirely sure he wasn't dreaming or that he hadn't gone mad, yet the snakes ran from him.

"It's real, Patrick," a man said. "It's all real. They fear you more than you fear them."

Pat tried to find the source of the voice in the pitch-black room. It was behind him, coming from the bathroom, its own darkness outlined by the frame of a behemoth.

Samuel.

"Well, shit, look at that." Randy gave a low whistle. *"The plot thickens, Patty Cakes. Let's see what he wants."*

"How? Why?" Pat demanded.

He searched for anything he could use to defend himself from the monster staring at him from the shadows. Daylight or not, he knew what that suit meant. His dad had told him so.

"I told you, he's far more powerful than you could ever imagine. I didn't believe it once upon a time, either. But he's given us far more than I bargained for."

The teeth of his grin glinted in the darkness, yet his eyes did not. The true nature of what he had become was apparent— no longer a man but not *quite* whatever Louie was.

"I'm sick of the games," Pat said. "Why do you all have to be so damn cryptic? Where's Lorenzo? He didn't do anything wrong. I begged him to help me. After you all burned that man, I just couldn't do it anymore."

"Despite your beliefs in good and evil," Samuel replied, "we aren't sadists. The man who burned deserved his death, but it's not for me to say why. Come with me. You have decisions to make, Patrick. Important ones."

Pat very much didn't feel up to following him. He'd grown tired of having no clarity, no answers.

"No. I don't think I will."

Samuel stepped from the shadows, his shining teeth gone as his smile disappeared behind his lips. There was no joy to be found here, artificial or genuine. "Excuse me? I didn't ask, Patrick."

"And? You can't kill me." Pat folded his arms, looking back at the bed and then to the outline of the man, which he could finally make out details of. "You people have a flair for theatrics. Take it from someone who knows the stage, this is preamble."

"We don't need to kill you. You didn't come here alone. C'mon, Patrick, we have a boat to catch. Just like last time."

Lorenzo. Then they *had* taken him. Why? If they weren't as evil as they claimed to be, why punish him? Especially for something that was Pat's fault? No matter what Samuel said, it didn't matter if they were evil or not. They were going to hurt a man Pat cared deeply for. A spade was a spade. It didn't matter if it claimed to be doing so for honorable reasons.

"So, you'll kill him if I don't? Didn't you just get done saying you're not the bad guys? You aren't making a lick of sense."

Samuel said nothing.

Pat looked at the doorway. Samuel could move quick, but Pat was a few steps closer to freedom. He leaped for the exit, but Samuel noticed his shadowy figure moving and gripped his ankle. Pat fell to the floor, his chin scraping ragged carpentry as he gripped the side of the door. Samuel was far stronger than he could've imagined, and yet he clung to the door like his life depended on it.

"Let me go!" Pat shouted.

He kicked at Samuel's skull, but with his grip on Pat's ankle, the force of it was muted. Still, there was a dull thud, though it did little to deter Samuel.

"You can't leave! Not until it's done. Not until it's done!" Samuel's calm, apathetic tone was gone, replaced with one of concern and genuine fear.

Pat kept kicking. Pangs shot down his armpits and through his rib cage as he felt himself being stretched away from his grasp on the door. "Let go!" he cried again.

Pat looked back at Samuel, who must've decided that pulling was not enough. He crawled up Pat's leg, his weight slamming it to the ground. Pat's kneecap ground into the carpet as he contorted his body, twisting and wrenching as hard he could to get away. Samuel's breaths were disturbingly warm against Pat's bare back as Samuel ascended, inching closer to where Pat held on for dear life. Arms wrapped around Pat's elbow, pulling it inward, and he finally had to relinquish his grip on the door.

Samuel looked down at Pat, flipping him over. "I told you, you can't leave until it's done."

Pat's hands were pinned to the floor. Samuel's face shone in the moonlight pouring in from the awning. His eye was swollen from Pat's kicks, blood trickling down his cheeks and past his mouth until it dripped off his chin.

Pat closed his eyes, prepared for whatever came next. He'd done his best. He'd fought as hard as he could. What was left? What else could he do?

A loud ringing filled his ears as copper trickled into his nostrils. At first, he thought it was just the blood from where he'd battered at Samuel's face in his attempt to flee. But when he opened his eyes, he knew this wasn't the case. Samuel had fallen to the side, pieces of his skull on the floor, coated in blood and brains. Pat looked up at a tall figure casting a shadow in the doorway above them.

It was Lorenzo. Sweat dripped from his brow, and his breaths labored in his chest as his hand shook. "Was only gone for fifteen minutes. That's it, Pat. I had to make a call. Sorry. I'm sorry. I didn't see it. I didn't stop it."

Pat crawled over to him and stood, his body trembling as he tried to process everything. "Thank you. I was...I thought they got you."

He gripped Lorenzo's back tightly, sobbing into his shoulder. He didn't know what Samuel wanted with him, but he doubted it was good. In that moment, only one thing really mattered. Lorenzo had come back. He could've left. It would've been much easier, much simpler. But he'd stayed. He'd saved Pat.

"It's okay, Pat. It's okay. He's done. He's not getting back up."

Their embrace broke as Lorenzo made his way to the closet and pulled out his suitcase, the one filled with cash—their ticket to escape, to start anew.

"YOU CAN'T LEAVE! NOT UNTIL IT'S DONE!" Samuel roared, rising from the ground. The bearish man's knees scuffed against the rug as he flung himself upward. "NOT UNTIL IT'S DONE!" His words were agony pouring through his lips. When he was fully on his feet, Pat understood why.

The eye he'd been shot through was nothing more than plasma and gelatinous goop oozing down his face. In its place was a crater of crimson and copper, the smell coming from the blood and bullet all at once. He snarled and gnashed his teeth as he stalked forward. Regardless of his ruined vision, he had one goal in sight, and they would not deter him.

Lorenzo gave Pat a terrified look, then back to Samuel, mouth agape.

"*Fuck.*"

27.

A lot could happen in fifteen minutes. A person could die, they could run a mile, make a meal. Hell, if they so desired, they could even take the first steps towards a new life, although, in reality, it was often shorter. As if to spite this, men almost always insisted it was longer. Life is, after all, a balancing act of truth and self-delusions converging to a happy middle ground that was not quite either.

As Pat had woken up in an empty hotel room, snakes surrounding his bed, Lorenzo was dealing with his own personal hell. He'd snuck out after they made love, leaving Pat to sleep, to dream of a world better than the one in which they lived.

Despite the day's heat, once the sun set, there were no trees or plants to block the cold, harsh winds in the mountain valley the motel was tucked away in. Still, chilly or warm, barren or not, Lorenzo had a phone call to make. He wasn't in charge of everything. They'd never let a non-Italian have too much power, doubly so since he was also a gay man. Neither of those facts had barred his entry into the Mob. If you could earn, it didn't matter to them who you were. Long-held beliefs caved in in favor of the almighty dollar.

There were limits to that, however.

Lorenzo stood at a pay phone. The booth shone brilliantly defiant in the desert night, surrounded by the shadows. His palms itched, sweat leaving him clammy with nervousness. He dialed, calling one of his colleagues, Matty Mariano, formerly of Kansas City, currently of Sin City.

The phone rang, each rattle reminding him of serpents under duress. *Rattle, rattle, hisssss!* He felt the urge to look around, to check if there actually was a snake nearby, but it was just static.

On the other line, it sounded as though a man was wrinkling plastic for a moment or two until his voice filled the receiver. "Who's callin'? What'cha want?"

"It's me. Lorenzo. Sorry, got ambushed outside the Lounge. That Native guy brought them bald-headed pricks. Had to skip town to lose their trail. I'm comin' back in, though. I'm comin' for them. Did they push at you guys? Do we even know who they are?"

Lorenzo knew the truth now. They weren't men. They weren't mobsters. Their goals didn't mesh with what he knew of the Mafia. Louie's guys weren't here to make money. They wanted to make waves, to make change.

He heard some indecipherable chatter between Matty and someone else before he answered. "Yeah, think that news down in Cuba has them confident. Ain't nobody lookin' this way. All the cops on the payroll are out in droves, lookin' for that Indian guy. Others gotta keep optics." The unknown man sighed. "Look, this war is real bad. They shot up the Pelican Lounge, for God's sake. Went in like they were Al Capone. Some bald broad shot a few innocent elderly folks. These guys, they ain't like us. I don't know what they are."

Lorenzo looked at his feet, anger boiling to the point that he thought steam was going to pour out of his ears. "*Animales.*"

This was Lorenzo's fault. They'd taken up a war at his request. They hadn't even questioned his motives. Once they knew about the burning church, that was it. The Italian mob fed into the hand of religion and vice versa, until the end of time. They could barely come to terms with a gay man within their ranks, even one who earned well above the others. But when a man burned down a church, even because of suspected pedophilia, that was a step too far.

But now innocent people were dying.

"I'm coming back," Lorenzo promised. "Where did you guys want to meet? What's the plan?"

"Yeah?" Marty sounded skeptical. "I was worried you got cold feet and skipped town with your lover boy. An Irish kid no less. Figured you'd go build your life somewheres else, eatin' potatoes and whatever it is you people eat." Now his voice had a sinister tinge. While it could just be interpreted as edgy humor, Lorenzo knew better.

Matty and the others didn't care that men who looked like Lorenzo gifted their chocolates to them or that the polenta they loved so much would have never been born without Mexico, without its natives. It didn't matter that Lorenzo barely spoke the mother tongue. The white man would never accept him as anything other than a burden. To the White Man, Lorenzo was another reason they couldn't succeed despite every single benefit gifted to them. The same gifts those of color would never experience.

Lorenzo sighed into the phone. This brought the ire of Matty, laced with enough humor to create reasonable doubt in someone who didn't know him. "Hey, hey, buddy, I'm only teasing you. I don't care what you stick in your ass. Listen, tell us where-abouts you are. We'll come getcha and fill you in on the plan. Don't sweat it. We'll take care of you."

He doubted the man's sincerity. Matty wasn't the worst of them, but rarely was he the one to make promises. "What if I come back into town?" Lorenzo asked. "Don't want you guys leaving in case those bald freaks try to pull another stunt. Need every man we can get."

"No, no, don't worry about us. We'll be alright, Lorenzo. Let me send some guys to get you. Can't risk you being tailed."

Lorenzo's heart sank. The offer seemed innocuous, concerned even, but he knew better. Rarely did they roll out the red carpet. The more likely outcome was duplicity, lulling their prey into a sense of security, drawing them out where it was easier to strike at them. They'd be buried or in the lake by night's end. He'd been on the winning end of that ploy more than once.

"Yeah, yeah, I'm about thirty miles north of town, on the road toward Reno. Bright red motel on the right, can't miss it. I'll see you when you get here, yeah?"

He looked back at the moss-green exterior of the motel. It was a lie but a necessary one. He didn't want to be another hole in the ground, at least not yet. His time hadn't come.

"Oh, yeah, I think I know that one," Marty said. "We did some work outta that back in '59. Okay, yeah, I'll be there. Wait outside with bells on, alright?"

His voice radiated smugness as though he'd won, even if Lorenzo knew better. This was good. It gave him time to get out of town. He was at the end of the road. War had come, and Lorenzo was without friends, caught in a crossfire beyond his wildest nightmares.

"See you soon."

Lorenzo hung up the phone and stared at the roadway, listening to the sounds of the desert around him, the crickets and scarce animal life buzzing in the distance. It was then he heard the faint sound of a rattlesnake—no, a *lot* of rattlesnakes. And the noise became progressively louder and louder.

His ears twitched as he tried to understand where the noise was coming from. It sounded like...

Pat. Shit.

Lorenzo turned back toward the motel and did a double take. Parked outside of it was a car he hadn't seen pull in, its passenger door still open. His room door was open, too, snakes fleeing into the parking lot. He reached for his firearm as he scanned the ground. The snakes pushed past the parking lot into the desert next to the hotel. Where had they come from?

After the snakes had slithered into the shadows, another commotion broke out from inside his room. Between his confusion and the pounding of his heart, Lorenzo couldn't discern what was being said, so he couldn't tell who had broken in. He doubted it was the Mob. They'd only just learned where he was, and they wouldn't have wasted manpower trying to find him on their own. That left one option.

Louie's guys. They found us. Fucking freaks.

His safety was off now as he made his way over to the room. Somehow, the other motel guests were sleeping through the chaos, no voices raised or heads poking out of doors to make sense of what was going on. As the shouting from his room grew louder, Lorenzo barreled faster towards the door, wondering how long it would be before more innocents got caught up in this mess.

Pat was gripping the doorway, yelling as he tried to escape. Lorenzo looked around, making sure nobody else was lying in wait, and then sprinted forward, his pistol aimed at the door. As he stood in the doorway, he saw the lanky shadow at the edge of the room rising as it gripped Pat's ankle. His boyfriend didn't look up to see his salvation. Instead, he desperately held on to the door frame, screaming as loud as his lungs could manage. Samuel got the upper hand and tore Pat from the door, flipping him over and staring him down. His bald head reflected the moonlight, and he didn't yet notice Lorenzo standing in the doorway.

Rage filled the caverns of his heart, pumping blood to his brain, clearing his thoughts, fueling him as he fired his gun. The bullet entered through Samuel's eye, splattering it out the other side. A loud boom filled his ears, and Pat's eyes opened wide in shock.

"Pat, it's okay! It's okay!"

He wasn't sure if Pat could hear him. He could hardly hear himself over the ringing in his ears. Lorenzo felt sweat coat his chest hair, sticking to his shirt as his breaths grew more labored. Between the anxiety and his mad dash from the phone booth, he was practically hyperventilating.

"Was only gone for fifteen minutes. That's it, Pat. I had to make a call. Sorry. I'm sorry. I didn't see it. I didn't stop it."

Pat embraced him, and he hugged him back tightly. The two of them exchanged words, but Lorenzo's focus was on the suitcase, their chance to start anew. He hurried to grab it out of the closet, certain this nightmare was over and they could get the hell out of here. It wasn't like a guy with a bullet through his brain could tell them no.

A lot could happen in fifteen minutes. Lorenzo's life, the one that had taken him away from Arizona backwaters and led him to Sin City, had come crashing down today as earthquake after earthquake ripped through the foundations of everything he'd built, everything he'd earned. The one thing he'd salvaged from the rubble of his life was that briefcase. It was his chance to escape with his gem in his arm, Pat's soul illuminating like the verdant fields of shamrocks his ancestors left for promises across the ocean. Lorenzo had passed through a sea of his own, a sea of sand, for his opportunity. He understood the allure, the luster of a fresh start. It had worked out once before, and with this briefcase, history would repeat itself.

But, even more could happen in fifteen seconds.

"YOU CAN'T LEAVE! NOT UNTIL IT'S DONE!" The bald man—no, not a man—rose, relinquishing the human veneer it had maintained for so long. Ichor dripped down its cheek in a mocking facsimile of tears. "NOT UNTIL IT'S DONE!"

Within fifteen seconds, fears could become reality, and nightmares could manifest, transforming from the abstract to the tangible. There was only one word on the tip of Lorenzo's tongue as the tsunami of reality battered the shores of his sanity.

"*Fuck.*"

28.

Samuel had been born with cerebral palsy. It was a mild case compared to others, but it was bad enough that bullying and ostracization was as commonplace as dinner or a shower in his daily routine.

He knew other people with the same disorder who didn't let it affect them, who refused to be defined by it. Samuel didn't share their drive or motivations. He couldn't square away the cognitive dissonance reverberating throughout his head whenever the magnifying glass of adolescent wrath found him. Life at home was no better, his parents hardly different from the bullies he had known day in and day out, well intentioned, but often just as cruel.

Adulthood provided no respite. He could walk, albeit slower than others, and his speech came out slightly slower. Kids were cruel, and adults even more so because they'd developed "justifications" for their biases. But whether it was eugenics, racism, or a twisted sense of moral superiority, their rationales didn't need to make sense to anyone but them. Human minds were exceptional at crafting narratives to prove their biases were correct and their lack of empathy divinely ordained.

So he left home for a city of hope, somewhere he could begin anew. It wasn't what he'd hoped; he was poked fun at once more, and while Samuel no longer carried that same childhood shame over his disorder, he knew the world would continue to be cruel, lambasting someone they'd never understand, mistaking bravery for weakness. It's courageous to wake up every day and walk through that front door knowing nobody will treat you with dignity, with respect. Yet Samuel carried on, his existence a brave act of revolutionary defiance against their preconceived notions of what he could be—what he was *supposed* to be.

That didn't mean he was above trying to cure himself. He wished he could be braver than he already was, that he could ignore their insults, their discrimination, but he needed to survive. He needed to eat.

Opportunity came the day he met the Devil in his khaki suit. His gold teeth glinted in the desert sun, a shadow cast from his tan Scala fedora.

Samuel could see the tattoos through his white dress shirt. Fate was knocking at his door, and he wasn't one to waste his chance.

"Tired of them makin' fun? Tired of them underestimatin' you? I could make them fear you, make it so nobody would *ever* say anotha' word to you besides, *Yes, sir; no, sir; thank you, sir; sorry, sir.*'" His words flowed like the waters of a collapsing dam—forceful yet effortless, as though this was how nature intended. "I know I look seedy and shifty, don't I? Looks can be deceivin', Sammy Boy. What say you? Fixin' to join the undesirables?"

Louie clearly wasn't what he appeared to be, but what did that matter? Who really was what they said they were? Louie offered a fairy tale promise. He didn't see how any man could change him, what he was. But Samuel also didn't know if that was a human staring back at him from behind the figure's eyes. He doubted it, but somehow that made the proposition all the more appealing. And part of him liked the idea of exacting revenge on those who'd disregarded him as less than a man—less than a person.

"What do you need from me?" Samuel asked. "I learned a long time ago that nobody in this city gives anything for free, least of all an offering like that."

"I'd say this world needs a revolution, don't you? I am but one *man*." The last word came out as a whimsical farce, a thinly veiled lie. "I need other people to join the fight."

"What are you fighting? What do you need from me?" Samuel asked, not blinking.

The smolder of Louie's eyes negated the wrinkled corners of his mouth. He was chaos personified. In those eyes, Samuel could see the implosions of empires, the destruction of countless tyrants, and the desecration of those who had desecrated. All at once, he understood everything to be nothing.

"Everything."

***

It was an easier choice than he'd imagined. Civility was only a veneer to obstruct the cantankerous masses that formed in the gums of humanity. Samuel only needed to look outside. Men fought in pointless wars for pointless ideologies. People labored under oppressive systems that served to keep them docile, pliant. Missiles pointed at each other, threatening to snuff out the flames of life, its vibrancy falling under a nuclear winter that would freeze even the brightest optimism.

He learned all this and more from Louie, a man who existed outside of such order—a man who was no man at all. He was an agent of chaos to some and an agent of justice to others. It really was a matter of perspective. To the downtrodden, he was their failsafe, their insurance that they too would not end up as coal in the chimneys of the elite, their life force burned to allow the chosen few to pretend they were the sun itself, their radiance turning those deemed beneath them into ash. To the elite, he was a menace, a wrench that threatened to lodge itself in the industrial machine that kept them in power, a warning that their empire would fall, just as so many others had.

But to Samuel, he was so much more than that. Louie was a new lease on life, a symbol of change on a visceral, personal level. Not a man. Not a devil. Not a god. No, Louie was something else, a blend of all three and none of the above all at the same time. And Samuel was loyal to him, would always be loyal to him, until the very end.

"NOT UNTIL IT'S DONE!!" Samuel howled.

He rose, feeling the bullet make its way through his head to the other side and out to the wall behind him. It was then he understood the full extent of Louie's power. Neuron pathways were reconnecting themselves, slowly eroding the trauma to his flesh from Lorenzo's firearm.

"*Fuck,*" he heard the Latino man call out.

Samuel rotated his neck several times as the healing of his injury quickened in pace. He reached up for the bed, gripping part of its frame to help himself to his feet.

"I'll shoot him again," Lorenzo said.

Samuel wasn't dead—hadn't even questioned whether or not death was an option for him— and he held a hand up, gazing at it, getting used to his new range of vision. His eyeball wasn't coming back. It had fully been separated from his body, and he could sense there were limits even to this newfound power.

"If I wanted to kill you," Samuel said, "you'd be dead. You can't leave without me. You need to come with me."

Patrick looked at him, hesitating. Samuel understood. Pat was certain his death was assured, stamped into the bullet that took Samuel's eye. "Why the snakes? Why all the theatrics if you're not trying to kill us?"

Samuel shrugged. He hadn't sent the snakes after Patrick. He suspected Louie had, though to what end, he wasn't privy. He'd held up his part of the bargain, played the role he'd been assigned, which didn't include being Louie's secret keeper.

"I am but a pawn," Samuel said, his speech coming out meticulous but tired as he stood tall now. "I merely serve him. If I knew, I'd say. They're here for you." Samuel pointed at Lorenzo. "*He* led them here. They followed you, waiting for more to show up. Reinforcements."

Samuel's brow furrowed. *How do I know that?* He wasn't sure, but he suspected this brief omniscience was another gift from Louie.

Lorenzo gripped his boyfriend, trying to shake some sense into him. "I don't trust him, Pat. I don't trust anybody but you. We need to get out of here."

Samuel's gunshot wound had healed by this point, and as he suspected, his eye didn't reform. His ears worked just fine, however, and there was the unmistakable noise of chatter and closing doors funneling in from the U-shaped parking lot for the motel. His hunch had been correct.

Samuel took his wallet out of his suit jacket and tossed it at the feet of the two men. "There. Directions for where to go from here are written on the back of a Lounge business card. Take it. And give me your firearm, please."

Lorenzo looked at Samuel as though his head was still split open. "Listen, I get it. You're not quite human, and you could kill us if you wanted to. But there's no way in hell I'm going out there without my gun."

The din from outside was growing, and Samuel could hear more cars peeling into the parking lot.

"They know you lied," Samuel said. "Those aren't Louie's people, Lorenzo. They're yours."

Samuel found his firearm in his waistband and checked that it was loaded. He'd rather have two, but it was clear by how tightly Lorenzo gripped his own that the other man wasn't going to give it up for anything.

"Keep your gun then," Samuel conceded. "But when we go out there, you run to your car and drive as far as you can. He needs Patrick. *We* need Patrick"

It was obvious that neither Pat nor Lorenzo understood why he was helping them, that they couldn't wrap their heads around it. It wasn't his place to explain, and he doubted they'd understand Louie's crusade, anyway. They were empathetic and capable, but were they hungry enough? Or had comfort made them complacent with the status quo? These were questions he knew better than to ask and the answers to them were above Samuel's place in the hierarchy.

Louie had given him everything, so he would return the favor. His hand gripped the wood of his gun handle as the air filled with the sounds of loaded firearms cocking outside. Lorenzo and Pat backed away from the door, peeking through a window in their room that overlooked the courtyard, the scene playing out behind the milky film of a white mesh curtain. They were scared. Samuel didn't need two eyes to see that much.

"I gave them the wrong place," Lorenzo said, clearly trying to convince himself more than Pat. "Said we were on the opposite side of the outskirts. There's no way they should know I'm here. There's no way."

Pat turned to Samuel, looking up at him with hard, angry eyes. There was no love lost between them, Samuel knew. Their relationship had always been a contentious one. Such was the way of things when you were only permitted to give half-truths.

"Did you do this?" Pat demanded.

Samuel just shook his head. He wished he could say more, but his mother always reminded him, no matter how cruel the bullies were: *"Actions speak louder than words. You're perfect the way you are, baby."* Samuel hoped his actions would speak volumes. He began a slow walk to the door, the chatter of mobsters filling the night sky beyond the motel room.

His body bulwarked the lovers inside. "Louie sends his regards!" Samuel yelled into the night.

A man in the crowd, who appeared to be the leader, raised a brow as he stepped forward. His tartan suit glinted in the moonlight. His own frame was anything but small in its own right, though Samuel was still bigger.

"Oh, yeah?" The man sneered. "Do you know who the fuck we are? We took a lot of you bald-headed freaks down back in town. What's to stop you from being another one? Who are you to threaten us?"

The man chuckled, the laugh of a bully. The ringing in Samuel's ears was familiar. He was the butt of the joke again. His hand gripped his gun as he heard the hissing. In their laughter, they drowned out the snake's rattles. There must've been at least a dozen of them, and not a single one noticed the sneaking serpents underneath their cars.

"Look down."

"If you think I'm gonna fall for that, you're even duller than you look."

Fire churned in his stomach, and his ears grew red, but he didn't react. His vindication slithered underfoot now. The man just didn't realize it yet.

Another mobster, however, did notice. "Boss, boss, he ain't joking. Look down."

A large rattlesnake rested by his ankle, looking upward, the venom in its eyes only rivaled in potency by the poison of its fangs.

"Fuck! *Fuck!* Get it away! Kill them!"

The mobsters looked down, saw the snakes, and then stared back at Samuel. They looked confused about the order in which the slaughter should occur. Half decided on the snakes, and the other half chose the giant man.

Samuel was quick. His gun had already fired two shots before anyone else even figured out what was going on. With that, at least one man lay dead on the ground, snakes encircling the corpse before biting into him in a theatrical display of the fate that awaited the others.

Samuel ducked behind a car as the men started shooting at him. He held his hand up, his gun pointed at them, and fired at random. He still had one good eye, and out of the corner of it, he saw Lorenzo and Patrick creep behind a car parallel to his own. The snakes were thrashing, and screams filled the night. Guests of the motel were waking up, lights in their rooms turning on as the chaos outside disturbed their slumber.

The mobsters were closing the distance, and Samuel could hear the gravel displace as at least two made their way to his car. Gunshots filling the night suggested that while the snakes had provided a distraction, they were by no means an assurance of victory.

"Get up!" someone shouted. "C'mon, coward, stop hiding!"

One man had taken the lead, firing through the car. Its windshield collapsed in a downpour of glass, some of which bounced off the hood and onto Samuel. He had since drawn his hand back, reloading his firearm with the only other magazine of ammunition he had. He stood up to fire but was too slow. Samuel slammed to the ground as a bullet struck him, the sheer velocity of it throwing him off balance.

The man who'd shot him yelled in excitement as he approached. "Got him! Got the prick!"

Samuel could already feel the fibers in his shoulder begin healing. Still, he stuck to the ground. Best to let them think he was down, anything to let the other two escape. He didn't know if they would heed his words, but he trusted them. Besides, things had escalated, and he was neither immortal nor all-powerful, so keeping low was his best bet.

Motel room doors flung open. As if reacting without thinking, the mobster turned his gun and fired at the first door to his left. A woman's scream filled the night air, adding to the chorus of chaos. An innocent person had been shot.

Samuel jolted to his feet. His body was still healing, but he only needed one good arm.

"What the fuck? I shot him!" The mobster turned his firearm on Samuel, not giving a second thought to the innocent person he'd almost assuredly murdered.

Samuel gripped him with his good arm, strong enough to pull the man off his feet with relative ease. When he'd pledged his loyalty to Louie, the not-quite-a-man had made it clear that transforming Samuel into a monster of a man wasn't about fixing him. He was being given the tools for his retribution, destroying the bullies of the world at their own game.

His strength blew away even his loftiest expectations. The man he held by the neck was well upwards of two-hundred pounds. Yet Samuel held him in his hand like he was nothing more than a baseball, pale with red stitches of veins zigzagging across his face as he desperately tried to inhale air. But Samuel was unrelenting, keeping his neck squeezed in a vice-grip.

"Let him go!" one of the mobsters cried, gun shaking in his hand as he attempted to find an opening to get a shot off. "Let him go!"

"Poor choice of words."

Samuel threw the man in his grasp into the other with such force that they smacked together, falling to the ground. Before either could make sense of the situation, Samuel towered over them.

"No, no!" the second man yelled, as his friend coughed and gasped for air now that the death grip had been relinquished.

Samuel didn't hesitate. Their shrill screams were met with the sound of a slug smashing the earth beneath their flesh. The other motel patrons scrambled toward their respective cars as the remaining mobsters finished off the snakes still attacking them. Their ringleader still stood. Samuel stepped toward him, stopping briefly to look down at the one he'd thrown by the neck. He was still gasping for air but slowly stabilizing.

"F-fuck you!" the guy sputtered out in defiance.

Samuel looked down, seeing not the mobster but an amalgamation of all his bullies through the years—children, teachers, even family, all resembling a melted candle of paradoxical facial features.

His foot came down hard on the man's head, stomping it into the earth as he peered over the battlefield. The mobsters took notice of him, especially now that their slithering attackers had been neutralized. His foot pressed down harder, and he heard a crack. Their leader looked him dead in the face. Even at this distance, Samuel didn't need two eyes to see the fear mixed with animalistic hatred.

Samuel blinked once and felt the holes in his flesh that told him he'd been shot. There was no pain, only the cold air pouring into his innards as they peppered him with bullets. He fell back, his black shoes flinging the brain matter of his last conquest into the air. He landed with a thud and struggled to breathe. The wounds were healing, but not as quickly as they had before. As they kept firing at him, a piece of his foot flung into the air, and he had a feeling it wouldn't regenerate, just like his eye.

The earth shook as cars rumbled out of the lot, desperate to avoid the shoot-out. Though he couldn't see them in the fleeing crowd, he hoped Lorenzo and Patrick had escaped. He heard faint screams as a dull thud filled the air—somebody had been run over. There was yelling and more gunshots, but they sounded far away, like they were happening around someone else.

Perhaps he wasn't immortal after all. There were limits to the power that had been granted. On the surface, it seemed like a massive ask. But it made a lot of sense. Louie would give you what society wouldn't; in return, he requested loyalty. He never made any qualms about his militant nature, never sought to deceive you about his agenda. Some people wanted to burn it all down and start anew; others wanted to fix things on a more personal level. And Louie would give it to them...for a price. He was almost assuredly not a man, but he had the heart of one. He had the duplicity and savagery of a human but not their zealotry. He cared not to separate those who were different; inclusion was his goal. But that didn't mean his gifts would last forever.

Samuel's mind raced as his lungs deteriorated and his world grew black along the edges, the darkness creeping to the center of his vision.

"What are you fighting?" he asked the night as footsteps inched towards him. He couldn't make out distinct features, only shapes, a dark silhouette hovering overhead, looking down upon him.

Another gunshot rang out as Samuel's flame was expunged. Louie's voice rang in his ears as the bell to place beyond tolled for him.

"Everything."

29.

When Samuel had gotten back up, Pat did not expect reason to be the next course of action. But as the snakes descended from the desert, they escaped. He tried to put it all together.

"Why?" Lorenzo swerved across the road to avoid the other panicking patrons of the motel. "Why did he help us? He was trying to kill you. I had to shoot him to get him off!"

Pat was going through Samuel's wallet. A faded photograph of a child and a mother stared back at him. The face was undeniably Samuel's, but he wore braces on his legs, and his head was full of hair.

"We might be wrong," he admitted. "What if the crew at Louie's Lounge aren't the bad guys? What if they're cruel, but they have good intentions?"

It didn't make sense. How could anybody be good when they were willing to burn men alive? How deeply had they sunk into depravity to ensure their aims? Their agenda was still foreign to Pat, a puzzle he couldn't quite unravel. But the facts remained, indifferent to his biases: something had happened at that motel, something that made him doubt his fears about Louie and his organization.

Lorenzo was proving more closed off to Pat's new theory, a look of skepticism etched on his face. "That's ridiculous."

"Is it?" Pat pressed. "He had a gun, right? You saw the way he pulled me from the hinges of the door. If he wanted to kill me, why not fire the gun? Why not just end it? We knew there was more to it. But now...I just...I just don't know."

As Pat's thoughts swirled, Lorenzo said, "I don't trust nobody, Pat—just you. Four months ago, if you'd told me a stranger could've meant more than the world to me, I'd have called you a liar. I live in Las Vegas, but that doesn't mean I gamble with my heart. But you...you mean everything." He nervously checked the rearview mirror, then added, "Samuel's an acolyte of something far beyond what either of us can reckon with. Let's just leave. I have my suitcase. It ain't much, but we can settle in and find new gigs. Start fresh. Just you and me."

Lorenzo spoke with the meticulousness of someone trying to suppress the surge of sadness on the horizon. In twenty-four hours, his life had collapsed, his world held hostage by a crisis of two powers far beyond his reckoning. Just like Pat, he was caught in the middle of a spider web woven long before either had ever settled in. Wrong place, wrong time.

Pat gripped his thigh as they drove on into the night, the screams and gunfire from the motel drowned out by the slicing wind through the open windows. "Listen, I came here to escape the past. Shit happened. It wasn't my fault, but I was there. I saw things no man can unsee. I had to leave and be who I was meant to be." He rested his head against the back of his seat, sighing. "And now I'm in over my head. We're both drowning in an ocean of sand. Ain't that a fuckin' irony?"

"How does that help us now?" Lorenzo asked. He didn't sound testy, just tired.

"My point is, I was naïve. Even when I saw something cruel, I ignored it. I wanted to believe in the best of humanity, but Las Vegas taught me I'm only one step away from being the bad guy and that looks can be deceiving. I was warned you were a monster, and maybe to some people, you are. But I don't see that. I see a man trying to survive in a world built on the presumption of his failure. I see a man who made mistakes trying to stay afloat."

Lorenzo nodded, biting his lip as he waited for Pat to press on.

"I'm a man," Pat said. "Nothing more, nothing less. I watched them burn someone alive when I stepped on that boat. Why? Why would they do that? Why would they kill a man and then turn around and give a homosexual a chance in a world that'd rather we go quietly into the night? And then what happened with Samuel...I understand, I think. I think I get it."

"What do you mean? Because I'm not seeing it, Pat. All I see is death and destruction. Yeah, the Mob, they kill, but they have reasons. There's money to be made. That's what matters to them. That's all that matters to them." Lorenzo gripped the steering wheel tight. "They don't care about people. I never mattered to them. I knew that eventually I'd be replaceable, that they'd throw me to the bottom of Lake Mead like so many others who'd hit their expiration date. And Louie? Bet he's the same, through and through."

"No, I...I think whatever Louie is, he stands opposed to who they are." The moment Pat said it out loud, the more deeply he believed it. "Y'know, when I was working there, I found out why there were so many people at the casino. Why Louie's was always so packed. People won more there. They never left broke down to their last coin. At least that's what I heard."

"And you believed that?"

Pat shook his head. "Not at first, no. I thought it was just old people spinning fairy tales about being big winners. But what if it wasn't? What if Louie's Lounge...what if they're nothing like the Mob? What if they don't give a fuck about money? What if they don't care what society is *supposed* to be like?"

"C'mon, Pat," Lorenzo said, darting a quick look over at him. "Don't start buying into their lies now."

"No, think about it. A Negro and a homosexual both on stage back-to-back? An Indian running the books? It doesn't make sense. They don't make money with the types of checks Hyland signs. There ain't no way."

"So they're Reds?" Lorenzo asked. "They're making their move because of Cuba or whatever? What does it matter if they care about money or not? You said you saw them burn someone—alive. That ain't moral; that's evil."

"No, maybe they're sympathetic to the Reds. But those ain't Soviets." Pat stared out the window, catching sight of a snake. It wasn't a rattler, but he still shivered. "Look at Samuel. If they could do that to people, we'd be speaking Russian. I don't pretend to understand who they are. But from where I am standing, they're at least more complicated than we gave them credit for. We wanted to simplify them, to hate them. Because we were scared. *I* was scared."

"Pat, it doesn't matter," Lorenzo insisted, turning down another empty desert road. "Fuck them. If they needed you, they should've asked. They chose to do this tap dance. They decided to put us—to put *you*—in harm's way." He rolled the window up a little, almost like he wanted to make sure Pat could hear what he said next. "Maybe he needs you, but you don't need him. You don't need anybody. Least of all, someone who can't tell you the truth. I wish I learned that lesson before I hurt you."

Pat looked away, digging through Samuel's wallet as he said, "You did what you had to. I was cold. I judged you too harshly. You didn't ever put me in a bad situation. As I said, people are complicated. Good people do bad things for good reasons, and even bad people do good things. Nothing's clear-cut; nothing's simple. I reckon if it was, we wouldn't be here. World wouldn't need to prop up mirages like Vegas, drawing in the desperate with the promise of hope."

He looked through everything Samuel had collected over the years. A wallet said a lot about a man, a lot more than he was willing to admit outwardly. And cards told a story, where a man had been, what he'd done.

Samuel's wallet was no exception. Business cards from specialists in New York and Washington, D.C., lined each pocket. Some had dates written on them going back years; others had a giant X scratched into them in pen. There was also, however, a card without anything printed on it. Instead, someone had handwritten a note on the cream-colored paper: *"Where it began, take the coin inside."*

Pat popped open the largest pocket, which ran against the shell of the wallet. Inside was a coin, much like the one he'd been forced to give the Ferryman the night he saw the other man burn. He stared down at it, rubbing the face of it with his thumb.

Lorenzo's focus was still on the road stretching out endlessly in front of them. "Pat, we don't need to be here. Let's go. I get it. You're an idealist. You need answers, but there are no answers there. Just more violence, just more death. We don't need him to make a better world. We can build our own. Just the two of us."

Pat looked at him, this man he'd grown to care about so deeply. He knew they could do it, that they could build the life they wanted together. Lorenzo was a man of tenacity, unwilling to bend the knee and give up. There was no doubt in his mind that, together, the two of them could forge a new world.

But then Pat thought of Tommy on that dark night, the bony clutches of death clawing at his feet with a feverous cadence. He thought about what Tommy had sacrificed for him, for his future. Pat had been saved and given a chance to live. And maybe Lorenzo was right. Maybe there was only death, even for those who wanted to fight against a cruel world never meant for them. But that didn't mean running away was the right thing to do.

"A world separated from it all doesn't exist," Pat said. "We'd just be lying. We could have amazing happy lives, living day in and day out the way we want. But at night? When the lights go down, I'll just hear them screaming, desperate to live the life we so cowardly shut ourselves away in." He closed his eyes, then popped them open again when the screams started up in his head.

"I've lived a good life, better than many who love the way I do. Maybe Louie's evil. But I want to know for sure. I don't want to run again—*ever* again."

"Pat...what if we die? What if it's a trap? What if we lose?" Lorenzo pleaded, his voice teetering on the edge of tears. He was confused. He was unsure what to make of it all, his eyes transparent as a window. Fear of the unknown was bred into the American psyche from birth. Lorenzo undoubtedly had seen firsthand what such vitriol produced.

"Then it's over," Pat said sadly, "and none of it matters." As he turned a dial on the car's dashboard, he added, "Besides, if you listen to the radio, the world's not far behind."

Lorenzo opened his mouth to protest, but as his eyes met Pat's, he closed it. There was a look in those eyes that all at once frightened and excited him:

Conviction.

30.

Time became an abstract concept as they progressed toward Lake Mead. Pat hadn't put the coin back in Samuel's wallet yet, just turned it over repeatedly, observing the same features, hoping for new insight.

"Louie changed him," Pat said, slipping the coin into his pocket. It tinkled against the shamrock ring, which Pat had pried off his finger and stashed in that same pocket after they fled from the hotel. "Hyland was right. I didn't want to believe in something so whimsical, so ludicrous."

He looked up when, outside the window, the noise of sloshing waves grew progressively louder. They were close and only getting closer.

"I'd believe anything now." Lorenzo tapped his steering wheel with his index fingers as he gripped it, a nervous tick that Pat had succumbed to many times himself. "Before? Honestly, I didn't think much of Louie and his guys. It's a big country, lots of people doing terrible things. It's not unheard of to encounter an organization you didn't know about. It wasn't until I met you that I really started to pay attention—and even then it was more about you than about them. But once Samuel shot back up..." He shook his head. "I don't miss, Pat. I got him right in the fucking eye. Make sense of that. You can't. Then the snakes? Where the hell did they even come from?"

Pat didn't answer him. Instead, he looked up at the sky. At this very moment, millions and millions of unheard stories were playing out concurrently with his. It was humbling, but he also had to acknowledge how silly it felt. Everything was so big that nothing really mattered. All the wars, the fighting, the posturing and back and forth would be lost to time.

The car slowly stopped as the headlights revealed a makeshift pier—the same one Pat had departed from the last time he was here. Its tide moved at the discretion of the brightest object that hung overhead—a full moon. The stars around it gave way to hues of purple in the cosmic constellations peppered throughout the otherwise void-tinged heavens above.

"It's beautiful, isn't it?" Pat said. "If you looked from far enough away, you wouldn't know everything is on the brink of exploding. I bet there's all sorts of turmoil out there."

He pointed at the stars. Lorenzo gazed upward, too, in silence.

When something caught his eye closer to Earth, Pat looked over at the wharf. A boat from a bygone era was docked, and a lamp hung from the front of the ship. The Ferryman was basking in its orange glow.

"It's a lot to think about. We'll have time to ponder everything soon enough, Pat." He pointed at the boat. "I think that guy's waiting for you."

Pat nodded, then felt his pockets to ensure he had everything he needed. He also checked that his firearm was on his waistband. Reaching into his blazer pocket, he felt the cold nickel of Samuel's coin in his clammy fingers. Anxiety shot through his veins, from his head to his toes, and back again, over and over.

Why am I here? he wondered. *I saw what they do to people who stand in their way. Even coming into town, they buried that guy, and I took his ring. What if they don't like what I have to say? What if they just want to kill Lorenzo and me?*

Doubt had returned. The old Patrick was back, desperate to hold onto the security of a life that was mundane but predictable. The damnation of others meant little to that Patrick, so long as he was comfortable, so long as he was in control.

No, no, Pat! This was the voice of the new Pat, the one who had left his small hometown behind, looking for success but only finding more trouble. *Samuel could've killed you. It would've been so easy for him. But he didn't. Even the snakes backed off. It defies our understanding of the world, but cause and effect remain. They don't think like you, but that doesn't mean you can't change. That doesn't mean you can't burn it all down with them. Nobody was born starting a revolution. Nobody saw the world for what it was the first time they stepped outside. They tried to bring you here. Samuel said you have a choice to make. That's more than anybody else ever gave you.*

And there was a third voice, now, the voice of a man who had nearly taken his life. Randy was back to haunt him. *"Which way, Patty Cakes? Want to come back to Clinton, spend the rest of your days with Tommy and your mother, pretending you didn't watch him kill me? Pretending my body isn't floating at the bottom of the dam, my body feeding the fishes you used to fry at the end of a long summer day?"*

Pat couldn't see the entirety of his figure, but Randy's blonde hair was on the fringes of the lamppost at the end of the pier. His voice was in Pat's ear despite the apparition being at least thirty feet away.

Randy gave a menacing chuckle. *"Or do you think you two are the next Bonnie and Clyde? Lorenzo's tough, but he can't run away forever. With all the chaos you've sown, do you think the Mob will ever let you live peacefully in Alaska? No, you'll return from a long day of sledding and open your front door to a flash. I'll see you on the other side, and we'll be best buds, just you and me."*

After all this time, Pat still wasn't sure if Randy was the manifestation of vague threats from something deep inside him or the first signs that the world was full of things he once thought were fairy tales. Either way, he wasn't going to let it bother him anymore.

All of that happened in the blink of an eye. Pat followed Lorenzo's hand to where he was pointing: the Ferryman giving them a wave.

"The last time I was here," Pat said, "Samuel led the way. But I think I know what we have to do."

Pat beckoned Lorenzo onward, and the two of them traversed the swaying pier, passing Randy's shadowy specter as though he wasn't there.

The voice of the bearded Ferryman boomed in the silence. "Ye have yer coins?" As he stepped out onto the pier, his galoshes squished. He looked impatient. Clearly, he had been waiting for some time. "Bald fella ain't comin' with? He was supposed to bring ye here." He scanned both faces before nodding as though he had deduced what had happened. "Good lad, good lad. Heart of gold in him. Ye have yer coins?"

"Just the one," Pat said. "It's all Samuel had in his wallet. I don't even know where to get these."

The man hovered over him. Taking the coin greedily into his paws, he looked it over before smirking. "Ye still have the ring? A token suffices in place of the coin. A toll is a toll, just the same."

Pat wasn't sure how the man knew about the ring. He couldn't recall if he'd been wearing it the last time they met. He reached into his blazer, searching for it, and felt the cool bronze graze his finger. An unexplainable swell of pride surged over him. He hesitated momentarily but pulled it out. The green gem shone even in the darkness.

Lorenzo gave Pat a curious look but said nothing.

"Aye, that ring," the Ferryman marveled as Pat swept past him and onto the boat. "Shine's brilliant. 'Member first time I ferried ye 'cross the lake. Told me I sounded like one o' dem Glouchstah fishermen. Ain't forget a fellow New Englander so easily. Ain't been nothin' more than a few months, anyway."

Lorenzo climbed in, leaning on Pat's arm as he tried to steady himself. The boat began to move, and within the blink of an eye, the Ferryman stood at the front, hands gripping the steering wheel.

"Y'know," he said, "Samuel said you'd be here for a year and off ta greener pastures. Didn't think much of him, did ye? Ain't blamin' you, mind. Many fear Louie and his bald acolytes, but they're good as people come."

"I don't understand," Pat told him. "If they're all so good, why are they this way? Why all the antics? We've seen them hurt people, innocent people."

The Ferryman held back a chortle, snorting. "Innocent? Word gets thrown 'round lot. Everyone thinks they ain't got no blame. We all do. But them who live a lie? They ain't like people who put their comfort first."

Lorenzo looked like he wanted to say something, but Pat held up a hand to stop him. He could sense the Ferryman wasn't done yet.

"I'm not different than his Chosen, save the pact," the man at the helm said. "Don't got nothin' 'bout myself I want to change—least nothin' I can't do myself. I just wanted to help. Tired of seein' the world as it is." He waved a hand back towards the shore, though there was nothing there. "Look at them government folk, them men in the suits, lyin' to your face. And just as quick to throw you into the meat grinder. Them folks did it to my boy. Died on some field in Belgium I can't even pronounce. Hell, they don't even know. First, it was Bruges. Next thing, it was Brussels, then some field outside there. We're just pawns to them. Never was nothin' more than that."

"I'm sorry for your loss," Pat said sincerely. "My father came back from that war and wasn't the same. A few years later, he died." He stared down into the dark water. "We just don't understand. About Louie's crew. The first time I met one of them, he was waiting in my hotel room, sitting on my bed when I opened the door. Threats and promises are woven together in the same sentence. Contradictions. They don't make sense."

"Sounds like them. Samuel, was it?"

"Yeah. Did Samuel have you wait for us here?"

The Ferryman nodded. "Aye, he did. Heard about the ruckus in the city. Lots of fights broke out. Missiles down in Cuba ain't doin' much ta bring down the hysteria. Louie felt it was his time to move, I guess. I ain't privy to their plans. I'm just the Ferryman."

Pat doubted he didn't know more, but what was the point of prying? The truth would come out soon enough. The glow in the distance from a large ship ensured that.

"Why?" Pat asked. Though he'd already started to convince himself of what he was being told, he still had to ask. "Why do you work with them? You know what they're doing here. I still smell that burning man. His screams fill my ears when I sleep at night. How could Louie be good? How could any of them be good?" Pat had already begun to convince himself, but the Ferryman didn't know that. He wouldn't share that either.

"You're here, ain't ye? Seen somethin' amiss on yer own accord. His methods ain't mighty ethical, but neither is this world."

It made sense. It was the same conclusion Pat had come to on his own. Even as doubt tugged at him, he couldn't shake this feeling that consumed him. Louie's Lounge had given him a far greater opportunity than any of the "moral" establishments dotting the strip.

"You're right," Pat admitted as their boat neared the larger ship. "But I'm scared I'll end up like that other man, tied to a chair burning."

From this distance, he could see that it was the same ship, the *Underworld*. That undeniable fear welled up inside of him, but he suppressed it, morbid curiosity taking the place of self-preservation.

"Yet ye came nonetheless," the Ferryman said. "We're approachin'. If ye don't mind, get yerselves ready. Got a busy mornin' ahead-a me."

Pat hadn't really thought about it. The sky had become decidedly less dark as the impending sun crept over the horizon. In the dying night, the red glow of a lit cigarette gave confirmation there was life aboard the ship, waiting for them.

"Here? Is this where we get off?" Lorenzo asked, finally speaking.

Pat gave him a weak nod. "Yeah. Last time I was here, someone let us aboard. Looks like they've been waiting for us."

The cigarette flame went down as the shadow approached the Ferryman's boat. Lorenzo tensed up. His fingers brushed against the grip of his firearm with each silent step toward them.

"Relax, you'd be sinking to the bottom if you were here to die," a tall brown man said, emerging from the darkness. His face hardened into a scowl of confusion as he stepped into the moonlight.

Hyland.

"Sorry if I am a bit red 'round the ears," Lorenzo said, gripping the handle tighter. "The last time we talked, you were shooting at us through a casino. Doesn't exactly seem like a partnership worth savoring."

Pat grabbed his free hand before stepping up.

"I am sure you've noticed, but I'm not bald," Hyland replied. "I'm not superhuman like Louie's Chosen. That means I wasn't privy to the plan. And if you recall, your people were waiting in my living room to kill me the night before. Suffice it to say I wasn't in a loving mood. I wouldn't have done that if I had known what Louie wanted." He gave a dry smile devoid of authenticity. "We make mistakes."

"Lorenzo, let it go. We aren't here for him. We're here for the truth."

Pat lovingly patted his lover's lower back as he stepped forward. Hyland moved to the side to allow them to enter the ship.

"Fine." Lorenzo offered his hand to Pat, who took it. "Let's get this over with."

The Ferryman cleared his throat, and Pat looked back at him as he said, "I knew the lad who had this ring, y'know. Took him here to this ship meself. Bright eyes, green 'round the horns like yerself the day ye first came out here. Good luck in there, lad. Louie's a complicated fella, but so aren't we all."

The Ferryman bowed his head, and the small vessel pulled away from the *Underworld.* Pat looked over the horizon as the Ferryman became nothing more than a speck in the distance. Fear rumbled and rattled around his ribcage like a morbid pinball game as he thought about how isolated he was, how alone. He was in the middle of a lake with people he didn't know if he could trust, people he'd seen commit atrocities.

But another thought cut through that fear, and the tenseness in his shoulders eased. He wasn't alone. Not this time. He had Lorenzo. And together? Together, they could do anything.

31

Hyland had only voyaged onto Louie's boat once before, back when it was first acquired. So when he arrived with Rosaline, he found himself in awe of what it had morphed into. The original luxury of it had been considerably undone. Now it looked more like a Pacific theater battleship than a millionaire playboy yacht. Just another reminder that looks could be deceiving. Louie was far more than a millionaire.

Each hallway Hyland was led down reinforced the militant nature of Louie's crusade. Fancy wallpaper had been scribbled over, black and red drawings covering intricate patterns with depictions of uprisings. Images of churches blackened by flames mixed in with other art showcasing various revolutions.

"He really isn't wasting time anymore with keeping up appearances," Hyland explained. "I suppose the truth comes out eventually. If it's any consolation, I still don't know the full extent of everything. I'm friends with Rosaline, but she's only one of his Chosen. Hell, even she couldn't tell me much. All I know is he thinks Pat is integral to his plan and willing to upend it all for him." Pat didn't fancy himself much a chosen one. His life had no sense of destiny, only close calls and deep regrets.

"Seems a bit misplaced," Lorenzo said. " Don't get me wrong. Pat's a good man, and I love him. But he isn't like us, Hyland. He doesn't kill like you and I have."

Lorenzo had no way of knowing what Hyland had done to survive. How could he? Still, he knew what navigating a white man's world was like.

"Everyone thinks they know someone until they don't," Hyland replied. "I thought I had him figured out, too, but people surprise you. Maybe he has a trick or two for you left up his sleeve."

He looked back at Patrick, who was walking stoically. He was anxious. He hadn't even bothered to comment on what they'd said about him, nor had he seemed to notice Lorenzo had said he loved him.

Hyland turned the corner. This hallway had been narrowed by makeshift barricades of kitchen equipment on the sides. Ovens became shields in preparation for a conflict Hyland doubted would ever come. Who would be so foolish as to try and raid Louie's yacht? At the end of the hall was a tall cherry door adorned with a bronze crest shaped like a snake split evenly down the middle. Each doorknob was one half of the serpent's head.

"Well, I thought *I* was into the drama," Pat said, seemingly coming back to his senses.

Hyland chuckled as he gripped the door and tugged the handle. "Would you like me to go first? Just to prove you're not walking into a trap?" he asked. When Pat nodded, he said, "Sure thing, Pat. Step back, just in case."

The door creaked open, its immense weight taking more effort than Hyland had bargained for, but he pushed through. Light poured into the barrier-riddled hallway, as did the smell of smoke.

Hyland peered into the room. Braziers lined the sides, and a massive desk was on the opposite wall parallel to the door. Sitting at it, puffing a cigar, was the man known simply as Louie. Rosaline stood to his left, and to his right, another of his Chosen, an African American man. He stood tall, staring at Hyland as the accountant entered the room, beckoning his procession to follow suit.

Pat and Lorenzo stepped inside the room, Hyland moving to their side as the figure lurking at the desk stood up. His golden-grilled teeth resembled a maw of fangs, gnashing at the chance to savor his esteemed guests.

"I'm sure there are so many questions on both of your minds. Yet, you came nonetheless. Without Samuel." Louie's smile was gone for a moment, his head bowed as he nodded, whispering to himself.

Hyland moved behind the couple, closing the door to Louie's chamber as Pat tentatively stepped forward. By the time Hyland had turned back to the conversation, Pat had found his words.

"I don't understand," Pat said. "Everything you've done makes no sense. If you wanted me, you could've approached me like anybody else. Why all the theatrics?"

Hyland stifled a smile. It wouldn't have been *his* first question, but he hadn't been so dramatic a courtship. No, when Louie met him, it was straightforward, a deal for a deal. A few weeks later, he simply asked. He offered Hyland what he'd offered to Samuel, Rosaline, and countless others. But the things Hyland wanted, no man could give. Those were things he'd have to take.

"You know, I'm not a man Patrick," Louie said. "I grant many wishes, but I don't ask for souls. What would I do with them? Waste my time burning them so they atone? Being the jailer for that prick up there? She wouldn't know good sense if it hit Her in the head with a brick. Believe me, I've tried. How d'you think I ended up down here with you all?"

As Louie flashed a devious smile, Lorenzo grasped his crucifix necklace and held it upward like a weapon.

Louie laughed and shook his head. "C'mon. You think She's going to protect you from me? She sent me down here to corrupt you. Self-righteous bastard died for your sins? No, no, no. She didn't even create you. Who do you think made us? She doesn't know either."

Hyland himself was still processing everything Louie was saying. He'd only heard it for the first time hours prior when he and Rosaline were escaping the all-out war in Las Vegas. Some of it made sense, but some of it? Well, perhaps it would make sense in time.

"Why?" Lorenzo demanded, still clutching the crucifix. "Why Pat? There are a lot of desperate people out there, lots of people dying. You ain't doing anything for them. Instead, you're sitting here playing mind games with a comedian. And for what?"

Louie puffed on his cigar, then blew a long stream of smoke out. "Your friends are waging war on me. They're afraid of me, Lorenzo, for the same reason you wear that cross on your neck. They kill in Her name, and they pray to her, wanting forgiveness for their transgressions. They think they'll burn in an inferno, turning the day-to-day for the downtrodden masses into a living hell on Earth. It's been going on for a long, long time." He tapped the ash from the end of his cigar onto his desk. "I'm no angel. She stripped me of that right. I make mistakes. After all, I'm only *human*."

"So you want me to fight them?" Pat asked, standing in front of his boyfriend as if to protect him. "When I met Lorenzo, you thought I could pull them into fighting you? Why? The Devil has an issue with the Mob? That's absurd."

"It's not them," Louie said dismissively. "They're pawns. They protect Her order—'God's order.' I should like to remind you that it's the very same order that believes you two should be dead in the ground, buried like the man you saw when you first showed up in Las Vegas."

Hyland gripped his rifle tightly. He didn't care that they were homosexuals, but Louie's words rang true. And yet, Hyland wasn't compelled to help them simply because they were downtrodden. A poor white man was still worth twice someone with native blood. They'd sooner exterminate Hyland's kind before they'd ever turn on the poor peasant homesteaders.

"Why Las Vegas?" Pat asked. "If you're the Devil, why here? You could go anywhere in the world. The priests out here aren't the ones influencing people."

Louie stood up and started pacing behind his desk, waving his cigarette around as he walked. "This city was built on the suffering of man, funded by the biggest agents of oppression. They built weapons to kill thousands in a mere second in this very lake's backyard. Where else would I go? What other wretched city would open the eyes of the world to the ugliness you people inflict on each other in the name of God? In the name of tradition? *I'm* the evil one? Why? Because I'd rather burn down a church than reason with a zealot?"

There it was. Louie's crusade was founded on personal grievances. It was undeniable. But that didn't mean good couldn't come of it. That didn't mean he was wrong. The world had denied many the chance to live with dignity, just as he had been denied.

"So you're the good guy who does the right thing the wrong way? You're the victim here?" Pat asked, his voice raised in accusation.

Louie leisurely limped over to Patrick, a man trying to make sense of things that defied logic. "Victim? No, no. I made my choices. I was in the sky, looking down upon you all like the ants you are—just like She does, just like Her other 'angels' do. They say I was kicked out of the pearly gates for my hubris, yet I operate in the shadows?" He shook his head, waggling his cigar at Pat. "I could spend the rest of my life explaining the contradictions to you. But you feel them yourself, don't you, Pat? Isn't that why you're here? St. Patrick himself questioned the word of God. How does someone chase the snakes off the island if they're in suits? Shaking hands can only go far if you're playing by their rules in a game designed to make you fail."

Hyland could see his eyes now, how strikingly human they looked, how much pain Louie carried in them. If he could see them, he could only imagine how intensely they appeared to Pat, who was caught in their gaze.

He was a deer in headlights, unaware of how fragile his life was. On the other side of the windshield was a driver, separated from the elements by a glass pane. It was only when a collision shattered that glass that he realized he was nothing more than an animal, too, his own life fragile. Louie was in the driver's seat, but his car had been through many accidents. He knew how to pump the brakes.

There was movement. Pat stepped up to Louie, proving that the deer was less of a doe and more of a buck, really. "What do you want? You could've asked anything. You could've talked to me anytime. Blood is on your hands. I'm not like you."

Hyland doubted the sincerity of the statement. Pat and Lorenzo had shown up without Samuel, after all. It didn't take a rocket scientist to figure out what happened there.

Louie sniffed the air as though he had caught the fragrance of deception. As he slowly circled Pat and Lorenzo, horns manifested out of his forehead, as though they had always been there. His silver suit reflected the flames of the braziers, and the heels of his dress shoes clacked against the flooring.

"He haunts you, doesn't he?" Louie asked enigmatically. "They looked for your secrets. They dug so deep. A mysterious man comes into town just wanting to peddle jokes and bring joy into people's lives. But surely there had to be more to it than that."

"I don't know what you mean," Pat said unconvincingly.

"The man at the bottom of the lake haunts you. I can see it in your eyes. I can see *everything* in your eyes." Louie's voice wasn't menacing, but it still sent a chill through the room. "But his death isn't your fault, even if you hold that guilt over yourself, taking responsibility for *his* transgressions. Her church has filled you with guilt, indebted you to an entity that wouldn't let you grovel at Her feet. Self-loathing makes you repent for being earnest, for being the way you were born. Comedy is your way of brokering peace in a war whose enemy is without a face. The guilt will consume you, Patrick."

Lorenzo gripped Patrick's arm, his free hand holding his firearm tight as he stepped forward. Louie's gaze drifted from Patrick to Lorenzo, the former letting out a deep gasp of air as though he hadn't been breathing this whole time.

Hyland hadn't seen Louie in his truest form until now. He was a sight to behold, indeed. Hyland could understand why people would promise him everything. The Devil in disguise, the silver serpent, was a cunning linguist, but it seemed there was no venom in his bite, at least not toward the common man.

"And you, Lorenzo," Louie continued. "You feel the Ides of March burst through your back, don't you? You thought your colleagues were indebted to you. Just twenty years ago, their parents prayed every night that Mussolini would come to this country and exterminate the Coloreds after he was done with Europe." He held Lorenzo's cold stare, and it was like he was reading his mind, his thoughts laid out before him like a picture book. "You were never going to be one of them. You thought they'd accept you because you earned them a few dollars and prayed to the same God? Earnest to your core, but you're not evil. Not like them."

"You think you know me?" Lorenzo spat back at Louie. "Do you think I'd ever fall for your evil whispers? No way, you're playing games. You burnt a man alive in front of Pat. You call that the moral high ground?"

"I don't pretend to be an authority on morality. I don't pretend I'm some valiant hero. Would you prefer I indulge in superficial pleasantries?" Louie turned to Pat now, ignoring the way Lorenzo was shaking his head. "Patrick, your father once told you the bad men are the ones in suits, that they come out during the day rather than hiding under your bed. I'm in a suit, and I'll admit that I'm a naughty, naughty boy, but I champion a good cause. Nothing gets achieved through civility. Look at them now, pointing missiles at each other. That had nothing to do with me, kid. Humans did that to themselves."

There was silence as the two men stared at each other. Hyland shifted uncomfortably, contemplating how much of his life Louie had seen laid bare, whether he could see the guilt Hyland carried about leaving his home. It scared him that no amount of self-assurance could bury the truths he hid from himself.

"You don't know who you are, Pat," Louie said. "That's why I chose you. That's why I *need* you. You stopped in that desert the very first day you came into town. You checked on that burning car. Fifty other people drove right past and didn't give it another thought. You have a heart in a world that'd sooner bury you than lift you up. You'd rather risk your life to liberate people than to oppress them for your own gain."

Hyland had heard about Pat's last encounter on the ship, how he was willing to throw another man who was to die under the bus for self-preservation. Surely Louie could see that. Surely Louie could see the darkness in Patrick's soul, the stain such an act left.

Pat apparently had the same thought because he said, "I'm not who you think I am. The last time I was here, I was willing to let that man die to save myself. Rosaline was there. She saw how I goaded him. I'm not a hero, and neither are you."

"*Hero?*" Louie scoffed. "God's fucked you up, Pat, huh? She wants you to believe in good and evil, the chosen and the miscreants, the degenerates and the faithful. There is no hell. Don't you think I'd be there if there was? Don't think *he'd* be there?"

He pointed toward the corner of the room, a vacant space outside the shadows the flames cast against the wall. Pat must've seen something there because he nodded. Hyland had to concede that Louie was far more than he could've imagined. There was a hypnotic truth to his words, which made sense if he was some sort of higher being, a term Hyland found himself discomforted by.

Pat's vision momentarily hovered in the corner of the room before he turned back to Louie again. "What do you want from me?" His voice was full of acceptance. Even Patrick, the man who could talk up a room, was reduced to basic questions in the face of the ultimate talker: Satan in the flesh.

Louie opened his mouth to speak, then stopped. He sniffed the air, a smile oozing over his face. "Oh, there it is. The one thing I admire about mankind, the one thing God and Her 'infinite' wisdom always underestimated, is your tenacity. You don't give up." He cracked his neck, pushing his chin upward into places a regular neck wouldn't allow.

Gunfire filled the corridor on the other side of the serpent door. Louie raised his shoulders up to his earlobes before lowering them again. Through his clothes, Hyland saw Louie's back stir. In the blink of an eye, the fabric of his suit jacket tore with an audible rip. Hyland's jaw slacked in shock as the sound of flapping echoed through the chamber.

Wings?

Fleshy flaps covered in singed feathers moved through the air, gusts of wind disseminating the overpowering scents of burnt flesh and sulfur. It flooded into Hyland's nostrils, turning his stomach. Louie's feet lifted slightly off the ground in a twisted impression of his adversary. Patrick and Lorenzo stood staring in disbelief, and Rosaline put herself in front of them, her hand outstretched to prevent them from jumping in.

As Hyland ducked out of Louie's way, he could see the full glory of his wings. They fluttered at least three feet above the being they were attached to and stretched down to the back of his knees. They were damaged, set aflame at one point, as evidenced by the rolling folds of black skin beneath the scorched feathers. With each flap of the wings, scabs ripped open and beads of blood dripped out of them in reddish-black rivulets. Louie, however, showed no outward signs of pain. If anything, he carried his head high.

Hyland raised his rifle as he stepped behind Louie, who was now at the door. His well-manicured hands had been replaced with talon-like nails, though they retained their distinctly human quality.

"I hope they know how to waltz," Louie said. "I got two left feet."

With that, he flung the door open to the chaos awaiting them on the other side of the breach. Hyland knew what was coming, could feel it thrumming through his veins.

War.

32.

The sounds coming from outside in the hallway were gut-wrenching. Pat clung to Lorenzo, burying his face in his lover's shoulder, trying to drown out the screams and roars and blood-curdling howls. Every gunshot reminded him of Randy, who he could still feel watching him from the corner of the room. Every hastily uttered prayer scored into his heart, reminding him of what Louie really was, of the secrets he'd revealed.

Just when he thought the one-sided massacre would last forever, it was over.. Shaking, Pat pulled away from Lorenzo, drawn by morbid curiosity to peek out into the hallway. What he saw made him sick.

Only one of Louie's Chosen was counted among the bodies on the floor. There was a slug in his chest, which Louie dug out with a claw. Lying beside him was another man, this one a mobster. His emerald tie met at his waistband, and pink-tinged innards gave what was once a white linen dress shirt a more vibrant and infinitely more intricate pattern. The others who'd had the misfortune of encountering Louie were practically unrecognizable as being human. They were so dismembered and ripped apart that Pat couldn't even tell how many there were. Pat retched as the smell of copper hit his nostrils.

Lorenzo gripped his shoulder, pulling him back, saying, "I know these guys. They must've followed us here." There was pain laced through his voice. What Louie had said about how little his colleagues valued him must've been both humbling and mortifying all at once, and now he was having to come to terms with it.

Louie rose from his knees, gently patting the head of his fallen Chosen before returning to the opposite end of the hall. From somewhere nearby, Pat could hear gunfire and shouting. Louie's wings flapped once more as he floated toward the sounds coming from the left, but Pat could only stand there in stoic shock, jolting out only when he felt someone's hand on his shoulder.

"Wake up, or you're going to be dead," Hyland said.

He pushed forward past spent shells, leaving Lorenzo and Pat behind. Rosaline also rushed past them, a pistol in her hand as she followed after

Hyland, who was facing the opposite end of the hall that Louie had flown down. They were being attacked from both sides.

A chorus of agony rang out from Louie's side of the hall. Firearm muzzles flashed, then died, the shadows they'd cast across the wall slowly dissipating until an eerie silence descended.

"Holy shit, I can't...I can't believe this is happening," Pat whispered to Lorenzo as they ducked behind one of the makeshift barriers in the hallway to catch their breaths.

It was clear now why Louie had rearranged the ship like this. He'd expected this to happen; he'd prepared this space to facilitate a war zone.

Lorenzo grasped Pat's hand as a wave of blood spurted overhead, landing nearly ten feet away on the bronze snake door handles. Pat closed his eyes. He could feel his heartbeat throughout his whole body, each throb pushing through the tips of his toes and the top of his scalp.

This is all too much, he thought, gasping for air. *When Louie looked into my eyes, I could see him going through every memory, every moment I thought I'd locked away. He could see everything. He's the Devil himself. But he doesn't feel evil—if anything, he's the most sincere person I've ever met.*

Pat's thoughts raced through his mind as Lorenzo held him tightly. Even though his eyes were closed, the sound of blood splashing like paint against the walls was undeniable.

"Pat." Lorenzo shook his arm. "*Pat!* Open your eyes. Listen to me. We need to leave. He's the literal Devil. Nothing good can come from knowing him, from listening to his lies. We need to skip town. This war isn't our burden. We can't save anybody but ourselves." Lorenzo gave one last desperate plea.

They were out of their depth, that was for sure. Pat wasn't a man of war. He'd never seen bloodshed like this. His stomach was weak, and it churned from the smell hanging heavily in the air. Thankfully, the tortured screams were becoming more distant as Louie mowed through the poor souls sent to kill him. But that didn't erase the horrible memories Pat knew would be forever seared into his brain.

He wanted to go with Lorenzo. He wanted their quiet life together more than anything—but it wasn't about him. *Not anymore. It's bigger. It's so much bigger. I can't turn my back on people suffering like I used to. I can't leave them for dead. Tommy came for me in the dead of night. He risked everything just to give me a chance in front of that microphone, just to give me an opportunity to be myself.*

For a moment, it all stopped, Lorenzo's face frozen in time. Even the barriers they hid behind began to fade as though they'd never existed. When Pat blinked, the whole setting changed. In front of him was the familiar silver of his microphone, bright lights reflecting off it, daring him to be something, anything more than the timid man he'd chosen to be for his entire existence.

"What is a dream if everyone around you is living a nightmare?" a disembodied voice said. "I don't know if this is a dream. I've been asleep for so long that nothing makes any sense."

Pat twirled around the stage, trying to find where the voice was coming from. With each spin, the room contorted, morphing from the ship he was cowering in into Louie's Lounge, the place where he'd lived out his dream, even if it was only for a few months.

"You know who I am," the voice said. "Turn the lights off."

Pat took a step back in deep confusion. Was he dead? No, he could still see Lorenzo sitting as if frozen, could still smell the blood and the sweat and sorrow. This was something else entirely. The voice sounded familiar but distorted, as though filtered through a radio, but he knew who it was.

The lights came down, but in the shadows, a figure approached. It was his father. His silhouette looked no different from how Pat remembered.

"How?" Pat asked, trembling. "How is this happening? I-I was—"

"If I knew, I'd say." His father shrugged. "Like I said, I don't even know if this is real. I've seen blackness for so long that I can hardly make sense of anything." His father took a step toward the microphone. Without the lights, Pat couldn't see into the audience. He assumed it was empty and that he and his father were alone. "Where is this place? I never thought I'd see you grow up."

"I don't—I can't rightly say," Pat admitted. "I'm not sure why, but this looks like the club I perform at. It doesn't make sense. We shouldn't be here. I need to go back."

He missed his dad, even though most of his memories of the man came secondhand. But this wasn't the man he remembered. His father's face was wrinkled in ways it hadn't been in life. He'd aged considerably, a gift taken from him and stored in the clutches of the black void that warmly embraced every man when his time came.

"You don't trust him," his father said. "Louie. I don't blame you. I met him once, y'know. I thought I was mad. I thought there was no way I was seeing Lucifer himself in a French village on the outskirts of Paris, but there he was.

"And you know what, Pat?" His father looked at him over his shoulder. "He was right then, but I was too cowardly. I walked away, and I went home to my wife. Hitler was dead, and the big evil was gone. I'd given enough of myself. I'd done everything I needed to, right? So I didn't listen to the Devil."

He looked at the crowd, the back of his suit glinting with the hints of glass jutting out in the backlights. It was the suit he had died in, his back smacking against the windshield as he flew out onto the street toward his death. Pat had not seen, but he had heard rumblings. Clinton was a small town, and the morbid fascinations of untimely death led to gossiping in dimly lit dive bars after the factories let out.

Pat struggled to understand what he was hearing. "Dad, what are you—"

"I came home to a country that invited them in. We needed to beat the Reds. I told Tommy, I told your mother, it was all lies. Nothing changes with the men in the suits. I can't escape the smell of decay, not even in death. I saw what they did, the worst acts humanity ever committed. And we let them off? Why, so we could fly to the moon? There is no God. There can't be. I earned a good death, but it's been blackness until now, and now they tease me with my son. Now they show me what he could be, my legacy."

His father moved toward center stage now, his foot dragging, his ankle shattered in a way Pat hadn't noticed before. He was reverting back to his final state. It wouldn't be long before he was bone. His words sounded less composed, as though the mouth forming them was rotting from the inside.

His father had met Louie in the war? His mother had always said he was a changed man, but he thought it was like everyone else who went to war. The Devil was all around them on the battlefields. He burrowed between pink-tinged ears exposed to the elements of a harsh Rhine winter. He was in the face of young men who feared the unknown, many who let perversions whisper justifications for the evil they carried out.

Yet those same evils felt absent in Louie's eyes. There was a pain in their place, the agony of watching collective failures over millennia. Pat did not know if the Devil was what he thought. He didn't know if the Devil was evil. The saint had driven snakes from the island, yet this Patrick couldn't help but feel drawn to the hissing of the world's most infamous serpent.

Pat wanted to go to him, but he held back, saying, "Dad, I don't know if this is real. Two weeks ago, I thought I was in with a bad crowd. I thought I made a deal with the Mob. But nothing makes sense anymore. Even two minutes ago, I was with my boyfriend—"

His father shifted, and the lights over the crowd returned. His flesh had since rotted from his face, and insects pushed through skin flaps on his cheeks before crawling into the small opening where his nose had once been. His hair glowed like a campfire atop his head in the illumination of the stage. The only thing that hadn't gone, the only thing that hadn't died, was his eyes.

"They will never accept you, Pat," his father said. "Don't make the mistake I did. We all die. It's inevitable, but don't die for nothing. I loved you both—you and your mother—but I failed you. I walked away from that field even though he saved me. He saved so many that day. We kept his secrets. Who would believe us? Satan saving innocents from Nazis? I'd have been in a padlocked cell with the loons."

Pat's stomach soured as he took in the decayed husk that was his father, but he resisted the urge to step away. There was love in those eyes. He didn't know, he couldn't understand how this was real, but some looks don't fade as memories do. His father was distant for the few years he lived after the war. But he loved his son. Pat was reminded of that daily by his mother and Tommy.

"Join him, Pat."

"I want to, Dad, but...I am not you. I'm not a soldier. I can't kill. I can't be the man you want me to be." He sighed, hanging his head. "I just wanted to tell people jokes, to make them forget about everything. Even if it was for forty-five minutes, I could help them escape. That's all I know how to do. I'm no hero."

Pat had wanted such things for selfish reasons: fame and fortune. He'd wanted to be more than a name on a tombstone, to be more than his father.

The shame he felt now paralyzed him, and he was lost in the stare of someone who no longer lived but refused to truly die.

"You don't need to kill a man to be a hero," his father assured him. "The bravest soldiers I ever knew refused to take another's life. He's marked you, the way he marked me. I can see it in you. That must be why I'm here. He's brought me here to tell you the truth. Maybe he hopes I'll nudge you to his cause."

Anger burned in Pat's chest. Louie's plight might be genuine, but he clearly wasn't above underhanded tactics. Then again, wouldn't Pat do the same? What was a tearful reunion in the face of what Louie saw as the ultimate struggle? Who wouldn't manipulate someone if it meant a benefit for the greater good? Pat himself had let another man die simply to save his own skin. Did that make him worse than the Devil?

Pat wrestled with the duality of his thoughts. At another point in his life, he'd have spurned his father and Louie out of spite. But he'd grown. And the stakes had grown. Whether his father fully understood what was going on or was simply another puppet in the game mattered little. He was right. And so was Louie...even if he went about it the wrong way.

"I only ever wanted to be my own man," Pat said. "My whole life—it's been spent trying to make everyone else comfortable. I came here to be my best self. I came here to escape my past. I nearly died. Tommy saved me. I owed him to do right by the second chance he gave me."

He was losing steam. He didn't even believe his own words anymore. Chasing your dreams was a good use of a second chance, but using your second chance to make a difference? That was everything.

"What did I tell you, Pat?" his father asked. "What did I tell you that night you looked at the night lights?"

"The men in the suits. I remember it like it was yesterday. It never made sense to me. I never understood it, but I do now. I understand it more than I could've ever imagined."

That snapped him back to reality, and he realized that he'd nearly forgotten about Lorenzo. Though he'd never forgotten about Las Vegas. In his heart, he wished he could stay. He wished he could look upon his father's face for days—weeks, even. It didn't matter. He was nearly a skeleton now, his eyes the only flesh remaining in his skull.

"I don't think we have much time left," Pat said sadly. "You're rotting away. Can I do one last thing for you before I'm pulled back? Before you return?" He asked it in a way only a child could of a parent, as though it was a talent show in some dimly lit auditorium and not the grandest stage most comedians aspired to.

The rest of his father's stripped flesh had fallen to the floor. His skull reflected the light in its pristine white crown, yet the eyes hadn't dulled—would probably never dull. Even in the blackness and emptiness of death, everybody was able to hold on to one thing: their soul. And the eyes were nothing more than windows to it.

"Of course. I'd love that. What do you have in mind?" His father looked down at the rows of vacant seating. "Oh, I see." He'd come to the conclusion on his own, and Pat nodded with eagerness as his father limped toward the front row.

Pat turned away from the invisible crowd, his foot tapping as though there was some metronome he was trying to match. On the sixth tap, he shifted back toward the audience, his hips swinging as though he was going to move into a dance number, his face contorted until his mouth resembled an Elvis-like jawline.

"Thank you all for coming out today. My name is Pat Gallagher, and I'm your Irish Elvis for the evening. Viva Las Dublin! Hope you like potatoes and whiskey because that's all they're selling at the concessions."

He looked out toward the back. There was no vendor. There was nobody else but Pat's father, and that was okay. They could have this moment. Whenever he woke up or returned to reality, he'd remember this. He'd remember it until he met the same silence his father had known all these years.

For a moment, he wondered if he could make his father laugh since he was all bone, but he soon had his answer.

Turns out you don't need lungs to cackle, after all.

33.

Hyland didn't believe in the White Man's God, but as he watched Louie slice through men as though they were weeds to be pruned from a garden, he realized he *did* believe in their Devil. His jaw was slack as Louie pushed on. The sheer amount of mobsters he'd mowed down was immeasurable. Hyland had given up after the tenth casualty.

"Pray to her. May she save you from me." His voice was dry and smug as he hovered over a man he'd just decapitated.

A shot rang out behind them, and a bullet sliced through one of Louie's wings. Sinewy flaps wrinkled over at the impact, but Louie hadn't reacted save a sinister smile as he turned toward the gunfire.

"No, keep pushing the other way," Rosaline said. "They're mine."

Hyland's mind was swimming. The world had flipped upside down, and he hadn't even noticed her, his only friend in the unholy militant pact he'd enlisted himself in.

"Go, " Louie said. "Go with her. She's your friend. I can handle myself."

He could feel Louie's eyes burrowing into the back of his skull, as though he was reading his mind. Hyland knew it was paranoia and nothing more. Louie wasn't omniscient. He couldn't be. Otherwise, he wouldn't need help from mankind. Otherwise, as he put it, he wouldn't have been cast down to their mortal world.

Louie flapped away toward the sound of sporadic gunfire. Hyland gripped his rifle, moving behind Rosaline. His gun was pointed just above her shoulder, using her decidedly more durable Chosen body for cover.

He pulled back the bolt of his rifle as it rested on her shoulder. "His healing cover ruptured ear drums?" he asked as she knelt behind a filing cabinet that'd been thrown into the corridor.

"Only one way to find out, don't you think?" she retorted.

He dropped down behind her, his gun protruding from behind where they were taking cover. Through the scope, he could see three mobsters hovering over the carcass of a fourth, who'd died in a fistfight with one of the Chosen. Both had perished, but the mobster came out far worse in the end, his skull no longer resembling anything close to a human shape.

"Just duck. I got this," Hyland said.

Despite everything he'd experienced in life, everything he'd learned in just the last couple days, he was still unsure about many things. But there was one belief he held onto in the tumultuous times, a conviction he felt far deeper than any other: he was not the prey; he was the hunter.

In days gone by, he'd hunted deer. Today, he was hunting an Italian American in a maroon suit who was smacking the barrel of his jammed Tommy gun. His two lackeys were trying to help him, and they seemed unaware of their surroundings. Or perhaps reality had set in. They knew they'd become playthings in a maze of bourgeois opulence that had been retrofitted into a slaughterhouse for the devout and zealous.

Their faith in God would only go as far as they could hold up their rosary beads. She wouldn't protect them from Hyland, especially when they hid their bigotry behind a crucifix. And so, Hyland struck down the first one. The roar of his rifle reminded him of a regal lion, but its claws had been replaced with bullets. He pulled the bolt of his gun back again as a blood-curdling screech filled the air and the casing fell to the ground.

Right in the back of the head. Hyland smirked. *Maybe they'll notice now.*

Pride swelled in his chest. It'd been a long time since he'd hunted, and his hand had remained steady.

Rosaline gripped his shoulder. "You don't miss, do you?"

Hyland turned toward her, a smirk replacing what was usually a sullen disposition. "Can't say that I do."

The mobsters had taken notice. The one with the Tommy gun heaved his firearm like a rock. Rosaline turned, and the wooden handle crunched her nose. She fell back, gripping it as the inevitable gush flooded out of her nostrils.

"I'm fine. I promise I'm fine," she said, her voice muffled behind her hands.

Hyland didn't doubt her words. He'd seen Samuel come back from things that would have killed another man. He doubted she was all that much different.

He turned back to the mobsters, vengeance still stirring within him. They'd taken his home—his life—from him, the life he'd built up from nothing back when Las Vegas was hardly more than a pit stop on the way to Los Angeles and the glitz of Hollywood.

The mobster in the maroon suit flashed his pistol, pushing his friend backward. Unfortunately for him, Hyland was too quick, firing a round that tore through his thigh. His heightening screams of agony were only overshadowed by the crunch of bone turning to dust.

"So dramatic," Hyland muttered as he pulled the bolt back.

The other mobster fired at him, and Hyland ducked behind the cabinet to avoid the bullets that clanged against the metal drawers.

"My turn?" Rosaline asked.

She crinkled her nose at Hyland, who saw that, sure enough, the blood had dried and stopped gushing down her black suit. She tossed her firearm to the ground, sliding it to Hyland.

"Watch my back?"

She stood before he could answer, her bald head shining in the reflection of the overhead lights. The last mobster was frantically searching for a weapon, having expended his ammunition.

Rosaline gripped the muzzle of the Tommy gun like the handle of a bat. "Need a gun? Maybe I can help with that."

The mobster's face was frozen in fear as the stock of the gun smacked into his skull. He fell to the ground, holding his hands up in a futile defensive gesture. It was a dance Hyland had seen on occasion, but Rosaline rarely attacked with such detachedness. She knew one blow to a temple would end the man's suffering, but she wasn't interested in mercy today. With each strike, Hyland winced, as though it were his ribs being shattered, his teeth being crushed into dust.

So consumed was he by the carnage that he didn't notice another pair of mobsters turning the corner at first. He didn't see that they were armed, a third wave of desperate men who knew death was coming swiftly but who still marched on toward the trenches.

His mouth formed the shape of words, but nothing came out. Things moved slowly, far slower than reality should allow. He could see the flash of a muzzle as Rosaline turned to him, a wicked smile on her face. She didn't see the bullet coming from behind her. Pieces of skull flew across the room like cranial shrapnel as the smile turned to a frown, frozen halfway in the process as nerve ends were served.

The image burned into his brain, and his heart ached. He leveled his gun at the men as she dropped to her knees on the floor. Though her brain had been severed from her spine, her body was still trying to fight the inevitable. Her guttural, gasping breaths haunted him, but they were joined by jeers from the man who'd killed her, and rage momentarily drowned out any sorrow he felt.

"Hey, Chief, come on out so I can scalp yer ass, too." The man's accent was thick and his tone taunting.

Hyland dropped back further, trying to not close his eyes. He didn't want to see her like that again, and yet he knew he had to. Louie's powers could heal, but he doubted Rosaline, his closest friend since he'd left home, would recover from such a fatal wound.

The mobster fired another round. This one clipped the top of the cabinet, a piece of metal lodging itself into the wall as it chipped away. "C'mon Geronimo, you ain't escaping this one. Come out, you prick."

Hyland heard the taunts, but his heart weighed heavy, pulling him to the floor as if he were sinking in a bog. When he caught sight of Rosaline again, though, his guilt subsided briefly, replaced by a surge of untethered primal rage.

"You fucked up. You died the second you stepped foot on this boat."

Hyland could feel the energy shift. The jeering man who'd once been so confident was now considering the reality of his situation. Perhaps he hadn't seen Louie, the Fallen Angel. Maybe he didn't yet know precisely what he was up against. Whatever the case may be, Hyland resolved to make sure he never made it that far. This prick was going to die, and he was going to die now.

Hyland stood tall, his rifle pointed at the man. There was terror in his beady eyes, but the mobster stood his ground, his hand wrapped around the undercarriage of his own gun.

A standoff.

"You're going with me then, Chief. I don't miss." His words pushed through his teeth like a whining taunt from a child. It didn't matter if he sounded scared. A gun was a gun, all the same when it was pointed at you.

Hyland grinned grimly. "Good luck."

He squeezed the trigger before the last syllable left his mouth. He heard the yelp but felt his arm buckle, the gun sliding out of his arms and falling to the ground. He reached for it, but his arm wouldn't cooperate.

Shock dulled the pain, but it didn't desensitize him to the reality that he'd been shot. The boat's stale air stuck to the warmth of his oozing blood, which ran down the course of his arm and past his fingertips, dripping onto the floor. With the loss of movement, he was certain tendons and nerves had been entirely severed.

He could hear groans of pain and the sound of shoes scraping against the floor, followed by agonized cries. *I must've got him in the leg, but he's still powering through. Shit.*

Pushing up with his good hand, Hyland managed to crawl in the opposite direction. He hoped and prayed that Louie would see and intervene. He couldn't fire back with his shattered arm.

"I may be a dead man walking," the mobster taunted, "but at least I'm still standing. Guess you ain't so good after all, Chief."

Hyland held back a laugh. His shot had gone right through the guy's leg. Once the shock subsided, he'd be a dead man. Hyland needed to escape him long enough for the blood loss to take its toll.

He crawled, all his might pushing him forward as he heard another bullet sizzle past his ear. The guy had clearly missed on purpose, a teasing warning shot meant to remind Hyland that he was at the man's mercy. He could see the mobster's shadow cast against the light, hanging over his frame like the specter of Death himself.

"Look at me," the other man growled. "I want to see the fear in your eyes. I want to see the life leave your face."

Hyland flipped himself over, not to oblige the man but for his own self-determination. He was unafraid of death. While he wasn't Chosen, his pact with Louie would only end one way, even if that fate seemed far removed from the heights he'd enjoyed in his tenure. It'd all come crashing down into a man-made sea, a reminder that no pact with the Devil, no matter its nobility, would ever be given the graces of floating in the skies with cherubs and saints. Such was the penance of self-autonomy.

But afterlife be damned, Hyland did it his way.

A distant rifle fired, like divine intervention. The mobster's face didn't change so much as wilt, his smug grin remaining despite the top of his skull bursting apart, skin folding upon itself as the body collapsed to the side, his legs twitching as the last neurons fired off.

"We're even."

Lorenzo's voice rang through the halls as though he were God. Hyland stared agape at the man, whose gun was still trained on the dead mobster.

"I need your help," Lorenzo said, offering a hand. "Something's happening to Pat. He won't respond."

Hyland grabbed hold of the hand and let Lorenzo tug him to his feet. Then he looked at his other arm. It hung limply, pain slowly creeping in as shock and adrenaline subsided.

"Thought you two would've made for the boats. Didn't seem too keen on Louie's offer," Hyland grumbled as he swayed in place.

He winced and closed his eyes, the dire reality of his situation dawning on him. Not even twenty-four hours ago, his savior had been an adversary, perhaps the only roadblock to making sure Patrick played whatever greater role Louie had deemed him worthy of. Now, Hyland had been rescued by a man who'd tried to have him killed just the other day.

He rested on Lorenzo, who helped keep him up as they slowly made their way toward where Patrick had been taking cover.

"We were talking," Lorenzo explained, "and next thing I knew, he passed out, convulsing. I looked for help, but Louie...well, I don't know where he is. And I didn't want to venture too far."

Hyland felt a pang in his heart, and he stopped short, looking back at the bloody mess behind them. "Thank you for your help, but...but I need to...I need to be here. Louie will come back. There's none of them left. He'll return. He can help."

"I saved you, Hyland. I need your help. Please."

"Rosaline..." The word choked out of him. "I...failed her. Please, let me...I need to be with her."

The world had left him to the dogs, but Rosaline hadn't. He could feel himself dying. No amount of medical care could fix his wounds. Perhaps Louie's power could, but then he'd have to live knowing he'd failed her. She'd given everything just so he could breathe a moment longer.

Perhaps she'd protest that he was throwing her sacrifice away, but he didn't care. They could argue and bicker about it together, whether it was in the White Man's heaven or the White Man's hell. Whether it was the afterlife his tribe had envisioned or whether it was blackness. Their two lights would burn bright, no matter what awaited them on the other side.

Lorenzo bit his lip, looking like he was biting back a rant, but he took a step back. No matter his desperation, he could see there was nothing Hyland could do to help him. So he backed away, leaving the man to die on his own terms, a gift that God, the creator, had denied many who'd come before.

After Lorenzo was gone, Hyland crawled toward Rosaline's body. Her face was marred by the bullets of bigots, yet despite the stench of blood and copper, her perfume reigned supreme. He could hear her talking to him now. The words were unclear, but the warmth of her voice filled him as his life ebbed away.

In the face of death, introspection was inevitable. He'd played the White Man's game better than anyone else he'd ever met, and yet, despite the tens of thousands in the trunk of his car on the shore of Lake Mead, it didn't matter. Here he was, dying, holding the hand of a woman he'd loved but had never made time for, not the way she deserved.

Hindsight was 20/20, and he was seeing so clearly now. The world they could've had felt so tangible, but never actualized. Regret filled his heart, but he accepted it. He could die without the possessions that'd ruled his life now that he held the cold hand of a warm heart on his own. He could die with dignity beside this amazing woman.

The bulwark he'd built up over the years collapsed, and his spiraling thoughts devolved into a flood of emotions that crashed through his decaying psyche. His brain began to shut down, and yet, the dream carried on. Louie and his crusade made sense. It all finally made sense. He'd just been too foolish to see it, too lost in his own head inward, to see it.

He smiled, not looking upon the destroyed face of Rosaline, instead letting her perfume waft over him with the remaining sense of smell he had. It enveloped him in a comforting embrace as he bled out, the crimson splashes on his skin feeling neither cool nor warm. Though he didn't fear death, he always assumed he would be wracked by anxiety in his final moments. Instead, he drifted away peacefully, his mind untroubled.

Within a moment, he had also fallen to the floor, the blood feeling neither cool nor warm on his cheek as the last thoughts of his brain assuaged any of the anxiety he thought would come for him in death.

Born alone, die alone. It's everything in between.

The thought carried him to the other side as the curtains fell on the talent manager of Louie's Lounge for the last time.

34.

Pat wasn't sure if this was damnation or not, but the world was oppressively gray. The flickering flames of artificial lights danced in his periphery as sense came back to him. His body ached as though it had been tensed up for the entirety of existence itself. He blinked, trying to recall why he was here in this unknowable place. Hell, even remembering his name would be a tremendous accomplishment.

Pat. Your name is Pat, he remembered. Things started flooding back to him after that. *You must've passed out. You were on a ship with the Devil. He was making you an offer. You already took an offer from him. You just didn't know it.*

He shook his head. He knew the words were true, but on the surface, it all sounded absurd. Hell, it sounded beyond absurd. A deal with the Devil? He wasn't real, right? The flapping of wings in the distance answered his own inquiry—no avian beast or flying mammal he'd ever heard of could generate the noise these wings did.

He tried to sit up, but his body failed him. His pectoral muscles pushed forward and failed like he had just bench-pressed the entirety of the world. Luckily for him, his jaw muscles had slacked enough that he could talk.

"Help."

It wasn't loud, but he couldn't have yelled if he wanted to. As the fuzziness of his stupor began to recede, he questioned the authenticity of his dream. Had that really been his dad? Or was it just one of Louie's tricks? Both? He didn't know, he couldn't know, and that frightened him all the more.

"Did you do this?" a man said. "Did you make him collapse?"

The familiar voice was coming from the other end of the hall. He couldn't move from behind the makeshift barricade to see who was speaking, but he remembered the voice.

Lorenzo.

"No, no. I was occupied with those mobsters," another voice said. It was also familiar, though he'd only recently heard Louie speak. "You think I'd spend so much time and energy bringin' him here just to kill him? I might run a casino, but I don't gamble like that."

In spite of his dire situation, Pat was momentarily distracted by Louie's inexplicable New Yorker accent. Why would the Devil even have an accent? Perhaps he was just maintaining the illusion that he was one of them. Or perhaps it was to taunt those who'd tried in vain to make him abdicate his throne over Sin City.

"Help," Pat tried again. This time, he heard running coming toward him.

"Pat! He's awake! Are you okay?"

Lorenzo had turned the corner, dropping to his knees immediately, his hands grabbing each side of his lover's face as he pulled him into an embrace. Louie stood behind them, frowning, both his wings limp. Chunks of his face had been torn off, revealing a darker burnt reddish color underneath. The mask was peeling. Just because Man couldn't kill Louie didn't mean he couldn't be hurt.

"I had a dream..." Pat said blearily. "My dad. What happened?"

"We were talking, and you collapsed." Lorenzo fussed over him, then fired off several questions in a rush. "Are you feeling okay? Can you move? And what do you mean you dreamed about your dad?"

Pat wanted to answer all of his questions, but his brain fog only allowed him to cling to one of them. "Yeah, he was there, at the lounge. He wanted to see me perform. So I did."

He spared Lorenzo the gravity of their conversation, the details of which were slowly coming back to him.

The conversation was much graver than that, the show only proving to be a reprieve. Louie watched on, his face unmoving, a poker face not revealing how he felt about the revelations.

As Lorenzo helped him sit up, Pat asked, "What happened? Did they follow us from the motel? We made sure we weren't tailed."

Louie shook his head. "It doesn't matter. They came. I handled them. They won't return. Even Her most devout know when they're defeated." Pat had started to slump down again, and Louie leaned down to help him right himself as he said, "Listen, Patrick, that *was* your father. It was no dream, no trickery on my part."

Pat still couldn't read his expression, so he had no idea whether or not Louie was being sincere. But deep down, he hoped it'd been real.

"I never told you why it had to be you," Louie continued as he and Lorenzo helped Pat to his feet. "Why I fixated on you. I saw all the same qualities in you that I saw in your father when we met in France. I offered him what I'm offering you now. He spurned it to be with his family." His voice was somber. "I'm not God. I don't do divine intervention; I don't coerce. I let him live his life, knowing the good he could've done."

Pat was standing on his own now, though he still felt shaky. Lorenzo kept a hand hovering behind him in case he needed help, but when Louie beckoned them toward the room with the serpent door, Pat managed the walk without any aid.

"We aren't immortal," Louie continued, pushing the door open and leading them into the room. "At least up there, we aren't. I've been cursed to live forever amongst man, a punishment for my lack of loyalty to God. She smited me down, flung me to Earth to watch those who worshiped Her kill each other in Her honor."

Lorenzo bent down to pick up one of the chairs in front of Louie's desk, then helped Pat sit down in it. Together, the two of them quietly listened.

Louie lit a cigar, puffing it to life. "I have lived a long time, and I've seen countless civilizations fall. I'm not a fortune teller; I have no way of knowing how this conflict will end. And I had no idea when I watched your father walk away that I'd meet his son. Or that he'd come to Las Vegas, the city in which I'd prepared myself to attempt it all over again.

"They convince you when you're one of the many angels up in the sky that there is no fate, nothing above Her in the will of the cosmos." Louie's words flowed like a river, soothing in their rhythm, entrancing in their cadence. "There is only God. Yet here you stand in front of me, nearly nineteen years removed from the day I met your father, the same fire in your heart. How is that not fate?"

"I was just in the wrong place at the wrong time," Pat insisted. "There's no such thing as fate."

Louie jabbed the cigar at him. "No, you stopped. You came face to face with burning wreckage, and you stopped. You knew he was dead; his car was nothing more than ash. Everything in your being told you not to go down there, yet you did." Blowing rings of smoke into the air, he said, "You have your father's heart, but I think you have your mother's will. A woman who went across the ocean to a land far from her own, a land that would disregard her from the moment she opened her mouth. Why? Because she wanted to chart her own course. Patrick, you have a heart of gold in a world of plunderers. Don't you want to give back? Don't you want to stop the vicious cycles mankind perpetuates? Don't you want to end this and give people a chance to live their lives their way?"

He was a powerful orator. It was easy to see how he'd brought a band of misfits together, why they'd looked past his abhorrent actions. He promised to make the bigots who had oppressed and violated them taste the very same anguish they had peppered through human history. Moralistic arguments meant little when a boot was pressed on your neck. And Louie offered to relieve that pressure, to remove it.

Until now, Pat hadn't realized the strain he was under, the immense weight of the world pushing down on him for simply daring to live authentically. But suddenly, that weight was gone, and he practically floated. He couldn't ignore it now that it wasn't crushing him. Despite the exhaustion in his muscles, his mind had never felt freer. The rules he'd been made to follow broke down like the walls of a castle being raided. The veneer of civility used to exert society's will upon him no longer held sway.

He thought of his father. Unlike dreams, which faded over time, their meeting grew more vibrant and real with each passing moment. A skeleton laughing and applauding his son's dreams from beyond the grave in a reality that couldn't possibly exist and nevertheless persisted in doing precisely that. A man had healed himself in front of Pat's very eyes. The Devil had flown on battered wings, raining down hell on his enemies. And Pat had seen it happen.

He made up his mind.

"What do you need from me? What do you want from me?"

Pat stood face to face with the Son of Perdition, unrepentant in who he was. He only hoped Lorenzo would stand with him. He only hoped others like him could dream of growing old together in a cabin nestled in the frozen forests of Alaska. He only hoped Tommy and his mom would understand.

He was never cut out to be a monologist. For all the empty, hollow words he uttered, he knew he wasn't making a difference. It was but a distraction from the everyday oppression his audiences endured, those living with the hope that the next generation would have it better but never knowing for certain.

Pat had left enough things to chance. This would not be one.

Louie had won him over.

"Everything," Louie finally said, obviously realizing he was on the verge of victory.

His eyes glowed with the lust one would bestow upon a lover as he looked at St. Patrick himself. He offered his hand to him and Pat took it. The man who'd drive the snakes from Ireland was now making a pact with one. Such was life. It was all a gamble, anyway.

"Do you have a phone?" Pat asked as Lorenzo gave his shoulder an affirming clasp. "I need to make a call. I need to talk to someone."

Louie pointed at a bright red phone sitting on a coffee table, ringing despite not being obviously connected. "Go ahead, pick it up." He moved aside as Pat weakly hobbled to the phone, his footsteps echoing in the silence.

Pat stared at the ringing phone, hesitant to pick it up. Taking a deep, steadying breath, he reached for it but was stopped by an icy hand snatching hold of his wrist.

It was the specter of Randy. *"Fuck you, Pat! You think he'll save you? You think you can just forget me, Patty? Now that's a funny joke. Maybe you ain't such a bad comedian. You can't escape me. Ain't no chance in hell."*

They locked eyes, the noseless ghost looking at him with a furrowed brow, but the look on his face revealed everything.

He was afraid.

Pat smirked, buoyed by the energy radiating off of Louie, who was watching the interaction but saying nothing. Lorenzo stood on his other side, an outstretched hand on the small of Pat's back as he shuffled forward, looking down at the phone with a solemn glare. In the silence, the phone rang again.

"There is no hell, just the one we make in our own heads."

He lifted the receiver, and there was no more resistance, just the mortified face of a ghost from his past. With each fading second, Randy was eroding into obscurity.

Pat held the receiver to his ear, and before the voice on the other side could say anything, he spoke.

"Tommy, you're going to want to sit down for this one."